National bestselling author
BARBARA BRETTON
has been hailed as
"AN AUTHOR OF IMMENSE TALENT."*

*Romantic Times

Now she brings her award-winning talents to a touching new novel about life's difficult choices—and learning to live with them and try again . . .

Maybe This Time

Praise for the previous novels
of Barbara Bretton:

"This seductive novel simmers with international intrigue, sex, and betrayal."
—Publishers Weekly

"Magic, passion and spellbinding drama . . . A stunning, powerful, and enjoyable novel."
—Affaire de Coeur

"Filled with tears and laughter, pain and betrayal, love and hate. . . . Wonderfully romantic as well as sensuous, this fairy tale is one that should be savored."
—Rendezvous

"Barbara Bretton demonstrates a gift for giving readers an unforgettable one-night read that's guaranteed to . . . warm their hearts."
—Romantic Times

"[An] elegant, yet down-to-earth offering."
—Chicago Sun-Times

"Dialogue flows easily and characters spring richly to life."
—Rocky Mountain News

Berkley Books by Barbara Bretton

ONE AND ONLY
MAYBE THIS TIME

Maybe This Time

Barbara Bretton

BERKLEY BOOKS, NEW YORK

MAYBE THIS TIME

A Berkley Book / published by arrangement with
the author

PRINTING HISTORY
Berkley edition / May 1995

ISBN: 0-425-14724-X

BERKLEY®
Berkley Books are published by The Berkley Publishing Group,
200 Madison Avenue, New York, New York 10016.
BERKLEY and the "B" design
are trademarks belonging to the Berkley Publishing Corporation.

PRINTED IN THE UNITED STATES OF AMERICA

10 9 8 7 6 5 4 3 2 1

1

"It's the last house on Marlborough Road," Christine Cannon told the limo driver as they stopped at a traffic light on the outskirts of the small New Jersey town. "About a half mile from here."

The driver aimed his thumbs at opposite windows. "Right or left?"

"Two lefts, then a sharp right at the white church with the red door. We're at the top of the hill."

"Man," said the driver, shaking his head. "What made you buy a place way out here in the boonies, Ms. Cannon? I would've figured you for the Hamptons or something."

"Hope," said Christine softly. "Nothing more than hope."

Everyone had said they were crazy to buy a house, that it was the wrong time, the wrong place, the wrong price. And maybe that they were the wrong couple.

"It's the same as the stock market," her father had told them. "Buy low, sell high, not the other way around. All that fancy education and you two don't know that?"

"Location, location, location," said Joe's father. "And that ain't the right location."

Trouble was, none of that mattered when you were

looking for a miracle, and they'd been so sure that the house would be able to provide one. It was perched at the end of the block, situated on a slight rise, a surge of wood and brick that battled oaks and spruce and pine for bragging rights to the land.

The windows rattled in the frames. The floors needed to be refinished. The property taxes were outrageous, and flood insurance was out of sight.

"We'll take it," Joe had said.

Even the real estate agent had been surprised. "Oh, dear," she'd said, biting her lower lip. "Isn't this a tad hasty, Mr. McMurphy? You haven't seen the Webster house yet."

"This is the one," Christine broke in. "This is the one we want."

The real estate agent fiddled with her Multiple Listing Service directory. "There's new construction going up a few miles down the road. Huge picture windows, marble floors, the builder picks up the points. You could do worse."

"But we couldn't do better," said Joe. "That's the bottom line."

They'd needed a new start, a new way of looking at all that had gone wrong in their marriage. A place where they could heal their wounds and rediscover each other, and that wonderful house was where they would do it.

All in all, it had been a lot to ask of a house.

The limo turned onto Marlborough Road, and a thousand memories flooded in on her. When the real estate market fell apart at the same time as their marriage, they'd agreed to retain the house as joint property, renting it when they could, lending it to friends and relatives when they couldn't.

Joe had used the house a few times over the years during ski season—or at least she assumed he had—but Christine had stayed away until now. Maybe it had been her survival instinct kicking in, telling her that the memories she'd managed to dodge since the divorce were waiting for her there. Or maybe it was simply the fact that she'd left the past behind and wanted to keep it that way. Whatever the reason, she hadn't seen the house in almost six years, and suddenly she wondered if she wanted to see it at all.

This isn't a good idea, Christine. You should have sublet one of those trendy lofts in TriBeCa or a brownstone in the East Sixties.

Some place as hard-edged and modern as her apartment in L.A., with lots of glass and a few key pieces of art that meant more to her banker than they did to her.

But she'd wanted a few weeks to call her own, some time to catch her breath before she crossed the river into Manhattan and her new life. She'd worked hard for her success, but this sudden climb from journalist to television celebrity had left her gasping for breath. The view was great from the top rung of the ladder, but the air got thinner the higher up you climbed.

Although she wouldn't admit it to anyone, least of all to herself, there were times when she felt as if she'd left the best part of herself behind when she turned away from Joe and the dreams they'd shared.

The people they loved.

"Come out to see us," her father, Sam, had said when they talked a few days ago. "Your ma and I know you can't make it to the anniversary celebration, but you could stop by for a spell on your way east."

"Sorry, Pop," she'd said quickly. "I have back-to-back meetings scheduled. I'll try to get home for Thanksgiving." She regretted her haste but not her decision. She'd learned the hard way that the best way to stay on top of her emotions was to avoid the people she loved most.

"Here we are, Ms. Cannon." The limo driver brought the car to a halt at the top of the driveway. "Looks like it's been shut up a long time. If you'd like, I can open up for you, check things out."

"Just unload the bags," she said with an automatic smile. She gestured toward the man asleep next to her. "I'll see if I can rouse Sleeping Beauty."

The driver chuckled and climbed out of the car.

"Wake up," she said, gently shaking the younger man's shoulder. "Welcome to New Jersey."

Slade mumbled something and dug deeper into sleep. Small wonder, she thought, looking at the empty champagne bottle next to him on the seat. He'd downed enough bubbly on the plane from L.A. alone to float a destroyer, and he'd continued drinking in the car.

She switched on the opera light and watched as he flung one skinny arm across his face in self-defense. His veneer of sophistication dropped when he slept, which was probably why he did so little of it. Watching him like this seemed an invasion of privacy, and she switched the light back off. Joe would have appreciated the irony of the situation. After all, she made her living out of invading people's privacy.

"I'm not so sure you're going to thank me for this," her friend Terri Lyons had said one morning, "but I have a young photographer I'd like you to meet."

"Why won't I thank you?" Christine had asked, looking up from her tofu and sprouts salad platter. "Is he a bad photographer?"

"On the contrary," said Terri, who was also working for the Los Angeles affiliate. "Great photographer, rotten person."

"How rotten?"

"He's an opportunist."

"So is everyone in this business. Is he a talented opportunist?"

"Absolutely. He's going to go far, Chris, and I thought he might be right for that print piece you're working on for the sweeps-week magazine insert."

"Bring him in," Christine had said. "Let me see what I think."

That was two years ago, and Christine will wasn't certain if Slade was more sinner than saint, but that might have more to do with his age than his ethics—or lack of them.

When you came down to it, Slade wasn't much more than a kid, which was probably why Christine felt so protective of him. He needed a break, a little guidance, someone to give him a push in the right direction. He was a phenomenon waiting to happen, and Christine knew it wasn't going to take much to push him into the big time.

Right now he didn't have much of anything—no wife, no children, no apartment, no car. He bummed cigarettes off models and rides from assistant producers. He owned two pairs of jeans, one dress shirt, and all of his camera equipment could be stuffed into a leather satchel not much bigger than Christine's tote bag. He never had enough money or enough time but he had more talent than any three photographers put together.

And she loved him. Not the way he wanted her to, but the way she loved one of her younger brothers.

Or the way she might have loved a son.

"Damn," she whispered, pressing her forehead against the window, grateful for the darkness. She worked so hard to keep her emotions under control; sometimes months went by when you'd almost swear she didn't have any at all. Not the slightest tug of envy over the mothers racing home to pick up their kids from daycare or the dull ache deep inside her belly each time she went to a baby shower or a christening.

And then when she least expected it, when she was tired and her defenses were down, it would all come rushing back at her, sensation piled upon sensation, until she hurt so much she couldn't breathe.

But how strange that a smart-mouthed Brit with a roving eye would trigger it this time. Any one of her friends would be looking to jump his bones, not serve him milk and cookies. Obviously her hormones were skewed. Instead of looking to bed younger men, she was looking to adopt them.

You're a pathetic excuse for a woman, Christine. You wouldn't know an opportunity if it stripped naked in front of you.

If she said the word, Slade would let her toss him down on the leather seat and have her lascivious way with him. It had been a long time since she'd had her way with a man. Truth was, she couldn't even remember the last time she'd fantasized about wild sex with a stranger—or even average sex with someone she knew. Since the divorce, she'd put all her energy, all of her time, into her career. Work was her lover and her child, and if she wasn't happy, she was at the very least content, which was probably more than eighty percent of the population could say.

It should be enough. You tempted the gods when you asked for more. She should have learned that years ago, back when she and Joe were married and she still believed happiness was a right and not the miracle it really was.

"Come on," she said, louder this time. "The limo driver gets paid by the hour."

"Coffee," he said, stifling a yawn.

"Get out of the car, and we'll talk about it."

She left him to his own devices and climbed from the limousine. Quickly she signed a voucher for the driver, aware of Slade's grumbling as he gathered his belongings.

"It was good to see you again, Ms. Cannon," said the driver, doffing his cap. "We've missed you around here."

She didn't doubt it. She usually overtipped by five percent, then berated herself for it. The hick kid from a small town in Nevada was never far from the surface. Always trying to measure up to the city folk and always falling short. Joe used to tease her mercilessly over the western twang that reasserted itself when she was excited or angry. The fact that he had a New York accent thick enough to slice had never fazed him a bit.

But then he'd always been comfortable in his own skin, sure of what he wanted from life and how to get it. In school she'd alternately hated and envied him, wishing that she had a fraction of his confidence and talent. Everything she had she'd worked like a dog to get. She had to study twice as long, look twice as good, then work twice as hard every single step of the way.

Slade swung his legs out of the car, took a gulp of air, then fell backward into the limousine.

"I can get him inside, Ms. Cannon, but do you really want me to?"

"He's harmless enough," she said with her best TV smile. "He'll be fine once he gets some coffee into his bloodstream."

"I'll go give him a hand."

She walked up the path slowly, drinking in the smell of rich earth and wildflowers. The azalea bushes near the front door were badly overgrown, encroaching onto the path itself. She'd planted every single one of those fifteen azaleas, eight euonymous bushes, and the pair of dogwood trees outside the kitchen window. "Save something to plant next year," Joe had said, watching from his seat on the front step. "We're going to have this house a long time, Christie."

Which was true enough.

Their marriage was over, but they still had the house.

The second Mrs. McMurphy started crying as soon as they reached the West Side. New York was never at its best during rush hour on a Thursday evening in July, but, except for a few publishers en route to the Hamptons, Joe had never seen anyone cry over it.

The cabdriver kept stealing looks at them in his rearview mirror, and Joe had a pretty good idea what the guy was thinking. Cradle-robber. Pedophile. Woody Allen wannabe.

"You almost ran over a nun. Why don't you keep your eyes on the road?"

The cabdriver said nothing, which came as no surprise since the odds were he didn't speak English.

"What are you crying about?" Joe asked the girl sitting beside him. This was the first sign of life she'd exhibited since they changed planes at Gatwick.

"I hate you," she managed between sobs. "This is not what I wanted."

"It's not what I wanted, either," Joe said, "but it's what your old man wanted. We're both stuck."

"We don't have to be," she said, her boarding school British accent ruffled by her tears. She waved toward the street. "Let me go right here. I'm very resourceful. I'll find my way back home."

"How?" asked Joe. "You don't have any money, and your passport is in my briefcase."

"There are ways," she said darkly. "You would be surprised at how easy it is to circumvent bureaucracy."

He took a closer look at her. "I thought you needed my protection."

"Hah!" Amazing how quickly her tears dried up when she was angry. "My father is a power-hungry monster determined to make me bend to his will. I refuse to be like his lackeys, always—" She stopped abruptly.

"Hey, don't stop now," Joe said. "It's getting interesting."

She cast him a quick glance. "I can say no more."

"Must run in the family," Joe muttered. He leaned back and closed his eyes as the cab idled in traffic.

Twenty-four hours ago he'd been at an airport in eastern Europe, waiting to board the next plane out. For six months he'd combed the countryside looking for the man who could bring peace to the former Soviet bloc nation but with no luck. Adjacent to what was once Yugoslavia, the country had much in common with its wartorn neighbors. Better men than he had given up the search weeks ago, but not Joe McMurphy.

He'd always been a sucker for the underdog. He was the guy who cheered the prizefighter with the glass jaw, who bet on the oldest horse on the race-track, and each time he did he was somehow surprised by the absence of miracles. If he'd been alive during the Civil War, he would have cast his lot with the Confederacy even though he'd been born north of the Mason-Dixon line. There was something noble about lost causes, something that spoke to him the way nothing else could.

But finally even Joe had to admit defeat and say it was time to go home.

One minute he'd been sitting there minding his own business, dreaming about hot showers and cold beer, and the next he'd found himself standing in the middle of a bombed-out house in the center of town, being married to a plain-faced nineteen-year-old girl he didn't even know.

He was a journalist. He dealt in the facts. But even he was hard put to believe the chain of events that had led to this.

"I've been here since December, Ric, and nothing. Why didn't you wait until I was airborne?"

"Security."

Joe had lifted a brow. "Yours?"

"No," said his friend who would be king. "Yours."

"There's got to be another way. Another guy. I came here to get your story, not to steal your daughter."

"Marina is in great danger. It is imperative that she finds refuge in your country."

"Then I'll take her with me," Joe said. "I'll set her up in an apartment. I'll put her through NYU, if you want me to. But don't ask me to marry her."

"You are my last best hope."

"I'm nobody's last best hope. Don't you remember? I drink too much, smoke too much. I'm an arrogant SOB, who's—"

"Unmarried."

"Divorced." Six years ago. You'd think it would have stopped hurting by now.

"Circumstances were unkind to you. I understand that all too well, but the fact of the matter is that I saved your life a long time ago and now I am asking you to save my daughter's. It seems a fair exchange."

"You're not looking for me to consummate this, are you?"

"Try it, and I'll find another avalanche with your name on it."

"Come with us," Joe had said, grabbing his old friend by the shoulder. "Grab your kid, your crown, and kiss this place good-bye. The country you loved is gone, and it isn't coming back. Think of yourself."

"I cannot. All I ask is that you keep Marina safe until the situation here eases. I lost her mother to this civil war. I will not lose my child. Surely you of all people can understand—"

Both men fell silent. The words seemed to linger in the air, assuming shape and dimension. Joe pulled a packet of cigarettes from his jacket and offered one to his friend.

"Those things are deadly."

"So's life," said Joe. He'd learned that on a summer morning a long time ago.

The cab lurched across a major pothole, and his eyes opened. He turned toward his wife.

"Don't look at me," she snapped. "I don't like it."

"I don't like what I'm looking at," he snapped back. He wondered what trick of genetics had caused two great-looking people like Ric and his late wife to create such an aggressively plain offspring. Her hair was plain, ordinary brown. Her eyes were the same brown as her hair. There was nothing remarkable about her cheekbones or her nose or her mouth. She barely topped five feet tall, and dressed in camouflage-green cotton pants and a baggy beige sweater, she looked like a bad-tempered kid who should be sent to her room.

His wife? *Jesus.*

"Infidel," she muttered. "How much did my father pay you to marry me?"

"There isn't enough money in Fort Knox, kid. I'm repaying an old debt."

"Pah!" She bristled with fury. "That old avalanche story again? That was a lifetime ago."

"It's a pretty good story," Joe said. "You might like it."

"I'd rather eat ground glass."

"We've got action, adventure, and a heartwarming ending when the boy king saves the kid from Brooklyn from an icy death on a Colorado ski slope. There's never a dry eye in the house."

"You may wish to note that my eyes are dry."

"That's only because you've heard it before. First-timers are pushovers."

"I no longer wish to talk."

"Suits me," said Joe.

Ten minutes later the cabdriver pulled up in front of Joe's apartment building on West Seventy-second. Before Joe could reach for his wallet, Marina flung open her door and leaped into traffic, shrieking as a bus swerved in her direction. He had to hand it to the kid. She recovered faster than a sacked quarterback. She kicked off her shoes and took off down the street full speed with him in pursuit.

He was jet-lagged as hell, and it showed. He stumbled around a pair of old ladies, careened past a mother pushing a stroller, then almost collided with a guy flipping through a magazine at the newsstand on the corner. He lost a beat when he slowed down to take a look at the cover of *Time*. For a minute he'd actually thought that was his first wife staring back at him.

Get it straight, McMurphy. You already lost wife number one, and you're about to lose number two if you don't move your ass.

Marina was halfway to Central Park before he caught up to her.

"Let me go!" she screamed, kicking at him with her small and dirty feet. "Monster! Beast!"

He grabbed her by the waist, trying to keep those feet away from certain vital areas of his anatomy. "If you don't shut up, I'll—"

She screamed even louder. "I'm being held captive against my will! Somebody help me!"

Poor kid didn't realize this was New York City. Two women whispered together, then gave them a wide berth while a guy in a T-shirt and jeans stopped to check out the action.

"We're married," Joe said, throwing her over his shoulder. "Newlyweds."

The guy nodded as if that explained everything, then moved off down the block.

Manhattan wasn't going to cut it. She'd be trying to escape every time he went into the bathroom to brush his teeth.

"You cannot hold me forever," she said, punching his back with her fists.

"I'm thinking leg irons," he said as a bus pulled alongside them to discharge passengers.

"I'm a political prisoner. Torture is against international law."

"This isn't torture, kid. This is marriage."

The bus started to move off into traffic, angling around the cab waiting for them at the curb. A poster of a woman's face was plastered to the back end of the bus. Lots of white teeth, honey-colored blond hair, big turquoise-blue eyes.

It looked a lot like an airbrushed Christine with all of her fiery personality and heart softened and out of focus. COMING THIS FALL screamed the banner headline across the top of the poster. CHRISTINE CANNON!"

"Jesus!" he whispered as the bus made its way down the street. *His* Christine? He'd known she was doing well in California, but this was a shot right out of the ballpark.

"The blood is rushing to my head," his current wife said from over his shoulder. "Put me down this instant."

"Hold your horses, kid. I want to buy a magazine." He turned on his heel and marched back to the newsstand. "Gimme a copy of *Time*," he said to the owner.

The man complied. "Looks like you got your hands full."

"You don't know the half of it." He tucked the magazine under his chin, shifted Marina's position, then dug around in his pockets for American currency.

"Ouch!" Marina dug a knee into his chest. "This treatment is unconscionable."

Joe handed the newsstand owner a pair of singles.

"Who is she?" the guy asked, gesturing toward Marina. "Your daughter?"

Joe didn't bother to wait for his change. With his luck he'd be arrested for compromising the morals of a foul-tempered minor.

"Put the bags back in the trunk," he said to the cabbie, who'd watched the whole episode and still had no expression on his face.

Joe dumped Marina onto the backseat, then climbed in after her just in time to keep her from a repeat performance.

"I hate to do this to you, kid, but you don't leave me an alternative."

Her eyes widened, and she shrank back against the seat. No doubt she saw leg irons in her future. "You swore to my father that you would not lay a hand on me."

"What I have in mind is a lot worse," he said as the driver reclaimed his seat behind the wheel. "I'm taking you to New Jersey."

"Sad," Christine murmured as she ripped into the half-melted candy bar she'd discovered at the bottom of her totebag. "Truly sad."

Ms. Hotshot TV Star was reduced to eating an old Milky Way and a packet of honey-roasted nuts filched from the plane for dinner. She glanced over at Slade, who was sacked out on the sofa in a champagne-induced coma. Good thing he was four sheets to the wind. She wasn't about to share her bounty with anybody, not even a skinny photographer who didn't know where his next meal was coming from.

How on earth could she have forgotten the basics of existence, like food and transportation? She'd remembered to have the electricity and the telephone turned on. She'd arranged for delivery of every piece of office equipment she could think of, including a plain-paper fax and laser printer. Unfortunately all the other details of everyday life had slipped through her fingers. Tomorrow she would have to grab a rental car, then see about a major trip to the supermarket.

She'd grown accustomed to having other people around to see to those details, and it brought her up short to realize how far she'd traveled in the six years since she'd been under this roof. Last week she'd actually said, "I'll have my people call your people," to a Hollywood producer, then fallen over her desk in a fit of laughter. Her staff had stood silently at attention. No one had so much as cracked a smile. Joe would have been doubled over with laughter. He'd always had a keen eye for the absurd and liked nothing better than puncturing overblown egos.

She polished off her last packet of nuts, then walked into the kitchen for a cup of water. That was at least the sixth time she'd thought about her ex-husband since they'd arrived at the house a few hours ago. She supposed that was to be expected. How could she *not* think about Joe there in the house where they'd planned to raise a family, live out their lives?

The water pipes rattled alarmingly as she filled her cup with water. "Gonna need major work," the plumber had told them their first week in the house. "One day you'll turn on the faucet and nothin's gonna come out."

But they'd turned a deaf ear to his words the same way they'd turned a deaf ear to the rumbles within their marriage. If they didn't talk about it, the trouble would go away. If they pretended their hearts weren't breaking, they wouldn't hear the sound when they finally broke in two.

Carrying her cup of water, she wandered back into the living room. Slade was flat on his back, one long leg hanging over the side of the sofa. His face was mashed into a cushion. It was a wonder he could breathe. He looked dreadfully uncomfortable in his tight jeans and sweater, but no one had ever died from uncomfortable clothing.

She perched on the arm of the sofa and sipped her water. "So now what," she said to the sleeping photographer. "Feel like clubhopping?" Not that there were any clubs nearby to hop, unless you counted the Elks and Kiwanis.

He shifted position. A shock of hair fell across his forehead, and she leaned forward to push it back into place. His hair was silky against her fingertips. His skin was cool. She waited for something, anything, to happen inside her chest, but nothing did.

It didn't have to be fireworks. A small, steady glow would do. A tiny, flickering flame. Just enough to remind her that there was more to Christine Cannon than a Q-rating that went through the roof.

"Damn it," she muttered. Nothing at all. She was dead below the waist. Unable to forgo love in favor of lust, even though she knew the latter often outlived the former and was probably the better bet.

Joe was the first to admit he had a lousy sense of direction, but even he was surprised just how lousy it was. They ended up halfway to Princeton before he remembered they should be looking at mountains not ivy-covered halls.

"I think this is the exit," he said to the driver as the sign for Hackettstown appeared, illuminated by the cab's headlights.

The cabbie turned the wheel to the right and lurched off the highway.

After that it all came back to Joe. The bank near the church. The pizza place on the corner. The twisted, bumpy road that led up the hill to their house. *Damn road's gonna knock out our shocks,* he'd said the day they moved in. *Who cares?* Chris had said with a snap of her elegant fingers. *When we're rich and famous we'll have our own road put in.*

Five minutes later he and Marina stood at the top of the driveway and watched the cab's taillights disappear into the darkness. Her canvas satchel rested on top of his beat-up leather suitcase near the front steps. He made no move to carry them inside.

"This *is* your house, isn't it?" Marina asked, a note of petulance in her voice.

"Yeah, it's my house." He knew where she was going with this, but he'd be damned if he helped her.

"Then open the door."

"Can't."

"Of course you can. Just insert the key in the lock and *voilà!*"

"Smart thinking, kid. You find me a key, and I'll do it."

"Who needs keys?" she said airily. "I'll pick the lock."

She was as good as her word. Thirty seconds later she flung open the front door and waved him inside.

"You sure you're not from Brooklyn?" he asked. Ric had said his darling daughter had spent years in some fancy boarding school in England. He wondered if the proud father realized she'd majored in breaking and entering.

"The bathroom?" she said.

"Straight back, off the kitchen."

She nodded, then vanished. Joe ran his hand along the wall, feeling for a switch. The next moment the entranceway was flooded with light.

"Bloody hell," came a male voice from the vicinity of the living room. "Turn the bleedin' light off."

Joe was on the guy in an instant, yanking him to his unsteady feet, then shoving him up against the wall. He had a long, bony nose, punk-cut hair, and the oldest clothes Joe'd seen outside of a museum.

"You've got ten seconds to tell me why I shouldn't call the cops," he said in his most menacing tone of voice.

The guy looked at him through a pair of glassy hazel eyes. "Because I'm drunk."

"Not good enough."

"Because I'm brilliant."

"Five seconds," Joe warned, "and you're history."

"These hands are lethal weapons," the guy slurred over a belch. "Touch me at your own risk."

With that the guy slipped down the wall, then landed on the floor in a heap, right at Joe's feet.

He was an expensive drunk, Joe noted. An empty champagne bottle rested, bottoms up, between the sofa cushions. Joe checked the front and side windows and the backdoor, but there were no signs of forcible entry. A terrible thought popped into his head. Could the guy be a renter, complete with a binding lease and a hungry lawyer ready to sue his ass off?

"Son of a bitch." He headed down the hallway toward the bedrooms. One broken window, that's all he was asking for. Footprints on the sill. Anything to prove that the guy was in the wrong and Joe was in the right.

He checked the first bedroom. Nothing. Not even a dustball.

Same with the second bedroom.

That left the master bedroom, the one he'd shared with Christine. Call him crazy, but he hadn't checked out that room since their divorce, not even the time or two when he'd stayed at the house. Too many memories. Too many dreams. But this was no time for sentiment.

He cupped his hand around the doorknob and stepped into the room. The windows were open to the summer breezes. Pale curtains fluttered in the wind. The screens were in place and intact. For a moment he thought he smelled her perfume. He didn't want to look, but his gaze strayed to the flowered wallpaper, the dressing table in the corner, the woman asleep in the four-poster bed—

"Great," he said under his breath as he backed away. The damn place was being rented. He'd roughed up the guy in the living room, and now he was prowling around the bedroom watching a strange woman sleep. They'd be on the phone with Jacoby & Meyer so fast his flat-broke head would spin. He turned toward the door, then stopped, drawn back despite himself to the sight of the woman asleep in what used to be their bed. Not that he could see much of her, with her face pushed into the pillow and the covers up over her shoulders. It sounded nuts, but she reminded him of Christine.

Christine? Impossible. His ex-wife was back in Los Angeles, hobnobbing with movie stars. He'd just seen her picture on the cover of *Time*. What the hell would she be doing in their old house in Hackettstown, New Jersey?

He stepped closer to the bed. She slept on her side, the way Christine used to sleep, one knee bent, one leg extended straight, hugging the pillow close to her chest the way she'd held him before it all went sour. He bent down close to her and caught the scent of Bal a Versailles, and in that instant he was twenty-one again, head-over-heels in love with the woman of his dreams.

"Jesus," he muttered. It *was* Christine. Her hair was shorter, blonder. It fell across her cheek like a veil of silk. The quilt slipped, exposing one shoulder, the skin lightly gilded by the California sun. He wondered if she was naked beneath the quilt. Then he wondered why he should give a damn.

She stirred. The quilt slipped down another inch.

He stirred, but then he reminded himself that this was the same woman who'd walked out the door on him because the only way she could find herself was to lose everything they'd shared, everything they'd dreamed of, everything they'd ever wanted. She hadn't had the guts to face him. She'd packed her bags and moved out while he was in Washington interviewing the Vice President, leaving behind nothing but a brief note and memories he'd sell his soul to be able to forget.

Christine naked and willing.

Christine aglow with excitement over a new assignment.

She rolled over onto her back. Both the quilt and the top sheet slipped, exposing the slope of her breasts.

Christine naked . . .

He cleared his throat.

She murmured something in her sleep.

He nudged her hip.

She turned back onto her side.

"Christine."

"Go away," she mumbled, throwing her arm across her eyes. " 's late."

"C'mon, Chris, wake up."

Her mumbling grew louder but not more intelligible. In the old days he would have pulled back the covers and climbed in next to her, enjoying the warmth of her body while he eased her awake with his mouth and hands. He could feel her rump pressed against his stomach, smell the perfume of her skin, hear the soft sound of her breathing in his ear—the memories were right there just beneath the surface, so close that he found the dividing line between the past and present blurring dangerously.

*   *   *

"For God's sake, Slade," Christine murmured. "It's the middle of the night. Can't you amuse yourself?"

"Who the hell is Slade?"

Since when did Slade do an American accent? Even more to the point, since when did he have her ex-husband's American accent?

That, thank God, was impossible. Joe was thousands of miles away in some no-name country, fighting the good fight for truth and democracy while she fought for Oscar, Emmy, and Grammy.

She opened her eyes, took a good look at the man standing by the bed, then closed her eyes again. A dream within a dream, that's what it was. Things like this didn't happen to her, not in her carefully constructed, orderly life.

"Too late," Joe said. "I know you're awake."

She caught the scent of his skin, and a voluptuous shiver rippled through her body.

Go away, Joe. I don't want you here. I want you on the other side of the ocean where you belong. She opened her eyes and sat up, leaning against the headboard with the sheet clutched under her chin. "What on earth are you doing here?"

"I could ask you the same thing." He looked older, which wasn't a surprise. Six years had passed since they were last together. There were lines on his face that hadn't been there before, and shadows beneath his eyes.

"I'm not the one who was running around Europe."

His left eyebrow lifted a fraction, just enough so an ex-wife would notice.

"Those were good stories you filed, Joe," she said. "I enjoyed them."

"You read them."

"I read them." The sheet slipped, and she grabbed for it.

"You're not naked," he said, "if that's what you're afraid of."

"How would you know?"

"I peeked."

"I don't think so. If you had you'd know I was naked."

Their eyes met. She felt a tingling in her chest, a heaviness that seemed to press against her heart, then push outward. He bent forward and looked closely at her face.

"Since when do you have blue eyes? They were gray the last time I saw them."

"I've always had blue-gray eyes."

"Not that blue."

She started to laugh. Not even her closest associates back in L.A. had commented on the dramatic change. "Contacts," she said, regaining her composure. "They can do wonders."

"I liked the gray."

"Blue looks better on camera."

"Is that why you bleached your hair?"

"I didn't bleach my hair." She paused. "I had it highlighted."

"It looks blonder."

"It's supposed to."

"For the camera?" he asked dryly.

"For myself."

"What else have you changed?"

"Nothing that concerns you." She caught the

sound of voices in the hallway. "Who is Slade talking to?"

Joe's jaw tightened noticeably. "Like I said before: Who's Slade?"

"Did you bring someone with you?" Joe with another woman, right there under the roof they'd shared as man and wife. It wasn't any of her business what he did or where, but still the idea rankled.

"You answer my question, I'll answer yours."

"I was here first," she said, sounding like a five-year-old child.

"Yeah," he said, "but I *asked* first."

"Smile for the camera, people." A light flared in the doorway, then died. "I said smile, Chris love."

"You should have knocked," she snapped, feeling suddenly put upon and overwhelmed. "This isn't Grand Central Station."

"Door was open," Slade remarked, stepping into the room as if he owned the place, which was no mean feat considering the amount of champagne he had consumed. "Besides, Rocky there and I already met."

She turned to Joe. "What is he talking about?"

"I decked him," Joe said evenly. "I thought he'd broken into the place."

"The bloody hell you did." Slade pushed up against Joe, righteous anger in his eyes. "I passed out." The jackass was proud of getting shitfaced and sliding down a wall.

Joe shoved the guy out of his way as if he were a pesky fly at a barbecue. "A liar not old enough to shave. Good going, Chris. You really know how to pick 'em."

"You son of a bitch!" Slade shoved back, careful to keep his Hasselblad chose to his chest.

Joe's hand curled into a fist, and he reared back, ready to deliver a blow, when Christine's voice split the air.

"Everybody out," she ordered, struggling to sound authoritative with a sheet clutched to her bosom. "This is a bedroom, not a conference room, and if you aren't out of here by the time I count to ten, I swear to God I'll call the police and have the lot of you arrested."

Not only did they not listen to her, but yet another person appeared in the doorway to her bedroom.

"Joseph," said a homely young girl in khaki pants and a ratty oversized sweater who had eyes for no one but Chris's ex-husband. "How dare you leave me alone with this inebriated fool."

Slade turned toward her and snapped two pictures in quick succession. "You forgot to smile, love."

She muttered something Christine couldn't catch, then grabbed for the camera. "Nobody takes my photograph without my permission."

Slade held the camera out of her reach. "Touch this camera and it's the last thing you do."

The girl's eyes blazed with fury, and she hurled herself at Slade like a human guided missile. She unleashed a chain of curses that had Christine staring at her in a combination of horror and admiration.

"Tell her who I am," Slade implored Christine.

"Tell *him* who *I* am," the girl ordered Joe as she kicked Slade in the shin.

Joe turned to Christine. "You first."

"That's Slade," she said, wishing she'd stayed in a nice quiet hotel with room service and a lock on the door. "He's my photographer." She gestured toward the plain-faced waif. "Who's she?"

"Marina," said the girl, striding into the room as if she had been born to the purple. "I am Joseph's wife."

2

Christine laughed out loud. "Very funny," she said, turning to Joe. "Who is she really?"

He didn't laugh with her. "She's my wife, Chris."

"You're kidding." He had to be kidding. The girl was young enough to be his daughter. Good grief, the girl was young enough to be *her* daughter. "What's the joke?"

"No joke," he said, still not cracking a smile. "Want to see the marriage certificate?"

"You carry your marriage certificate around with you?" She glanced over at Marina, who was watching them with open curiosity, then turned back to Joe. "All things considered, I can see why that might not be a bad idea."

"What the hell's that supposed to mean?"

She bunched the pillows behind her back and sat straight against the headboard. "Do the words 'jail bait' mean anything to you?"

"Jail bait?" Slade chimed in from the doorway.

"Go find some coffee," Chris ordered. "And put that camera down."

Joe lifted a brow in her direction. "That how you treat your boyfriends these days?"

"He's not my boyfriend."

"You're sleeping with him, aren't you?"

"None of your business."

Joe's expression darkened. "Yeah," he said. "You're sleeping with him."

Slade stepped into the room. "Want me to call the police?" he asked Christine. "They broke in. That must be good for a few nights in jail, even in New Jersey."

"We did not break in," said the girl. "The door suffered no damage. I picked the lock."

"So young and so funny," Christine observed dryly. "You're a lucky man, Joe."

"You can't be arrested for breaking into your own house," Joe pointed out.

"I thought it was your house," Slade said to Christine.

"It is my house," Christine said, growing more exasperated by the minute.

"Want to run that by me again?" Joe said, sounding pretty exasperated himself.

"Damn it," she snapped. "It's *our* house, okay?"

Slade made a show of looking Joe over. "You bought a house with him?"

"It seemed a good idea at the time," Christine said. "We were married."

"You were married to *her*?" the child bride asked Joe.

"I can understand the confusion," said Christine. "I'm old enough to vote."

"Lay off her, Chris," Joe warned. "This isn't what you think."

"You don't know what I think," she said. How could he when she didn't have a clue herself.

"So what're we talking about?" Slade broke in. "Bigamy?"

"Sorry to disappoint you, pal," said Joe. "We're divorced." He turned back to Christine. "Where'd you find him?"

"Slade's photographing me for a story in *Vanity Fair*."

"And?"

"And nothing. That's it."

"You wound me," said Slade. "I thought I meant more to you than a strobe and a rose-colored filter."

"Joseph." The child bride approached the foot of the bed. "I need to bathe."

Apprehension snaked its way along Christine's spine. "You and your . . . wife aren't planning to stay here, are you?"

He didn't look any happier about the prospect than Christine felt. "That's the general idea."

"Under the circumstances it doesn't seem like a very good idea."

"You and Glade—"

"Slade."

"Whatever. The two of you can find someplace else to stay." He paused. "On me."

She started to laugh. "I don't need your money, Joe. I've done quite well for myself."

A trace of the grin she'd known and once loved tugged at the left-hand corner of his mouth. "Cover of *Time*, Christie? Pretty damn well, if you ask me."

"You saw *Time*?" *Almost all of my dreams have come true, Joe. Can you tell me why I'm not happy?*

"I saw *Time* and a monster ad on the back of a bus. You've got yourself one hell of a PR firm working for you."

He looked genuinely impressed. Somehow that pleased her more than anything had in months. "The network is doing it all," she said, trying to act nonchalant. "All I have to do is show up."

They both knew that wasn't true. She'd worked hard for everything she'd achieved, and Joe had been around for much of it. Nothing in her life had ever come easily. He should know that. She'd had to study twice as long as he did, work three times as hard, just to keep even with him back in college. After they graduated it was no different. He did the meaningful stories, the stories that changed people's lives, while Christine got her first break covering movie stars at restaurant openings.

Joe's wife swayed on her feet, and he caught her, pulling her against his side. A simple act. She was a tiny slip of a thing, and he easily swept her into his arms, cradling her the way you would cradle a child. *How could you, Joe? Somehow I thought you would always belong to me—*

Stupid thought. She didn't want to pursue it. What he did and with whom were none of her business.

"She needs to sleep," he said without preamble. "Where can I put her?"

It took Christine a second to regain her bearings. "In the—in the back bedroom." She cleared her throat. "The one with the double bed."

He met her eyes. It took everything in her to keep from looking away. "We'll work things out in the morning," he said over the head of his sleeping wife.

Christine nodded. "Sure we will."

She wanted to snap her fingers and make everyone disappear. Joe and his little wife. Slade and his knowing eyes. This house filled with memories she thought she'd put behind her. She didn't want to feel vulnerable or needy or so lonely that she thought her heart would break.

"So that's your ex," said Slade as Joe's bedroom door closed behind him and his wife.

"I don't want to talk about it, Slade."

"Surly but photogenic. You could have done worse."

"Don't," she warned. "I'm not in the mood."

"What's bothering you, love? That he's married or that you're not?"

Slade didn't expect an answer.

He'd never prided himself on his sensitivity, but there was something about the look in Christine's eyes that made him back off for the moment. It had taken him all of ten seconds to realize this wasn't your average divorce. The currents running between Christine and her ex-husband were deep and treacherous. At least they were if you believed, as Slade did, that emotions could be turned on and off as easily as you turned off a light.

Too bad he'd polished off the champagne. The empty bottle winked at him from between the sofa cushions. Christine was too bloody controlled. A few glasses of bubbly, and he'd have her spilling her juiciest secrets.

He tossed the bottle on the floor and watched as it rolled under the dark pine coffee table. The house was quiet except for the creak of plumbing as someone flushed a toilet. He missed the punctuation of city life, everything from sirens to screams of screeching tires and curses in languages that weren't in any textbook he'd ever seen. He loved the anonymity, the way you could invent and reinvent yourself until you got it right.

The couch was too short for his lanky body, but he stretched out anyway, letting his feet hang over the arm. His Nikes were scuffed and scarred, marked by encounters at most major airports and celebrity watering holes in North America. He hated those fucking Nikes. People in Queens wore the bloody things, and early on Slade had vowed he'd never wear anything that was popular on the wrong side of the East River.

He'd considered switching over to Doc Martens, but they were too counterculture for his upwardly mobile tastes. His mother had bought into that whole reverse-chic thing back in the Sixties when she moved down from Scotland to experience the Carnaby Street scene firsthand, but Slade had seen enough of patched jeans and Jesus sandals to last him the rest of his life.

Even as a boy he'd wanted the things he couldn't have. He'd watched the toffs in their public school uniforms as they climbed into their fancy cars to head for the M-4 and a weekend with Mummy, and he memorized every detail. The bowl-shaped haircut. The tailored navy blazer with the discreet insignia on the breast pocket. The shiny shoes that probably cost more money than his mother paid in rent every month for their cold-water flat.

Sometimes he would lock himself in the upstairs loo of the boardinghouse and practice the tight-jawed speech that seemed to separate him from the others even more quickly than his shabby clothes. It didn't take long, however, to realize there was more to it than diction and wardrobe. He could be outfitted head to foot by a Savile Row tailor and amaze people with the way consonants tripped off his tongue and still find the doors that mattered locked against him.

Opening those doors with a telephoto lens had brought him a lot of satisfaction. Not enough yet to trade in his Nikes for a pair of Italian loafers, but soon.

He closed his eyes and saw Christine in front of him, saw the way she'd looked at her ex-husband, and he smiled into the darkness.

Gucci. Size 13 medium. The color of fine cognac. It was only a matter of time.

Asleep, Marina looked even younger, young enough that Joe actually felt something akin to paternal concern. He'd placed her fully clothed on the bed, then covered her with one of the blankets he found in the closet. She slept on her stomach, clutching the pillow to her as if she expected to have to fight for it during the night.

Ric had told him that she'd been living in the mountains with a band of revolutionaries. He had no doubt she made up in spirit what she lacked in size, but she was so tiny, so painfully thin, that for the first time Joe understood why Ric had been so desperate to get her to safety.

Not that he wanted to understand. The absurdity of his situation had hit him full force in the gut when he found Christine asleep in the master bedroom. Who the hell spent his wedding night watching wife #2 wrestle her pillow while wife #1 slept one room away? Geraldo and Phil would have a field day with the situation.

"Shit," he muttered. Who was he kidding? *Christine* would have a field day with the situation. She could even get Bozo the photographer boy to take the pictures, then air the whole goddamn thing on her own television show. One-stop shopping for Nielsen ratings. No questions asked.

He wanted to storm back into her bedroom, pull her into his arms, and kiss her senseless. He wanted to feel her breasts flatten against his chest, the length of her legs, the soft brush of her breath on his skin.

But mostly he wanted to forget her.

He'd worked hard and long at forgetting her. He'd tried booze, work, and other women and had yet to find the right combination that would drive Christine Anne Cannon from his mind.

Talk about being between a rock and a hard place. He didn't trust Marina in Manhattan. He didn't trust himself in New Jersey.

"Damn, damn, damn." Christine punched her pillow as she struggled with the tangled bedcovers. She considered the wisdom of punching her fist through the headboard but thought better of it.

Six years ago she'd walked out on Joe with no explanation, and now he'd walked in on her with a wife who looked young enough to be their daughter. There was probably a karmic justice to it all, but the universal pattern eluded her at the moment. She had the oddest feeling that God was exercising his sense of humor at her expense.

Less than twelve hours ago she'd been mourning the loss of her sex drive and wishing she could find it in her to be attracted to Slade. Slade was young, attractive, and frankly interested in her, and still she hadn't been able to work up so much as a degree of heat. Then along comes her newly married ex-husband, and she felt as if she'd fallen into a volcano.

"Sorry," she mumbled, kicking off the covers, "but I fail to see the humor in the situation."

She had no trouble at all seeing the danger, however. This was the shortcut to a broken heart. She'd left Joe the first time because her heart had been breaking apart like shattered glass, the parts scattering so far and wide she could never piece it together again. So she'd left. Packed her clothes, taken half of their money, and walked out. He deserved better than what she could give him. He deserved a woman who could be a wife to him and a mother to his children, not some neurotic overachiever who had the home phone numbers of the top five box office stars but could never give him a child.

Marina might not be her choice for Joe's perfect woman, but the plain gold band on her ring finger spoke volumes. She wasn't your basic fantasy, but she was young and probably fertile. It wasn't the girl's fault any more than it was Christine's fault life had dealt her a bad hand. You didn't hate a woman because she had blue eyes and blond hair. Hating her because she could do the one thing you couldn't was every bit as unfair.

But Christine didn't claim to be rational on the subject. She'd spent more years then she cared to count ducking baby showers and christenings, looking the other way when pregnant women walked down the street. Like it or not, Marina was the new Mrs. McMurphy, and the odds were that sooner or later, she'd give Joe a child. Christine entertained a swift, painful vision of Joe sweeping the girl off to his bed, his powerful body covering hers, limbs entwined—

She swung her legs out of the bed, shivering slightly

in the cool night air, then crossed the room to the dressing table with the stack of color-coordinated file folders stacked on top of it. When in doubt, work. For years that had been her philosophy, but lately that philosophy had been failing her. Success was sweet—she'd be the first one to tell you that—but it wasn't everything.

With all of her heart she wished it could be. She enjoyed being recognized on the street, signing autographs, getting the best table at the best restaurants. But it wasn't enough.

She grabbed a pile of folders and took them back to bed, spreading them out on the thin cotton spread. Clippings from a hundred different magazines and newspapers, all of them touting the wonders of Christine Cannon. *Mix Barbara Walters's eye for ratings with Diane Sawyer's nose for news, and you have Christine Cannon, the most bankable face of the upcoming television season.*

"Junk journalism," one of her friends had said behind her back. Christine couldn't deny it. Most of the time she was comfortable with what she did, proud of her climb to the top, and mellow in the face of her peers' criticism. But every now and again one of the cracks hit home with surprising force and made her glad her ex-husband wasn't around to see what had become of her idealistic plans to save the world.

Because you couldn't save the world. You couldn't even save a piece of it. The best you could do was help to lighten the load. And that's exactly what she did. The public's fascination with the rich and famous was as timeless as the elements.

Back in the days of Caesar and Cleopatra, servants

probably gathered around the fountains and speculated about what really happened in the royal bedchamber. What Christine did was give them that tantalizing peek behind the velvet curtains, and she'd be damned if she was going to apologize to anybody for being successful at it.

She'd spent a few lean years on a quest to save the world. She and Joe had shared a certain wide-eyed optimism when it came to the human condition, and that optimism had propelled them through grad school in a blaze of competitive naïveté. She'd lost her naïveté on a summer morning seven years ago. She wasn't entirely certain Joe ever had.

After the divorce she'd moved to Oprah territory in Chicago, signing on as a reporter for a local newspaper. While covering a brouhaha between a movie company and neighborhood residents determined to keep their homes out of the klieg lights, her telegenic looks and razor-sharp mind had attracted more than their fair share of attention. The next day she found herself signing a contract to be the entertainment correspondent on one of the local news stations. Her hip, slightly sardonic reports made more news than her subjects, and after a short stint on *E!*, she went to KABC in Los Angeles. Within days she was the talk of the town.

She knew who was hot before the temperature began to climb. She had spies at the DMV, at police stations from Malibu to San Diego, and at every AA meeting in a two-hundred-mile radius. No one was safe. She could tell a boob job at fifty paces, a nose job from across a crowded ballroom, and bullshit the second she heard it, even when she was the one spouting it.

But when you're sitting on the bed you once shared with your husband and he's down the hallway with his brand-new wife, it was hard to think of anything but the fact that you were sleeping alone and he wasn't.

They were in New Jersey, that much Marina knew, but once they had exited the tunnel that crawled beneath the Hudson River she'd found it hard to gain her bearings. She was reasonably certain New Jersey lay to the west, but her grasp of American geography was minimal.

If they had stayed in Manhattan, she knew she could have found a way to get back home. But, no. Her new husband might be a monster, but he wasn't a fool. He knew full well that her failed attempt at escape was only her first try, and so he'd exiled them both to the middle of nowhere.

The sprawl of highway and open land had made her want to weep with despair. Not that she was about to do so, however. She'd already cried quite enough in front of him and to no avail. Tears were a powerful weapon; she wouldn't waste them until she was more certain they would have the desired effect.

Still, despite her best intentions, the tears stung her eyes, and she blinked rapidly to force them back. In two short years her entire life had been turned upside down.

Her mother was dead. Her father tilted at windmills, looking to be a king in a world that no longer recognized the need for such things. Nobody on earth understood the aching loneliness inside her heart, the need to belong somewhere. To belong to someone. She had thought that by returning to the land of her father's birth she would discover a place for herself in the grand scheme of things, but even that had failed her.

Or at least that was what she had believed until she met Zee. He was everything she'd ever dreamed a man could be. Strong and passionate, committed to a cause greater than himself, a cause that quickly became her cause as well.

And he loved her. Plain, forgettable Marina. Somehow he saw that she had the spine of a warrior and the soft heart of a woman.

In the time she'd been with him, Zee had never been wrong about anything. Not for him the old ways of his father who had grown up under Soviet rule. And not for him the backward ways of his great-grandfather, a man who was willing to bend his knee before a mortal man simply because the man called himself a king.

"Your father was born with power," Zee had said, his beautiful mouth narrowed into a slash of anger. "The need to wield that power is in his blood. We fight for those who are powerless."

Something about that statement hadn't made sense to her, but Zee was as compelling as he was persuasive, and she loved him more than she'd ever loved anything or anybody.

She looked across the room at the man sleeping on a pile of clothing by the door. He wasn't her husband, he was her jailer, determined to keep her imprisoned against her will. His loyalties lay with her father, but he would soon learn that the daughter was a force to be reckoned with as well.

Joe woke up a little after dawn feeling jet-lagged and older than God. While Marina slept the sleep of the young and untroubled, he'd been stretched out on the floor near the door with his jacket bunched under his head for a pillow. He doubted he would ever walk upright again. As if there wasn't enough, his mouth felt like the inside of an ashtray, and his brain didn't feel much better.

Yawning, he unfolded his rapidly aging body from his makeshift bed and stretched. Another night on the floor and he'd be a candidate for the chiropractor. Hell, he thought as he rebuttoned his shirt. Another night in this house and he'd be a candidate for the psychiatrist.

Joe wasn't big on vibes, but there'd been no mistaking the currents pulsing through the old house last night. He'd spent a lot of time wondering if the photographer had found his way into Christine's bed after he'd left them alone together. Every creak of the floorboards had sent his imagination into overdrive, and then he cursed himself for giving a rat's ass what she did or where she did it.

He headed for the john. Wouldn't hurt to detour past the master bedroom and check out the action. If she was sleeping with the photographer, better to know it now than spend any more energy wondering about it. He was going to need all his energy to figure out where in hell he could stash Marina to keep her out of trouble.

The first thing he noticed was that the other guest room was empty. He looked longingly at the single bed pushed up against the window wall. Too bad separate bedrooms might make the newlywed concept hard to swallow. He went back into the living room, taking note of the empty champagne bottle lying under the coffee table. The sofa looked as if it might have been slept on, but then he remembered seeing the guy sacked out on it when he and Marina arrived. Just because he'd started the night there didn't mean that's where he ended it.

Christine's bedroom door was closed. He stood in front of it, debating whether to knock, call her name, or barge right in when the door swung open, and he found himself face to face with his ex-wife.

"Don't you ever knock?" she asked, tugging at the belt on her white satin robe.

He raised his hand and tapped on the doorjamb. "You beat me to it."

"A likely story." She pushed past him and started for the kitchen. "I don't suppose you started the coffee."

"Maybe the British wunderkind did."

"He's out running. By the way, he has a name."

"Glade, isn't it?"

"*Slade*," she said, glaring at him over her shoulder as they entered the kitchen. "It's not a difficult name, Joe."

"You're right," he said easily. "It's not difficult. It's stupid."

"Not everyone can be named Joseph." The way she said it, his name sounded like Englebert or Oscar.

He leaned against the counter and folded his arms across his chest. "Yeah, well, call me crazy, but I can't see naming a kid after a department store or an air freshener." Somewhere parents were debating the relative merits of Tiffany, Macy, and K-Mart.

"Not that it's any of your business, but Slade is his middle name."

He watched while she flung open the cabinet

doors, searching for coffee. "So what's his real name?" He paused a beat. "*Joseph*?"

She opened the refrigerator, mumbling something into the butter keeper.

"Didn't hear you, Chris," he drawled, thoroughly enjoying himself.

"Damn it his name is Rainbow." She spun around to face him. "Are you happy now?"

He couldn't help it. He started to laugh. "Rainbow?"

The corners of her mouth twitched. "His mother was a Scottish flower child."

"He's lucky she didn't name him Petunia."

"Don't think he doesn't know it."

"So where'd the name Slade come from?"

"His mother's favorite TV show."

"Gotta love those British traditions."

Her mouth twitch slid into a reluctant grin, then surrendered to a smile. "This from a man who was named after his father's favorite bartender."

"Bookmaker," he corrected her, smiling back. "I got the middle name from the bartender."

She leaned back against the refrigerator. "So how is your father?"

The question pinched. "Nothing's changed. Still alive. Still in Brooklyn. Still angry with the world."

"Have you seen him since you came home?"

"I haven't even been home twenty-four hours, Chris."

"What did you do, come here directly from the airport?"

"Just about."

"No wonder she was so tired."

"It's been a rough couple of days."

"You and your—you and Marina having troubles?"

"We haven't been married long enough."

Her smile tightened. "How long have you been married?"

"You're not going to like it, Chris."

"Try me."

"We got married yesterday afternoon."

"Are you telling me last night was your wedding night?"

"Yeah," he said, aware that he was on dangerous ground. "Technically."

Her jaw tightened to match her smile. "Technically? What does that mean?"

"Not what you think it means."

"How do you know what I think it means?"

He regrouped, then tried again. "You saw her last night. She was wiped out."

"You'll make up for lost time, I'm sure."

He thought of their own wedding night years ago. The words *exuberant* and *incredible* came to mind. "About that coffee," he said. "Why don't you check the fridge?"

"Nice try, Joe."

"I thought so."

"Do you love her?"

"What do you want me to say?"

"I don't know," she answered. "Maybe that you adore her, you can't live without her, that she makes the world a better place just by being in it."

"Been reading romance novels again, have you?"

"I want to hear you say that you love her."

"What I feel for her doesn't matter."

"Good God, Joe, she's your *wife*. If you don't love her, why did you marry her?"

"I didn't say I don't love her."

"And you didn't say you do."

He thought of the empty guest room. "Where did your friend sleep last night?"

"In the guest room, I suppose."

"Think again."

"Is this some kind of test?"

"You haven't answered the question."

She narrowed her eyes, but that didn't mask the dangerous glint. "I don't owe you answers to anything."

"Bingo." He jabbed the air with his forefinger. "Back off, Chris," he warned. "I'm not your next story."

His words hurt. Nobody else would know, but he saw it in the way she straightened her shoulders, regaining her legendary sense of control. He wanted to pull her into his arms and tell her everything, but he'd promised Ric he'd keep Marina's identity secret. Besides, telling Christine was like blasting it on the front page of the *New York Times*. The news would hit the tabloids quicker than you could say *paparazzi*, and Marina would be at risk.

"There's no coffee in the house," Christine said, moving toward the doorway. "I'll get dressed and go into town."

"You have a car?"

"I'll walk."

"It's over two miles."

"I can handle it."

"I'll come with you."

"Don't," she said, her tone deadly. "You'd better be here when your bride wakes up."

* * *

Newlyweds, Christine thought as she changed into jeans and a T-shirt. *They're newlyweds.*

Last night she wouldn't have believed anything could hurt more than the discovery that Joe was married. She was wrong. The thought that Joe and Marina were at the very beginning of their marriage made her feel sick at heart.

She sat on the edge of the bed and pulled on a pair of socks, then looked around for her loafers. One week earlier, even one day and maybe—

"Who're you kidding?" she said, looking across the room at her reflection in the mirror.

It was over.

Joe had a new wife and a new life, and before the day was over Christine would make sure he had a new place to live.

3

"I can't possibly be the one to leave," Christine said when they sat down in the kitchen later that morning to discuss the issue. "I have a full schedule of assignments ahead of me." Joe snorted, and she shot him a fierce look. "And I'm expecting quite a few deliveries."

Joe leaned back in his kitchen chair until he was balanced on the two back legs. "I'll have the deliveries forwarded to you in Manhattan."

"Why don't I forward you to Manhattan?" she shot back. "You're not expecting anything." She glanced pointedly toward Marina, who was fixing herself a cup of tea. "*Are* you?"

"Low shot, Christie," he said. "You can do better than that."

"You're right," she said. "Shall I?"

"Save your breath. I own half this house. I'm staying."

"I was here first." *Great going, Christine. Dazzle him with your elementary school logic.*

"And I don't mind if you stay here."

"How generous of you," she drawled, aware that Slade was standing in the doorway behind her.

The chair's front legs hit the floor with a bang as Joe rocked forward. He leaned across the table, all intensity and barely suppressed anger. "You're good at leaving, Chris. Why don't you show us how it's done?"

The silence in the room was powerful. Christine felt as if she were trapped in a freeze frame. Marina, teacup cradled between her small hands, stood by the stove. The little bride was taking it all in, every single detail of Christine's discomfort. And she didn't have to turn around to know that only fear of death kept Slade from snapping a picture of this ghastly scene.

Taking a deep breath, she slowly pushed back her chair and rose to her feet. "Do what you want," she said to Joe in a voice that sounded steadier than her emotions, "but don't expect me to cater to you and your . . . wife. Buy your own food, arrange for your own transportation, and stay out of my life."

Joe rose to his feet. "I couldn't have said it better myself. It's a big house. No reason we can't stay out of each other's way."

"We're adults, after all," Christine agreed. "We should be able to handle it." She extended her right hand. He looked at it, then at her, and an instant later she watched as her hand disappeared into his. His grip was firm, confident . . . warm. She remembered those big hands moving along her body—

"You okay?" Joe asked.

She nodded. "Fine," she said. "Just fine."

"Yeah?"

She forced a smile. "Yeah."

He released her hand.

She moved away from the table. "I have some work to do," she said, heading toward the doorway. "If anyone needs me, I'll be in the bedroom."

*   *   *

Joe looked up from his coffee at the sound of the bedroom door slamming shut. Christine had always been good at punctuation.

Marina settled down opposite him with her cup of coffee while the photographer helped himself to the bagels.

"Want one?" Slade asked Marina.

She nodded. "I would."

"Better not touch them," Joe warned the girl. "Knowing Chris, she took inventory."

Slade reached into his pocket and withdrew a quarter. He tossed it on the counter next to the bag. "It's on me."

The photographer placed a bagel down in front of the girl, then, balancing a mug of coffee and his own bagel, he sauntered from the room, leaving Joe alone with Ric's daughter.

She looked even younger by daylight. And, Joe noted, a hell of a lot more fragile. Almost demure, actually, although that was a stretch. It was hard to believe this was the hellion who'd kicked and clawed her way across the Upper West Side yesterday in her bid to escape. She wore black trousers that had seen better days and the same baggy colorless sweater she'd worn yesterday.

"Is that all you have to wear?" he asked, gesturing toward the sweater.

She took a sip of coffee. "Clothes are not important to me. Fashion is a bourgeois concept."

"I'm not talking fashion," Joe said. "I'm talking convenience. If that's all you have, you're going to be in trouble when it's time to get it cleaned."

Another sip of coffee. The girl had learned her

delaying tactics from the best. "I will see to it that I don't embarrass you."

"Embarrass me?" She was better at this than he'd first thought. "Why the change of heart? Yesterday you would have knifed me through if you thought that would get you out of here."

"Yesterday I didn't understand," she said, eyes downcast. "Today I do."

"All of a sudden you believe your old man did the right thing by marrying you off?"

"I believe that things happen for a reason." She met his eyes. "You will have no problem with me, Joseph."

"I must be crazy," he muttered. "I almost believe you."

A small smile curved her mouth. For an instant Joe saw a glimpse of her beautiful mother, but it vanished before he could be sure. "We do not have to stay here," she continued, breaking off a piece of bagel and dunking it in her coffee. "If Manhattan is better for you, we can—"

"Nice try, kid," he said, grabbing himself one of Christine's bagels. "I might trust you in Hackettstown, but Manhattan is another story."

Joe was laughing as he left the room, a fact that might have angered Marina just a few hours earlier. In her experience Americans did a great deal of laughing at that which they didn't understand—or care to deal with. It was a character flaw that she'd discovered in every American she'd met thus far, a certain unwillingness to face serious issues with serious thought. Her new husband was no exception.

He was a good deal smarter than Marina had first

believed, however. She broke off another piece of bagel and dunked it in her lukewarm cup of coffee while she considered the situation.

It wasn't as if she'd believed he would agree to her suggestion about Manhattan. That was more to cover her tracks than anything else, although she would not have complained if he had seen the wisdom of her words. Of course he had not, and so she was condemned to living with strangers in the middle of New Jersey.

But there were compensations. She smiled and took a sip of coffee. Zee had always said she was the most resourceful woman he had ever met, that despite her upbringing she understood the common people had needs that must be met, and she didn't hesitate to meet those needs at great risk to herself.

This plan, however, would require little in the way of risk.

This morning, before her bath, she had been rummaging in the huge hallway closet in search of towels and soap when she came upon a score of expensive perfumes, still sealed in their original wrappings. She stared at the bounty for what seemed an eternity, her mind trying to wrap itself around the outrageous excess the perfumes represented.

And the perfumes were only the beginning. Tucked farther back in the closet's depths were place settings of fine china, crystal goblets, a multitude of linens and laces. All in their original wrappings. All untouched. She wondered if other closets held riches that would rival Aladdin's Cave. It was a big house by American standards, and there was an attic and a basement and a garage all awaiting her investigation.

Nobody deserved so much when so many people in

the world had nothing at all. The worst of it was that no one seemed to know those items were even there.

Her temper grew so hot it was a miracle her bathwater hadn't reached a boil.

And that's when it occurred to Marina that no one would notice when they disappeared.

It would be a long process. A bottle of perfume here, a crystal goblet there. There was a false ceiling tile in the closet of the room she shared with Joe, the perfect place to stash her treasures until she could trade them in for money to help Zee and their cause.

Christine had arranged for a rental car while she was in town earlier that morning, and it was delivered not long after noon.

"A Buick?" Joe asked, obviously disappointed. "Since when do you drive Buicks?"

"Since that's all they had," she retorted. "Besides, what's wrong with Buicks?"

"Nothing's wrong with them," said Joe. "You just don't look like a Buick driver."

The clerk who'd delivered the car looked from Joe to Christine. "You don't want the car?" he asked her.

"Of course I want the car." She reached for the clipboard that held the receipt. "Let me sign it so you can be on your way."

"No Maseratis?" Joe asked the guy.

"Got a Corvette," he said, "but the lady didn't want it."

Joe looked at Christine. "You passed up a 'Vette?"

Christine ignored him. She signed the receipt, handed the clipboard and pen back to the clerk, then watched as the guy ambled down the driveway, climbed into the waiting car, and drove away.

Then she wheeled on Joe. "How dare you embarrass me like that!"

"Embarrass you? What the hell did I do to embarrass you?"

She had to hand it to him. He looked totally baffled. "You should've tried a career in acting," she snapped. "I'd almost believe you don't know what you just did."

"I don't," he said.

"He's going to go back to the rental car place and tell everyone that Christine Cannon is too cheap to rent a Corvette."

"You're paranoid. All we were doing was talking about cars."

"Maybe that's all you were doing, but that's not what he heard."

"You've been working in the trenches too long, Chris. You need a breath of fresh air."

"I know the way these things work, Joe. That's all it takes to get a rumor started."

He seemed totally unconcerned. "Who gives a damn?"

"*I* give a damn. I have my reputation to think about."

"Are you that careful with other people's reputations?"

"I never report anything that hasn't been verified by at least two sources."

"Right," he said dryly. "And pigs fly."

She flung open the car door and slid behind the wheel. "Why don't you go back inside and babysit your bride?"

He stood between her and the open door. "How about a lift to town?"

"It's a nice walk," she said. "Might do you some good."

Slade, ubiquitous camera in hand, appeared around the side of the house. "Christine, love!" he called out. "I need a jolt of civilization."

"You're sleeping with him," Joe muttered.

"Shut up!" Christine snapped. "I'm not sleeping with anybody." A statement she immediately regretted when she saw the look of satisfaction in her ex-husband's eyes.

Slade approached the car. "A Buick, love?"

Christine rested her forehead against the steering wheel and resisted the urge to scream. "I'm going into town," she told the photographer, "but if you say one more word about the car, I swear I'll leave you along the side of the road."

Slade dutifully climbed into the backseat.

Joe cupped his hands around his mouth. "Marina!" he yelled. "Get out here. We're going into town."

"He's coming, too?" Slade asked.

"He invited himself," she said in a sour tone of voice. She looked at Joe, who was still blocking the car door. "Why don't you at least let Marina stay here? The girl looked exhausted."

"She goes where I go," Joe said.

Christine tried to ignore the stab of jealousy his words evoked. She had been Joe's equal when they were married, strong and independent and very much in love. "How very caveman of you," she muttered.

"Yeah," said Joe. "We're inseparable."

Christine snapped to attention. It wasn't so much what he said as it was the way he said it. There was nothing of the bridegroom in his tone, nothing even remotely husbandlike. It occurred to her that so far she hadn't detected the slightest spark between them. Why hadn't she realized it before? They didn't steal kisses when they thought no one was looking. They didn't exchange longing glances. They didn't even hold hands. In fact, if they weren't married, she'd swear they didn't even like each other.

Marina appeared in the front door, looking as if she just woke up from a nap. Joe motioned for the girl to hurry, but she ignored him and took her sweet time ambling down the driveway. The shapeless sweater devoured her small figure, and with her hands stuffed into the pockets of her baggy pants she looked almost pathetic. Christine itched to unbraid that mane of mousy brown hair, chop off a few inches, add some highlights—

She almost laughed out loud. She wasn't an expert in post-divorce behavior, but she was reasonably certain ex-wives didn't oversee makeovers for current wives. Even if the current wife was badly in need of some serious beauty advice.

"I have no desire to go into town," Marina announced when she reached the car. "I would prefer to stay here."

"Fine with me," said Christine.

Slade shrugged.

Joe, of course, had other ideas. "In the car," he said. "I'm not leaving you here."

"No," said Marina.

"Listen, kid, you know the—"

"I think your wife's old enough to stay home alone," Christine interrupted.

Marina smiled at her. Christine smiled back.

"I love big black cars," said Marina.

Joe practically shoehorned the girl into the car next to Slade.

"Isn't this special?" Christine said as she backed the car out of the driveway. "Just one big happy family."

"Shut up and drive," said Joe.

Marina stopped dead in the middle of the produce aisle, a look of utter amazement on her face.

"So what's wrong?" Joe asked. "You've never seen a scallion before?"

"Green onions," Marina corrected him automatically. She gazed around like a child at Christmas. "Certainly never so many of them in one place."

Joe angled his shopping cart next to her. "I know you've been in the mountains for a while, but you grew up in London. Don't they have supermarkets?"

"Of course they do." Her look told him exactly what she thought of his level of intelligence. "We had people to do our shopping."

Joe frowned. "Where did I get the idea your father didn't have much money?"

"That idea stems from the fact that my father is a materialistic fascist with the humanitarian instincts of a wild boar."

"Like I said, Ric was rolling in dough."

She really did have that look of disgust down pat. "You needn't be rich to have the moral appetites of a social parasite. My father was raised to believe other men were put on this earth to do his bidding."

"Not doing him much good with his loving daughter, is it?"

She grabbed a zucchini. He wondered how death

by vegetable would look in his obituary. "This would feed a village in my country."

"Great," he said, refusing to rise to the bait. "We'll put you in charge of cooking."

"It's no wonder my father chose you to kidnap me. You are as insensitive and uncaring as he is."

He supposed he could list his credentials, from saving the whales to trying to save her country, but he doubted if she'd hear a word he said. And he also supposed it didn't matter much what she thought of him. He'd been her age once, burning with the fires of righteousness, and he'd watched as one by one those fires were extinguished by life. Sooner or later you stopped tilting at windmills. You chose your battles more carefully, usually with an eye toward spending your time on the battles you might actually win.

A kid like Marina might call it cynicism. Joe preferred to call it bowing to the inevitable. Life came with boundaries, time limits that, the older you got, the harder you found to ignore. So you narrowed your focus and poured all of your energy into one cause and tried not to notice when you fell short of your goal.

But you couldn't understand something like that at nineteen. Nineteen was about impossible dreams, like a love that would last forever.

Christine had been minding her own business, squeezing tomatoes and wondering if the melons were ripe, when Joe and Marina had their confrontation near the zucchini. Joe had never been able to resist a good argument, and it was obvious he and his new wife were at odds about something. Christine drifted toward the bananas, trying to hear what they were saying, but she couldn't make out the words.

She jumped when Slade dropped a pineapple into her cart.

"Trouble in paradise," he observed. "Might be a chance for you, love."

Her face flamed with embarrassment at being caught so obviously eavesdropping. "Don't talk like a fool, Slade. Joe and I are ancient history."

"Right," said Slade. "And that's why you're hanging on their every word."

"I'm a reporter. I find the human condition endlessly fascinating."

Slade was still laughing as he headed toward the gourmet foods aisle.

Marina stormed off in the general direction of the dairy aisle.

Which left Christine and Joe staring at each other across a pyramid of red delicious apples.

"Fancy meeting you here," Christine said breezily.

He grunted something noncommittal.

"I must say you two don't seem like a match made in heaven."

He tossed a bunch of scallions into his shopping cart. "Depends on your idea of heaven."

She rounded the apples and grabbed a bunch of scallions for herself. "I'm a trained professional, Joe. Sooner or later I'll get to the bottom of it."

"Great," he said, "and when you do, let me know. I need a laugh."

He started toward the potatoes with Christine hard on his heels.

"She doesn't like you very much, does she?"

He didn't seem terribly concerned. "She doesn't like anybody very much right now."

"She must miss her family."

No comment from Joe.

"Her friends?"

Still no comment.

"Damn it, Joe, what gives? You two act more like cellmates than newlyweds. You can't tell me this is normal behavior, not after the way we—"

He grabbed her by the wrist. "The way we what, Chris? The way we did nothing but make love for a week straight?" His fingers dug into her flesh. "Or the way we promised we'd be forever?"

"Times change," she said, trying to ignore the painful pressure of his grip. "You should be glad I walked out the way I did. You never would have met Marina."

"Yeah," he said, releasing her abruptly. "I owe you a real debt of gratitude."

"You're better off." She started down the aisle. Much better off.

His voice followed her. "You should've let me decide that, Christine. I think we had a chance."

"Can I help you, miss?"

Marina turned to see a middle-aged man peering at her from behind the meat counter. He wore a white, bloodstained apron, a paper hat, and a big smile.

"No, thank you," she said icily.

"You've been standing there staring at the round steak for the last ten minutes."

"And you have been staring at me staring at the round steak for just as long."

"If you've got any ideas about copping a steak,

forget it," he said, his smile fading. "We got security watching the doors."

She leaned across the counter, eyes flashing angrily. "You have a security force to guard the *meat*?"

"Damn straight, we do. Can't be too careful these days."

"Who on earth would steal a piece of meat?"

The big fat butcher shrugged. "Old people on Social Security, the homeless—"

"The hungry," she broke in. "The only person who would steal food is a person who was hungry."

"Not my problem," he said. "I only work here. You want food, you pay for it. That's how we do business."

"Trust me," said Marina, lifting her chin. "Your precious steaks are safe. I wouldn't think of touching them."

He didn't look as if he believed her. His gaze strayed repeatedly to her clothing as if he was mentally calculating her net worth.

"Americans are too concerned with externals," she said loftily. She could just imagine the way his jowls would drop if she told him she was the daughter of a king.

The butcher gripped his cleaver. "Says who?"

"Didn't you hear me?" She stepped closer. "*I* said that Americans—"

"Are a wonderful group of people, individually and collectively."

Slade lifted her off her feet and spun her around.

"I've been looking all over for you, love." He winked at the butcher. "She's a flirt but harmless."

He put her down near the baked goods. "Politics and supermarkets don't mix, love. The Yanks like to keep these things separate. Someone should have told you smart girls don't argue with men bearing meat cleavers."

"Did you see that man?" she sputtered, all righteous indignation. "How dare he look at me as if I were a bug beneath his shoe!"

"You were right about one thing back there," Slade said, brushing her hair off her face with a brotherly gesture. "Appearances are everything."

"Appalling!"

"Not to me," he said with a smile. "I have my eyes on a pair of Guccis that'll get me the best table in the best restaurants."

"You ask a lot of a pair of shoes."

He put an arm around her shoulders. "Christine and the Boy Scout will be in here for a while. Why don't we take a walk around town? Two kindred souls and all . . ."

She looked up at him and started to laugh. "I should love to see the train station."

4

They rode back to the house on Marlborough Road in silence.

Christine maintained a white-knuckled grip on the steering wheel even though the roads were free of traffic and the weather was sunny and bright. She was a little heavy on the gas pedal for Joe's taste, but he kept his mouth shut. He had enough to worry about. Rear-ending the eighteen-wheeler in front of them seemed like small potatoes compared to the disaster he'd averted at the train station.

He glanced over his shoulder at the co-conspirators in the backseat. Slade and Marina were quiet, probably crushed beneath the weight of Joe's watermelon and case of beer. It wasn't so much the fact that Marina tried to escape that bothered him; it was the question of how much the photographer knew.

Marina wasn't the naive young thing he'd first thought. Not by a long shot. She was as sharp and as cunning as her father, and she wasn't afraid to try a grandstand play if the situation warranted. The Brit bastard was an opportunist of the first order. All in all, a combination made in hell.

The silence was getting on Joe's nerves. He considered the wisdom of switching on the car radio, but the set of Christine's jaw made him decide against it.

Another problem added to the mix. She'd let her emotions get the better of her back there in the produce department, and now she was beating herself up about it. She'd always prided herself on her self-control in public situations. Getting weepy in Shop-Rite wasn't her style.

He found it hard to believe his marriage had her all broken up. She was the one who'd walked out on him, not the other way around. Except for the housing arrangements, there was no reason he could think of why she'd give a goddamn one way or the other about him and Marina.

She had everything she'd ever dreamed of: a high-powered, high-profile career, ass-kissing friends like the Brit photographer, a condo in L.A., a house in the country, and a Manhattan penthouse almost ready to move into. She might have rented a Buick in New Jersey, but he'd bet his favorite pair of jeans she had a Maserati or BMW in her California garage.

You've got it all, Christie, he thought, watching the play of light across her sculpted cheekbones. She had fame, fortune, beauty. Probably had to beat the men off with a stick.

Or maybe she wasn't beating them off at all. Maybe there was some guy back on the coast who had her heart. Some guy she thought about late at night and wished was lying there next to her in the bed she'd shared with Joe.

Not that it mattered to him.

He'd stopped loving Christine the night she walked out the door.

Now if he could just stop wanting her.

The delivery truck from Offices Extra was waiting for Christine when they returned from the supermarket. At last, something she could handle. She'd made an idiot of herself in Shop-Rite, and she was anxious to put that moment of vulnerability as far behind her as she possibly could.

"What about the food?" Slade asked as she leaped from the car.

"Oh, do what you want with it," she said over her shoulder as she headed for the delivery truck. Freeze it, boil it, bake it, stow it. She had more important things on her mind than groceries. Like her desk, her fax, and her brand-new computer.

It took two hours to find just the right spot for her goodies. She had the delivery men set up the computer and printer in the master bedroom, then had them assemble the stand for the fax and answering machine and set it all up in the living room.

"Think you'll get any hot gossip from Hollywood on this thing, Ms. Cannon?" asked one of the men as he plugged in the fax.

"We can hope so," she said, signing for the delivery.

"Man, what a job," he continued, giving Christine her copy of the receipt. "All you gotta do is sit around and wait for other people to do things that you can talk about."

"That's about the size of it," said Christine with forced sweetness. They said you were doing it right when the hard work didn't show. Sometimes she couldn't help wishing she dug ditches for a living, because if she dug ditches people would at least recognize the hard work that went with it.

"A fax machine," Joe said, wandering into the living room with a can of beer in his right hand and a huge sandwich in his left. "Great. I can send my expense account vouchers in to the paper."

Slade ambled out from the kitchen, carrying a bottle of Perrier water and a thickly buttered croissant piled high with raspberry jam. "Christine, love, you don't mind if I add a message to your answering tape, do you? I gave out this number to my associates."

"What about you?" Christine asked Marina, who was curled in the window seat with a cup of tea, a slice of Jarlsberg, and an apple. "I suppose you want to learn WordPerfect so you can type up letters home from my computer."

"I am already proficient in three different word-processing programs," said Marina to everyone's astonishment, "and would appreciate the opportunity to use your computer when you aren't busy with it."

Something in Christine softened. "We'll work something out," she said.

Again the quick smile that lit the girl's plain face then vanished before you had a chance to appreciate it.

"Thank you," said Marina.

"You're quite welcome," said Christine.

Joe looked over at Slade, who appeared to be as puzzled as her ex-husband. "Female bonding," said Joe. "Is it great or what?"

Christine glared at Joe, who managed to look incongruously innocent. Slade snapped a quick series of shots of them glaring and looking innocent, and Christine turned away from the all-seeing eye of his camera. For an instant she wondered if this was how Princess Di felt when the British press published the transcripts of her infamous "Squidgy" conversations. Hunted. Exposed. Vulnerable.

"Feels lousy, doesn't it?"

She jumped at the sound of Joe's voice low in her ear. "I don't know what you're talking about."

"The hell you don't. Makes you think twice about the tabloids, doesn't it?"

"It doesn't make me think about anything except why I'm letting you stay in this house with me."

"It's known as joint ownership," he drawled. "Think about that."

For the next week Christine did little else but think about the house. It was big but not big enough for four adults with different agendas.

Marina slept a lot and kept to herself. She ate little and spoke even less, although Christine had the distinct feeling her silence was more deliberate than the result of shyness. At times Christine forgot Marina was even there, and then she would see the girl moving down the hallway toward the bedroom she shared with Joe, and the pain was as intense as it had been when Marina announced herself as Joe's wife.

Terri Lyons called from her weekend home in the Hamptons.

"You're *what*?!" Terri shrieked when Christine broke the news of their slightly bizarre living arrangements to her friend. "Have you lost your mind, girl?"

"I know it sounds strange," Christine said, "living here with Joe and his new wife, but we're all adults. We can handle it."

"Dr. Joyce Brothers couldn't handle a situation like that. Throw them out," Terri ordered. "Rumor has it they still have hotels in New Jersey. Tell them to find one."

"We'll talk about it at lunch," Christine had said, lowering her voice. "You can read me the riot act in person."

"At the very least, get rid of Slade," Terri persisted. "Unless you *want* to find yourself on the front page of the *National Enquirer*. I can see it now: 'I Was Christine Cannon's Love Slave.'"

Christine had laughed at the absurdity of the statement. "Trust me, Terri. I'll explain it all to you at lunch."

Slade wasn't the problem.

Joe was. It didn't matter whether or not they were in the same room. She could feel his presence through the walls, coming up through the floorboards, sizzling through the very air she breathed. She tried to avoid him whenever possible. She ate breakfast on the patio, lunch on the porch, and dinner in her room. Not that it did any good. She found herself wondering about him at every turn.

On the third afternoon of their communal living experience, the housekeeper arrived. "Not a minute too soon," said Mrs. Cusumano, reaching for the mop.

Of course, Mrs. Cusumano found Joe utterly charming. Most women did. She fresh-squeezed his orange juice each morning and made sure his coffee cup was filled. Slade muttered something about preferential treatment, but Mrs. Cusumano turned a deaf ear to his protests. Joe became her special project and, by default, so did Marina. While Joe doted on the attention, Marina was having none of it. "How can you allow that old woman to wait on you hand

and foot?" Christine had heard Marina ask Joe. "Because she enjoys her work," was all that he said.

Marina didn't understand, but Christine did. Joe was one of those lucky people who found value in the most menial jobs. Plumbers. Waitresses. Every occupation on God's earth . . . except Christine's.

She took the car into Manhattan for an interview one day in an attempt to escape the currents flowing through the house, but the trip was a disaster. Slade hitched a ride with her and got into an altercation with one of the window washers who hung around the exit of the Lincoln Tunnel, looking to make a quick buck with spit and a rag, and they ended up explaining the situation to a cop who had better things to do.

"Next time keep your mouth shut," Christine said through gritted teeth as she angled the Buick up the ramp that led to the indoor parking lot. "We could've ended up in jail."

"Bloody fascist," Slade muttered.

"The cop or the window washer?" she asked with an arch of her brow. "You fought with both of them."

"Aren't we critical today, love. Are the Boy Scout and his bouncing baby bride wearing out their welcome, or is this PMS talking?"

She didn't answer. The truth was she couldn't. Maybe it was the crush of traffic that had set her nerves on edge or the fact that she was already late for her first appointment. Whatever it was, it made it difficult to take Slade's endless comments about Joe and Marina.

And it would make it impossible to explain the whole thing to Terri Lyons when they met for lunch later in the day. Christine and Terri had met as undergraduates. Terri had been in school on an affirmative-action scholarship and feeling combative about it. Christine had been there on scholarship as well, and felt apologetic. Neither one fit in with the privileged types who roamed the campus.

"Why does everyone find it necessary to tell me they have a black friend?" Terri had complained one night over pizza. "Maybe I should announce I have a blond friend."

Christine, the blond friend in question, tossed a mushroom in Terri's direction. "They want to let you know how liberal they are. That's better than being asked why you talk so funny. I'm from Nevada, not Mars."

"You do talk funny," Terri had said. "I think you've spent too much time talking to horses, cowgirl."

Their friendship had been born of their differences, but it grew with the knowledge that in all the ways that mattered, they were very much the same. They'd both shared a fierce ambition, a desire for family, and the belief that they'd been destined by the gods to have it all.

The fact that they were now both divorced didn't escape either one of them. But there was a difference. Terri had two beautiful daughters while Christine had no one at all.

"Okay," Terri said hours later as they settled down on their banquette at the Russian Tea Room. "Admit it. Our English friend is driving you nuts."

"No," she said, nodding her thanks when the Cossack-clad waiter handed her a menu. "It's not

Slade. It's the whole damn situation that's getting on my nerves."

Terri ignored her own menu. Her brown eyes were riveted on Christine with the same intensity she brought to her news stories. "So get out of the situation. You don't have to go back to Hackettstown. I have plenty of room. Come back to Long Island with me. You can stay until your place is ready."

For an instant Christine was tempted. "Are the girls with you for the summer?"

"Celina leaves for Maine next week to see her father. Ayeesha's with me in body only." Terri rolled her eyes. "She's nursing a broken heart, stays in her room playing music and writing poetry." She sighed. "I'd forgotten what sixteen was like."

"It seems like yesterday she was crying over her braces and wondering if she'd ever need a bra."

"It *was* yesterday, Chris. That's the scary part. Life keeps moving faster and faster. You really notice it when you have kids."

An uncomfortable silence descended upon the table.

"Most people have kids," Christine said to her friend. "I know that. I understand that."

"But it still hurts, doesn't it?"

"It still hurts." Terri had shared Christine's excitement when she'd discovered she was pregnant, and Terri had been there to help Joe take apart the nursery after the miscarriage. The bond between the two women was wide and deep.

Terri offered up a sly grin. "How about I send Ayeesha to stay with you for a few days? A touch of teenage angst might be just what the four of you need."

"We have enough teenage angst, thank you very much. Joe's wife isn't exactly a cheerful sort."

"Whoa, girl! Back up a minute." Terri leaned across the table. "How old is the blushing bride anyway?"

Christine cursed herself for bringing up the subject in the first place. "Nineteen or so."

"Male menopause," Terri said sagely. "Happens to the best of them sooner or later. I did a story on it last year at the Hartford station. Highest-rated story during November sweeps. Every woman in Connecticut recognized the symptoms."

"Joe's not old enough for male menopause," Christine said, laughing despite herself. "Besides, I don't think it's like that between them."

"Not like what?"

"I don't know." Christine fumbled around, trying to find a way to put her hunch into words. "There's just no heat between them. No spark." She leaned back against the banquette and shrugged. "Maybe it's just wishful thinking."

"That's it, isn't it? That's why you're letting Slade stay with you."

"Slade's staying because he's being paid to stay." She heard the way her voice had gone all tight, but she couldn't help it. "He's doing the photos for the *Vanity Fair* story."

"Uh-huh," said Terri. "And I suppose there isn't another photographer in New York who could do the job. Annie Leibowitz maybe or Jill Krementz."

"He's good, Ter. You were the first one to realize how good."

Terri wasn't about to be thrown off track. "Joe thinks you're sleeping with him, doesn't he?"

Christine felt her cheeks turn the color of the decor. "I have no idea what Joe thinks."

"This is me you're talking to, Chris, not one of your production assistants. The ex-husband comes back to town with a nubile young bride. Why not let him think you're hitting the sheets with a hot Brit photographer?"

She suppressed a grin. "I've told Joe there's nothing between Slade and me."

"Right," said Terri. "Then prayed he didn't believe a word you said."

Christine started to laugh. "I told him the truth. It isn't my fault he didn't believe me."

Terri laughed, too, but her concern was obvious. "I don't want to see you get hurt, Chris. We both know Slade's done work for the tabloids. What if he decides to make a few bucks talking about your ménage à quatre?"

"Never happen," said Christine, wishing she could knock on wood. "Selling to the tabloids isn't going to break him into the big time. *Vanity Fair* can do that, and he's too close to grabbing the brass ring to risk it."

"I hope you're right."

"I *am* right," Christine said. "Besides, why should I let Joe and Marina screw up my plans? That's my house, too, and I'm not going to be driven out of it because he decided to come back."

The waiter came to take their orders, and after he left they found themselves talking about everything but Joe and Marina. They covered politics while they waited for their lunch, race relations while they ate, then dissected the current state of the fashion industry while they dawdled over coffee.

"God, I've missed you," Christine said as she sipped the rich brew. "I'm glad we'll be at the same station again." She didn't make friends easily, and Terri was as good a friend as she'd ever had. Someone Christine could turn to when the going got tough and know she was there in her corner, ready to help.

"Slight difference this time, girl. I'm still scrambling for stories. This summer you *are* the story."

It was after three o'clock when they left the restaurant.

"Summer in New York," Christine said with a groan as the heat and humidity slapped her in the face. "How could I have forgotten?"

"The offer still holds," Terri said as they started walking in the general direction of Fifth Avenue. "Sea breezes, cool nights, a room with a view, and no ex-husbands for miles around."

"A tempting offer," Christine said, "but I'm staying where I am. I got there first. Let Joe and the little missus find somewhere else to go."

"Brilliant logic," said Terri. "Celina used it once." She shot Christine a sideways glance. "I think she was in fourth grade at the time."

"Very funny. I'm from Nevada," she said, "and we're very territorial. I've staked my claim. Let him move out."

They walked together for a few blocks, right past Terri's apartment building.

"You're not going home?" Christine asked.

Terri shook her head. "I thought I'd say hello to our little shutterbug."

"Great," Christine mumbled. "Just what I need."

As it turned out, she needn't have worried. Slade wasn't waiting for her at the parking garage. Terri hung around for a half hour, then had to make her train back to the Hamptons.

"Be careful," Terri said as the two women hugged good-bye. "Slade's only allegiance is to himself. Don't forget that."

Christine waited another hour for Slade to show, then finally gave up and drove back home, where she found him lounging on the front porch, cold beer in one hand and the Hasselblad in the other.

"Take one picture and you're a dead man," she warned as she climbed out of the car. Her linen blazer looked as if she'd slept in it, and her makeup hadn't survived an afternoon in Manhattan's humidity, both of which would look great on the cover of *Vanity Fair*.

"Say cheese, love." He snapped two pictures. "Real life and all that."

She sank down on the top step and leaned back against the railing. "If I wasn't so tired, I'd brain you for making me wait at that garage."

He smacked the heel of his hand to his forehead in a parody of dismay. "Sorry, Christine love. There wasn't much going on, so I thought I'd get back here."

"Right," she said, stifling a yawn. "Like you thought there'd be more going on around here."

He favored her with a cat-that-ate-the-canary smile.

"My marriage is off limits, Slade," she said evenly.

"Something to hide?"

"Joe's not a celebrity. He doesn't deserve having his life dragged through the pages of one of your tabloid rags."

"You wound me, love. You should know there's a

fine line between news and gossip." His smile widened. "The only difference between tabloid gossip and prime-time dish is the paycheck of the reporter."

Christine stormed into the house. What on earth was the matter with everyone? Slade, of all people, had no business slinging barbs in her direction. So far the man had made his living hanging out in front of trendy night spots and sleazy dives, hoping to see a celebrity with his or her metaphorical pants down. He was a hell of a lot more talented than his résumé might indicate, but that talent wouldn't have a chance to develop if he didn't get his attitude under control.

It was Joe's influence, she thought as she shed her city clothes in her bedroom. She and Slade had had no problems at all before her ex-husband showed up on the scene. Why, they'd understood each other perfectly well. They shared ambition and pragmatism, and she was hopeful that the *Vanity Fair* assignment would help launch the young Brit's career into orbit. Grimly she yanked on her favorite jeans and old NYU T-shirt. Another day like today and she'd launch Slade into orbit with her bare hands.

Joe's distaste for her career path was no secret. She could just imagine him holding forth for Marina and Slade, regaling them with stories from their salad days when they both believed they could change the world. Was it her fault that she found success in Hollywood instead of Beirut or Bosnia? She didn't see anyone knocking down Joe's door to give him his own prime-time television show.

She was on her way into the kitchen to tell him that when the telephone rang.

"For God's sake, Christie, where in hell have you been?"

"Hello to you, too, Natalie." Her sister had never been big on the amenities. "I take it you called before?"

"Three times," Natalie boomed. "Don't you listen to your messages?"

Christine took a deep breath and counted to ten. "I just walked in the door, Nat. What's up?"

"I'm about to spay an Abyssinian, so I only have a minute. Daddy's sick, and we need you here."

Christine sat down on the edge of the sofa. Leave it to her veterinarian sister to mention the cat before their father. "What do you mean, Daddy's sick?"

"We don't think it's anything serious, but chest pains always—"

"Chest pains? When did he start having chest pains?"

"Well, maybe I shouldn't have put it quite that way. Ma's afraid he might get chest pains if he goes on worryin' the way he's been doing."

"Did they run a cardiogram? A CAT scan? Does he need angioplasty?"

"Right now he doesn't need anything except to have his family around him at the party."

"I could kill you, Natalie!" Her own heart would take hours to return to its normal rhythm.

"It would do him a world of good to see you."

Christine felt the tug of home. "With all of you around him, I don't think he has time to miss me."

"You're his favorite, Christie." The tug of home grew stronger. "You know it won't be the same for the folks without you there."

"Don't lay a guilt trip on me, Nat. Daddy understands why I'm not coming for their anniversary party even if you—"

"What anniversary party?" Joe, munching on a handful of nacho chips, appeared in the kitchen doorway.

"None of your business," she said to him. Then, "This isn't a good time, Nat."

Joe brightened. "Is that Dr. Nat, the best vet in Nevada?"

Natalie said, "That isn't Joe's voice I hear, is it?"

Joe picked up the kitchen extension. "Hey, Nat! How goes it?"

"Joe! It *is* you! My God, boy, where have you been hiding yourself? It's been a dog's age since I heard your voice."

"Spent a few months in Europe—"

"Not in—"

"Yeah, right in the middle of the whole mess."

They were like an old married couple, finishing each other's sentences, laughing at each other's jokes. Christine found it patently disgusting.

"I hate to interrupt the two of you," she broke in, "but Natalie and I were having a discussion before you butted in, Joseph."

"Joseph," repeated Natalie with a laugh. "She's ticked off."

"So what else is new?" asked Joe.

"I'd be happy to tell you what's new with Joe," Christine said into the phone. "Why don't you tell Nat about the little woman?"

"What was that, Christie?" Natalie asked. "The connection's fuzzy."

"So what about that anniversary party?" Joe

asked. Laughing, he looked over at her. Christine wanted to leap for his throat.

"Mom and Daddy's fiftieth," Nat gushed. "Lord, Joe, I know they'd love to see you again. You were just like one of their own." Her tone grew downright coy. "Maybe you and Christie could—"

"Don't you have a cat to neuter?" Christine asked.

"Good grief! Spanky Baldwin's under and prepped. Gotta run. Now, you make sure to come, Joe. You know our door's always open."

"Give me the dates, and you're on," he said.

"August first," said Natalie, "but the earlier you can get yourself out here, the happier we'll be."

"Don't even think about it," Christine said to Joe after they broke the connection. "You're not going to my parents' anniversary party."

"You got a problem with it?" Joe asked, all mock innocence.

"You bet I've got a problem," Christine snapped as she stormed into the kitchen. "Doesn't this situation strike you as a tad weird?"

"Yeah," said Joe, "now that you mention it, it does. Why the hell aren't you going to your parents' anniversary party?"

"God knows I'd love to go, but with the show starting up and all, I just can't." Delivered with just the right touch of regret.

"Bullshit."

She busied herself at the sink, rinsing out an already clean juice glass. If you're going to reinvent yourself, she thought, make sure you don't have an ex-husband around to remind you of who you really are. "They understand," she said after a moment, hazarding a glance in his direction. "Not that this is any business of yours."

"I love your folks," he said with disarming honesty. "Losing them was almost as hard as losing you."

"Damn it, Joe!" She leaned against the sink. "I wish you wouldn't say things like that."

"The truth doesn't go away just because you won't acknowledge it's there."

"Thanks for the philosophical moment of the day."

"How long are you going to keep running, Chris?" he asked, moving closer to where she stood. "Don't you get tired of dodging your own life?"

"You've been watching too many talk shows," she said, aiming for cool disregard. "We're not all looking to get in touch with our inner child."

"Gotta hand it to you, lady. You've got flip down cold. Must make you a sensation on the Beverly Hills party circuit."

"It's part of my job."

"Sure it is," he said, starting to laugh. "Spago, the Monkey Bar, guys in Italian loafers with no socks—"

Christine poked him in the chest. "You're really getting on my nerves," she said, voice rising. "Keep your career comments to yourself."

He didn't stop laughing. "You and your seven-figure bank account should be laughing me right out of the room. Why do you give a damn what I think of your career?"

"Because you're obnoxious and annoying and you delight in making me crazy."

"Maybe it's because you know I'm right."

"Don't flatter yourself, Joe."

"Maybe it's because you know you can do more."

"You're really pushing it." She turned for the door.

"Good going, Chris. I'm glad to know some things never change. You still walk out whenever things cut too close to the bone."

"This is a ridiculous conversation," she said over her shoulder. "Go to my parents' anniversary party. Drink yourself blind. Ask them to adopt you. I just don't give a damn."

He grabbed her by the shoulders and spun her around to face him. "Son of a bitch. People don't live forever. One day you're going to wake up, Sam and Nonie'll will be gone, and you'll wonder why you let so much time slip away."

"Save your sermons for your wife. I don't have to listen to them."

"When the hell are you going to stop thinking about yourself and start thinking about what that party means to them?"

"Damn it, Joe. Let go of me!"

She struggled to break free, but he held her fast. They were close . . . too close. His intensity was overwhelming. He had the clear blue eyes of a dreamer and the determined jaw of a realist. She'd always envied him the ability to dream. It was one of the things she'd lost along the way. "Let me go, Joe," she said, more softly this time. "There's no point to this."

Joe started to speak, but the words caught in his throat. Beneath the sleek blond hair, behind the tinted contacts, the girl he'd fallen in love with on the steps of the NYU library was still there. And she still had the power to touch his heart in the way no other woman before or after ever had.

"Chris."

She met his eyes. He saw defiance—and he saw something else.

His grip changed as his anger veered toward a darker and more dangerous emotion. Six years hadn't dulled the pain, and they certainly hadn't erased the desire. There was no force on earth that could have stopped him from pulling her up against his body and claiming her mouth with his.

She tasted of lost dreams, angry and sweet and achingly familiar. Once upon a time she'd been the other half of his heart. She'd been his soulmate and his lightning rod, and when she walked out on him she'd taken away the sun. Everything he did, everything he was, everything he'd wanted to be—it was all somehow for Christine.

She wanted to hate him.

He had no right to touch her, no right to hold her that way, no right to leave her breathless with desire so fierce she knew she'd die if he stopped kissing her.

And she had no right to let him.

Feelings she'd believed were part of her past welled up inside her heart, and in an instant she was standing in the summer rain, laughing at the look on Joe's face when she said *yes*.

And she was in the bright Nevada sun, holding Joe's hand, while her father toasted the newlyweds and talked about the golden future that was theirs for the taking.

And she was standing in the doorway to their bedroom about to tell her husband that miracles sometimes happened long after you'd given up hope—

Anger sharpened his kiss, and regret shadowed her response. Nothing had changed . . . and everything had. She knew the swell of his lower lip, the smoothness of his teeth, the smell of his skin, and the sound he made in the back of his throat as he drew her in even closer. And she knew, beyond reason, that she wanted him.

Stop it now, Christine, her rational mind warned. *There's no future in this. . . .* They had too much extra baggage, too much pain between them to find a way to start again. But maybe, her heart whispered. Maybe there's a way. *Right,* said the voice of sanity. *Maybe if he weren't married to someone else—*

She placed her hands against his chest and pushed him away with what remained of her self-control. "This can't happen again," she said, her voice trembling with emotion. "I won't allow it."

"This has nothing to do with Marina, if that's what you're thinking."

"I'm *not* thinking," she blurted out. "If I was thinking I would never have let you kiss me."

"Your problem is you think too goddamn much. Just go with what you feel."

"If I go with what I feel, we'll end up in bed together."

"Would that be so bad?"

"If I have to remind you that you're a newlywed, then you're not half the man I thought you were."

"Things aren't always what they seem, Chris."

"They never are when a man's trying to get you into bed."

"Is that what you think this is all about?"

"If things aren't always what they seem," she countered, "why don't you explain them to me?"

His reluctance cut right through her. So much for fantasies. "Chris, I—"

"Don't bother," she said, aware of the ache in the center of her chest. "I get the message. A quick one for old time's sake, then it's back to the wife. You're not the first man to try that, Joe, and you won't be the last. I guess I just expected more from you."

Not Slade.

This was exactly what he'd expected from Joe. But Christine? Now, that was another story. The fact that she didn't land a right hook on the guy's nose told Slade everything he needed to know.

It wasn't over. Not by a long shot.

He heard Marina's footsteps in the hallway, and he stepped in front of her.

"Move, please," she said in that annoying tone of voice she used with everyone but Christine.

"You don't want to go in there, love." He placed a hand on her fragile shoulder.

She shook it off and sent him a vile look. "Move," she said again. "I wish to prepare my dinner."

"Not right now."

"I am trained in the martial arts," she said, her tiny face deadly serious, "and I would not hesitate to use my skills on you."

"You're a charmer, all right," Slade said, amused despite himself. "But I'm telling you to stay out of the kitchen for a few minutes."

She tried to dart around him, but he was too fast for her. She tilted her head and listened to the murmur of voices from the kitchen. "Christine and Joseph are in there, aren't they?"

Slade said nothing, just continued to block Marina's entrance.

"Fighting?" she asked.

He shrugged.

An odd look passed across her face. "Sometimes I wonder—" She shook her head. "It does not matter."

She suspected something. He could see it in her eyes. There were two ways he could play this. He could let her burst in on the guilty parties and watch as all hell broke loose. Or he could let the suspense build another week or two while he did a little digging on the boy reporter and his plain young bride.

He didn't have a chance to decide. The door crashed against the wall with a bang, and Christine rushed past them as if they weren't even there. She was angry, yes, but there was more on her lovely face than that. Her cheeks were flushed, her eyes danced with a dangerous light. *Alive,* he thought with a shock. Christine looked wildly, passionately alive in a way he'd never seen her before, and it didn't take a genius to figure out the reason.

The Boy Scout glanced over toward where Slade was standing in the doorway. "What are you looking at?"

Slade grinned. *Guilty bastard,* he thought with some satisfaction. Two wives under one roof. Maybe even in one bed. The possibilities boggled the mind. And with a little luck they'd fatten his bank account before the summer was over.

5

Marina stormed into the kitchen, hungry for blood.

Preferably her husband's.

"What did you do to Christine?" she demanded, blocking his exit. "Why can't you treat her in a civil fashion?"

"Mind your own business, kid," he said in a tone of voice clearly meant to cow a lesser woman.

"Answer me!" she snapped with all the authority at her command. Now and again she was grateful for the arrogance that came with being born royal. "Christine is a fine woman. She deserves to be treated with respect."

"That works two ways," said Joe.

"She was your wife. That entitles her to your respect."

"She walked out on me," he snapped back. "I don't owe her a damn thing."

"And I am your present wife. What do you owe me?"

"Your safety," he said. "It's what I promised your father."

"Your loyalty to my father is admirable," she said dryly, "but it is ill placed."

He gestured toward the backyard. "Sun's still shining. Why don't you go outside and play?"

"I am not surprised Christine found it impossible to remain married to you. The wonder is only that she married you at all."

He walked to the refrigerator and pulled out a bottle of beer and popped the top with a flourish. He didn't explain his behavior or apologize, and Marina's anger escalated another notch.

Dinner forgotten, she swept from the room, brushing past Slade in the hallway. In her opinion the world would have been better served if her father had let the avalanche bury Joseph McMurphy. She could see her husband now, slowly vanishing beneath a mountain of snow until the last lock of hair disappeared. The thought pleased her no end. He was a dreadful person. Christine was doing her best to accommodate him, and still all he did was peck away at her, morning, noon, and night.

He deserved to have lost Christine. He was rough and disagreeable while Christine was polite and considerate—at least, she was when not talking to her ex-husband. Of course, Christine was much more interested in fancy clothes and success than Joe was, but for once Marina was willing to overlook such signs of weakness.

The truth was Marina felt at war within herself, drawn toward a woman who represented everything she devoutly disliked. Was she as big a fool as most people who yearned for all they could not have, or was it just that she was more lonely and afraid than she cared to admit?

Marina pushed open the front door and stepped out into the blue light of dusk. A soft breeze drifted from the west, carrying with it the scent of roses and clover. She used to dream of being alone with Zee on a gentle evening like this, when they could forget the sorrows of the world they knew and pretend they were just a man and a woman in love.

She sank down onto the top porch step and wrapped her arms about her knees. Once she had whispered her fantasy to Zee, but he had looked at her as if she'd spoken in tongues. He only understood the greater good, the distant goal of freedom. Moonlight and roses meant little to him, and she'd been willing to accept what he could offer her and not ask for more.

Yet on a night like this it was hard not to think of starry skies and promises in the dark. She had few illusions about herself. She was as plain as her mother had been beautiful. Even as a little girl she'd recognized that whatever magic it was that made a female irresistible to the male, that magic had passed her by. When she met Zee, it no longer seemed to matter. He saw something in her that went beyond physical beauty, and in his arms she'd finally discovered the purpose to her life.

She closed her eyes and tried to imagine Christine and Joseph when they were young and newly in love, but no matter how hard she tried, she couldn't bring the picture into focus. It was hard to imagine Christine ever being shy or unsure of herself. And the thought of her hanging on to Joseph's every word made Marina laugh out loud. She was the kind of woman to whom men paid court. The kind of woman Marina would never be.

The door behind her opened, then softly closed. The scent of Christine's perfume mingled with the roses, then the step creaked gently as she sat down next to Marina.

"Did you eat dinner?" she asked.

Marina shook her head. "No, I did not."

"I don't know about you, but I don't feel like cooking." Christine jingled her car keys. "I'm heading out for pizza. You're welcome to come along."

Marina hesitated. Joseph had warned her that there was danger afoot from the opposition, danger that could extend across the ocean to America, but it was hard to believe anything bad could happen in this sleepy New Jersey town. Still there was his disagreeable temper to consider—

"No problem," said Christine, rising to her feet. "Just thought I'd ask."

"I love pizza," Marina blurted, "but Joseph won't let me leave the house without him."

If the girl had announced she was Satan's bride, Christine would not have been more surprised. "You're joking, aren't you?"

Marina's expression closed in upon itself. "I can say no more."

"You're not his property. This is America—you can do anything you want, whenever you want."

"There are reasons," she said mysteriously.

Those reasons were exactly what intrigued Christine. "Fine," she said, feigning indifference. "If you're content to be chattel, I understand." She started toward the car. *Come on, girl. You're not going to just sit there, are you?*

Marina beat her to the Buick. It took all of Christine's self-control to hide her smile. The girl was predictable, but there was an odd charm to her that touched Christine despite herself.

"Buckle up," she said as she started the car. She couldn't help noticing that she sounded like Marina's mother instead of her predecessor. *You're getting old, Cannon. What happened to the green-eyed monster?*

"I refuse to be shackled," said Marina, disdaining the seat belt.

"Don't we all. I'm afraid it's the law."

The girl refused again.

"You can always go back inside and eat dinner with the men."

Paydirt. Marina buckled her seat belt. Smiling, Christine backed the Buick down the driveway and headed into town and Angelo's Pizzeria.

"So tell me," Christine said as she and Marina took a table near the window, "was it love at first sight?" Conversation in the car had been less than scintillating, so she'd opted for the more direct approach.

Marina tilted her chin in a decidedly imperious fashion. "I do not discuss personal matters with strangers."

"I do," said Christine with her most disarming smile. The same smile that had brought Sylvester Stallone, Elizabeth Taylor, and the Princess of Wales to their collective knees. *"Tell me anything,"* her smile said. *"Anything at all."* The fact that she withheld more than she revealed was what kept her on top. She leaned forward across the Formica table and lowered her voice conspiratorially. "You must admit this is a very unusual situation, Marina. I've never shared a house with an ex-husband and his new bride before."

That brought a faint smile from Marina. "And I have never been married before."

"That gives us something in common, wouldn't you say?"

"Besides Joseph?"

Christine broke into a grin. "You have a sense of humor. I wasn't sure you did."

The smile narrowed. "Americans care too much about such things. A sense of humor is a luxury many can ill afford."

At last, the opening she was looking for. "And what is it you care about, Marina?"

"I care about the things that matter."

"Such as?"

"Freedom."

"From oppressive husbands?"

"From fear."

Christine's curiosity kicked into overdrive. "You strike me as the kind of woman who isn't afraid of much." There was an air of strength about the girl that had nothing at all to do with size.

"I am afraid of you."

Christine choked on her Diet Coke. "I'm not interested in your husband, if that's what you're afraid of." She knew she had no business kissing Joe. And she'd swear on a stack of Bibles that it wouldn't happen again.

"Joseph is not the issue." Marina waved her hand in the air in a gesture more sophisticated than Christine might have expected. "You are everything I dislike," she said bluntly, "and yet I find I admire you."

"And that frightens you?"

"Yes," said Marina. "You are a perfect example of wretched excess, and I have spent the last few years seeking to—" She stopped abruptly.

"Seeking to what?" Christine urged.

Marina shook her head. "It no longer matters."

Christine leaned back in her chair. "If you're afraid of insulting me, don't worry. I have a remarkably thick skin." She hadn't gotten as far as she had in tabloid journalism without taking a few sharp knocks.

"You lead a useless life," the girl observed, "yet you are most successful at it. I should like to dismiss you as a social parasite, but instead I find myself wishing I could be more like you."

"You don't mince words, do you?" Christine muttered.

Marina's brown eyes widened. "I do not mean to insult you."

"Right," said Christine with a shake of her head. "And I don't want to be around when you do."

To her astonishment Marina leaned forward and placed a hand on Christine's arm. "You are beautiful," she said simply, "and the world is different for women like you."

Christine struggled for words. "It takes a lot of hard work to make me look this way."

"Perhaps," said Marina, "but all the hard work in the world would not yield the same results for me."

"You underestimate the value of cosmetics."

"I am plain," Marina said. "You cannot understand how that is."

The counter clerk brought over their pizza and placed it in the center of the table. The two women directed their attention toward the food. Christine ate automatically, barely aware of the sharp tang of spicy pepperoni or pungent tomato sauce. Marina devoured her food with enthusiasm that bordered on the sensual.

Christine took another bite of pizza and studied the girl. Joe was a highly physical man, the kind who set off fireworks in a woman without even trying. Was it possible the newlyweds were setting off those fireworks every night and Christine was too blind to see it? She made her living noticing things like fireworks and sparks and chemistry. If there was so much as the slightest glimmer between Joe and Marina, Christine's radar would be on red alert.

No, this marriage wasn't about sex. Not entirely. And it certainly wasn't about love. Whatever it was that had brought them together was a mystery to Christine, but if she had her way, it wouldn't remain a mystery much longer.

Joe fixed himself a sandwich, gulped down a can of Bud, and listened to Slade curse at the stove.

"What the hell are you doing?" he asked as the Brit kicked the oven door.

"Bloody bangers spattered. Nearly blinded me."

Joe peered into the frying pan from a respectful distance. "Sausages," he said, stepping back. "We call 'em sausages here."

"Bloody bastards is what I call them." Slade stabbed a fork into one and winced as hot fat bounced off his arm.

Joe watched as Slade pushed the sausages to one side, then cracked two eggs into the pan where they floated in an inch of fat. "Those things'll kill you."

Slade grinned. "Want some?"

"Yeah," said Joe. "Actually I do."

Slade cracked a couple more eggs into the pan, and

the two men watched as the sausage fat bubbled and hissed.

"Disgusting," said Joe.

"Stomach-turning," Slade agreed.

"I'll ask Chris and Marina if they want to join us. Can't hog all that good cholesterol, can we?"

"Good idea," said Slade, reaching for more eggs.

Joe started off down the hall. He'd been trying to come up with a way to approach Christine. Kissing her had been a goddamn stupid idea, but there had been something irresistible about the moment, and he'd never known how to turn away from her. If he'd been trying to prove himself immune to her charms, he'd failed miserably. She still did it for him, still fired his blood and his imagination and made him believe happy endings were possible. Which, in retrospect, was a dangerous thing to believe. Bad food seemed as good a reason as any to approach her. She'd get off a few tart remarks, he'd fire back a few retorts, and things would get back to normal. Or whatever normal was, considering the situation.

And they'd never mention the kiss in the kitchen again.

He stopped in front of the bedroom he shared with Marina. "Hey, kid," he said, rapping his knuckles against the closed door. "How about some food?"

No answer.

He pushed open the door. The bed was neatly made. The window was open to the evening breezes. His laptop computer rested on top of the dresser where he'd left it. Everything was as it should be, so why the bite of apprehension as he moved down the hallway toward the room he'd once shared with

Christine? The kid was probably sitting outside on the porch, sulking over Yankee excess.

Christine's door was ajar. He leaned inside. "Chris?" No answer there, either. He stepped into the room, trying to ignore the faint scent of Bal a Versailles that lingered in the air. A pale pink nightshirt of some silky material lay draped across the foot of the bed. His fingertips grazed the soft fabric, and it didn't take a leap of imagination to imagine the supple curves of Christine's body lending their shape to the formless garment.

"Pathetic bastard," he muttered, turning away. He had a wife he didn't want, and he wanted the wife he no longer had. And neither one of them seemed to be anywhere around.

Apprehension nipped harder. He raced through the hall, through the living room, and out the front door. Christine's car was missing, and he didn't need to be Sherlock Holmes to know the Merry Wives of Hackettstown were together.

"Son of a bitch! I told her not to—" He caught himself just in time. Slade stood in the open doorway, spatula in hand.

"Cardiac special being served. Where's the little women?"

Careful, McMurphy. Things were bad enough. He didn't need to give the photographer any more ammunition. "Beats the hell out of me."

"Food's getting cold."

He pulled the car keys from his jeans pocket. "I'll be back." He started for his rented Lexus with the Brit bastard right on his tail.

"Don't you have some eggs to fry?" he asked as he slid behind the wheel.

Slade tossed the spatula on the dashboard and fastened his seat belt.

"I'm not taking any passengers."

"I'm not a passenger," said Slade. "I'm on assignment."

"Why don't you go back to picking through garbage cans like your other friends at the *Enquirer*?" The engine started on his second try.

"Why bother?" Slade countered as they roared off down the street. "Seems to me I've got the best story in town unfolding right under my nose. Teenage bride. Sexy ex-wife. Hot-tempered reporter—"

"Go to hell," Joe muttered.

Slade just laughed and settled back for the ride.

Marina polished off the last slice of pizza, then glanced longingly at the calzones.

"You're kidding, aren't you?" Christine asked. "Nobody could eat a calzone after four slices of pizza."

"I do not know what possessed me," said Marina with a sheepish grin.

"Look, I was only teasing about the calzone. If you're still hungry, we can—"

Marina raised her hand. "This is unlike me. I am not prone toward excess."

"Don't apologize for having an appetite, Marina. It's not like you have to worry about calories." As it was, Christine had had to pull off most of the mozzarella and promise to use the rented treadmill for an hour before bedtime.

The girl started to say something, then stopped herself.

"Marina? What were you going to say?"

"It is nothing." Color stained her cheeks. "A simple observation."

"I'd like to hear it." Actually she'd like to hear anything that would shed some light on the girl's Odd Couple marriage. All she had were bits and pieces that added up to next to nothing at all. Marina was beginning to let down her guard, if only a little bit, and Christine was known for her patience in pursuit of a juicy story. Unfortunately Joe chose that moment to storm through the door with Slade close behind. Her ex-husband looked loaded for bear while Slade looked much too happy for Christine's taste.

Joe saw them immediately and was at their table in the blink of an eye. "What the hell are you doing here?" he demanded of Marina.

"It's a free country, Joe," Christine broke in. The word *Neanderthal* sprang to mind. "She's your wife, not your possession."

He met her eyes. She knew that look. He wasn't about to give an inch. "This has nothing to do with you."

"The hell it doesn't. I'm the one who brought her here."

He gestured toward the tomato sauce stains on the girl's sweater. "Obviously against her will," he said dryly. "You probably force-fed her the pepperoni."

"She was hungry," Christine said. "She wanted to eat. Since when is that a crime?"

"She can eat at home."

"Marina said you forbade her to leave the house."

His head swiveled toward Marina, who met his gaze calmly. "That isn't what I said to you."

"Yes," said Marina. "That is exactly what you said."

Christine was not generous in her triumph. "You might be pigheaded, but you were never an autocrat. What gives, Joe?"

"Jesus Christ!" he exploded. "I was worried about my wife. Is that a crime?"

He really cares about her, Christine thought with utter certainty. Whatever the reasons for their marriage, whatever passion their union might lack, he was telling the truth about this. A pain gripped her chest, tighter and tighter, until she found it difficult to breathe around the realization that he and Marina shared something that was beyond her comprehension. *I wish you were sleeping with her. I wish you two were setting off fireworks like the Fourth of July.* Sexual combustibility was something she understood. That was a battle she knew how to fight. Joe was a crusader at heart, champion of life's lost and lonely souls, and he obviously saw something in Marina he'd never found in her. This deeper connection between her ex-husband and his new wife made her feel lost in a way she'd never been before. And more alone than she would have imagined possible.

Joe felt it like a punch to his gut. Christine's loneliness, her fear, the empty feeling deep inside that nothing could fill. He felt it and understood it and wanted to pull her into his arms and make promises that weren't his to make. But his wife was looking up at him with curious brown eyes, and the photographer was standing next to him adding up the clues, and he'd never been any good at sentiment and sweet talk and all the things women loved to hear. Which was probably one of the reasons Christine had walked out in the first place.

He could find the words to explain the pain of a hungry child to a world who didn't give a damn about small sorrows, but he couldn't find the words to tell the woman he'd loved and lost that things weren't exactly the way they seemed.

6

By the next morning Christine knew she had to get out of New Jersey as soon as possible. It was a big house but nowhere near big enough for the emotions battling inside her heart.

She'd lain awake the entire night alternately telling herself Joe meant nothing to her and then listening for the soft sounds of laughter from the bedroom he shared with his new wife.

When the sun came up and she hadn't heard so much as a sigh, she was too exhausted to be relieved.

"You can't go on like this," she said to her reflection in the mirror. Dark circles ringed her eyes, her hair looked like a rat's nest, and pillow creases zigzagged across her right cheek. Clay, her makeup artist, would have a field day with the number two base and porcelain concealer.

This vacation was supposed to rejuvenate her, not turn her into a hag. In less than three weeks she'd have to climb aboard the publicity bandwagon and begin a series of TV appearances designed to promote her new show. If she looked like this, she'd scare the viewers all the way back to radio.

As far as she could tell, she had two choices. She could stay here in Hackettstown in the most bizarre domestic arrangement since *Bob & Carol & Ted &*

Alice. Or she could go home for her parents' anniversary. Either way she risked a broken heart. It was just a question of degree.

"Coffee," she said to the old lady in the mirror. "First coffee, then decisions."

It was a little after seven. Mrs. Cusumano was working half days so she could be with her pregnant daughter in the afternoons. The smell of coffee floated down the hallway, and Christine greedily inhaled the caffeine. Trendy Kona and elegant espresso had never given her the same pure satisfaction that plain old Maxwell House provided. Especially at the crack of dawn.

When she was a little girl, she'd loved the early morning. She came from a family of early risers, but she'd been the earliest riser of them all. There was something so pure, so sweet, about first light that she'd wanted to be able to welcome the sun with open arms and embrace the day close to her heart with all the youthful enthusiasm at her command.

She smiled at the memory of cool mornings and the sweet sound of birdsong from high in the cottonwood trees. Invariably her dad Sam would find her sitting out by the stable, watching as the sun gilded the mountaintops. "Great time for dreamin'," he liked to say as he sat down beside her. He'd already put in a full day's work before dawn and had another full day's worth ahead of him, but somehow he always found time for Christine. Her hopes, her dreams . . . her fears. He understood her in a way nobody else ever had, except for Joe, and she had wanted so much to make him proud. If only—

No. She wasn't going to think about any of it. Not the tug of home, not the longing she felt each time she looked at Joe, not the inescapable fact that all the success in the world wasn't going to make her loneliness go away.

She hurried down the hallway, past the closed bedroom doors. Joe and his child bride would still be asleep. Slade had borrowed her car last night and gone off to check out some of the Manhattan clubs, looking to create photo ops for publicity-hungry celebs. She'd heard him come home an hour ago and doubted anyone would see him until noon.

Wrong again.

She found the lanky photographer standing in the center of the kitchen, breathing fire like Saint George's dragon. Mrs. Cusumano, breathing fire herself, stood by the door, poised for flight.

"I quit!" the woman declared when she saw Christine appear in the doorway. "I don't work for people who think I'm a thief."

"A thief?" A major upheaval before breakfast. She felt as if she were back on the ranch. "Who's calling whom a thief?"

Slade turned some of the trouble in her direction. "Three lenses are missing, not to mention the gold coins I picked up in San Juan."

"Have you seen his room lately?" Mrs. Cusumano demanded. "You could lose Macy's basement in there and not know it."

"Coffee," Christine said, heading for the coffee-maker on the counter. She poured herself a cup and took a long sip. "What makes you think Mrs. Cusumano has anything to do with the missing lenses, Slade?"

"Who else's it going to be?" he asked, his tone laced with fury. "The Boy Scout isn't a likely choice, and Lolita married herself a meal ticket. Figure it out."

"Maybe you misplaced them. You've never been known for your organizational skills."

"At least I'm not anal-retentive."

"Better anal-retentive than a slob," Christine shot back. "At least I know where my things are."

"Don't bet on it, love," said Slade. "Didn't you say you couldn't find your gold hoop earrings and the diamond bracelet the network gave you when you signed the contract?"

"I probably left them in the vault."

"You don't sound all that certain, Christine love."

"I'm not," she admitted, "but that doesn't mean Mrs. Cusumano swiped them."

"I want a lawyer," Mrs. Cusumano announced, marching across the room to the telephone. "I know my rights."

Christine took another gulp of coffee and wished it were Scotch. "Nobody's accusing you of anything, Mrs. Cusumano."

"He is," the woman said, pointing an index finger at Slade. "And I gotta say, Ms. Cannon, you don't look all that sure yourself."

"Sit down," Christine said, motioning the house-keeper toward a chair. "Let's try to talk this out. There has to be a reasonable explanation for these disappearances." She'd been able to get an interview with Hillary Clinton, for God's sake. Certainly she could handle a domestic crisis.

"You just don't want me to call my lawyer," said Mrs. Cusumano.

"That's right," Christine agreed, pouring the

woman a cup of coffee. "No one is accusing you of anything. We all need to talk."

Joe chose that moment to barge into the room. "Where the hell's my watch?" he roared.

Christine buried her face in her hands. "Mrs. Cusumano," she said with a sigh, "maybe you should make that phone call after all."

Marina shrank back deeper into the shadows and listened as the righteously angry housekeeper telephoned her attorney. This wasn't exactly the way she'd had it planned. Joseph hadn't worn his watch in days. She'd figured he wouldn't notice its absence before she found a way to turn it into cash for Zee's cause. Wouldn't you know her annoying husband would decide he suddenly needed to know the exact time.

As if time mattered. The days were running into each other in a boringly predictable pattern. Such empty, meaningless lives. Slade did little but follow Christine around, snapping pictures of her coming out of the loo or typing at her computer, and when he wasn't doing that he was lying on the sofa, staring at the telly.

Christine apparently spent much of her time thinking about famous people, trying to figure out their deep, dark secrets so she could expose them to the public. If there was a more useless occupation in this world, Marina couldn't imagine what it was.

And Joseph wasn't any better. Oh, her father had told her that Joseph was a man of conviction and purpose, that he would give his heart and soul to the cause of freedom against oppression, but thus far she'd seen no evidence of that conviction. He was ill-mannered and bad-tempered, going out of his way to snipe at Christine at every possible opportunity.

Last night she had told him for the hundredth time to leave his ex-wife alone, but he had laughed and said, "Mind your own business, kid," then retreated to his pallet on the floor of their bedroom.

The tension in that house was appalling. Sometimes Marina felt more hunted there in New Jersey than she ever had up in the mountains with Zee. At least with Zee the danger was recognizable: a bullet, a bomb, something you could see.

Here the danger manifested itself more subtly. Her own temper was growing shorter with each day that passed. She found herself alternating between fear and loneliness and everything in between. There were times when she was tempted to walk out that front door and somehow make her way back to Zee, where she belonged. But there were reasons why she couldn't, compelling reasons that not even her rebellious heart could ignore.

And so she stayed on, trying to convince herself that the booty she was amassing in her closet hiding place would make it all worthwhile. How she would manage to get away long enough to convert it into cash was another story entirely. She never seemed to have a moment to herself. Someone was always peering around corners or lurking in the shadows, same as she was doing right now.

In the kitchen Mrs. Cusumano was wailing into the telephone. "You gotta help me, Sol! I didn't do anything, but I know they're gonna call the police."

And then Christine's low voice, "Maybe we *should* call the police, Slade—"

You must do something, Marina thought, moving

quietly toward the bedroom. The housekeeper was one of the oppressed, doomed to go through life cleaning up the messes of the privileged. Never had Marina intended for that good woman to bear the responsibility for Marina's own actions.

She slipped into the room she shared with Joseph, then eased open the trapdoor in the closet ceiling. She considered the array of stolen treasure. Joseph's watch and one of the lenses. That should appease everyone. Christine's bracelet twinkled up at her, and for a moment Marina felt a pang of conscience.

Despite herself, she liked Christine. Christine was like the diamonds sparkling in the bracelet, brilliant and beautiful and admirably strong—even if she had chosen to waste her gifts on a frivolous and worthless profession.

Still, Christine had a queen's ransom in jewelry tucked away in the upper right drawer of her dresser. The loss of these pieces represented an inconvenience, nothing more.

Somehow Marina had the feeling that Christine would miss the plain band of gold Marina had passed over more than all the diamonds in the world. When she'd asked Joseph why he and Christine had ended their marriage, he had shrugged and muttered, "She ended it."

Which, considering his miserable personality, came as no surprise to Marina.

Still, watching Christine and Joe together, seeing the way Christine seemed to glow from the inside out whenever her ex-husband was in the room, made Marina wonder if Christine was still in love with the man Marina had married.

"You are welcome to him," she murmured as she

headed toward the kitchen with the camera lens and Joseph's watch clutched in her right hand.

If she could find a way to stop being Joseph's wife, she would do it in a minute. Then she could return to Zee, where she belonged, Christine and Joseph could remarry each other, and Slade could take snaps of everybody, sell them to those dreadful American tabloid newspapers like the ones she'd seen in London, and everyone would be happy.

They thought they were so sophisticated, so shrewd when it came to the world, its dangers and delights, but they knew nothing at all. They had no idea—no idea at all—how little it took to render a person invisible in the eyes of those who kept the world in motion.

Stripped of their identities, torn away from everyone and everything that mattered, Marina had seen doctors and lawyers, philosophers and teachers, reduced to moving through the back alleys in the dark of night in search of food for their families. How fragile was the network of people and places and things that gave you a place in the world and an identity.

But that was something these people would never understand . . . if they were lucky.

"I think she stole them," Christine said to Joe. They were standing on the back porch talking about Marina.

Joe gestured over his shoulder toward the kitchen, where Marina sat at the kitchen table under Slade's baleful eye. "Mrs. Cusumano?"

"Your wife."

"You've got to be kidding."

"Try me," said Christine. "I can buy the excuse about your watch being in the bedcovers, but Slade's telephoto lens? That's pushing it."

Joe had his own suspicions about his wife's honesty, but he wasn't about to let on to Ms. Sherlock Holmes here. "What would she do with a beat-up Seiko and a camera lens?"

Christine's eyes glittered the way they always did when she smelled a juicy story. He remembered a time when her eyes glittered like that for him. "There's still the question of my missing jewelry."

"Your safety deposit box in L.A."

"Maybe, maybe not. I think I brought those pieces with me."

"You don't know for sure."

"I'll bet I did."

"Let's say you're right and you brought the jewelry. It could be our pal Glade."

"Impossible. His lens was stolen."

Joe threw his hands in the air. "I thought you read Grafton and Parker. Maybe he was throwing us off the track."

"That's ridiculous," she said, bristling.

"So's blaming Marina."

"Maybe you should raise her allowance. Then she wouldn't have to resort to petty theft. Either way we've lost Mrs. Cusumano."

"Don't blame me," said Joe, grinning. "I'm the one she liked."

"You're on your own," Christine said to Slade as she threw some jeans and T-shirts into a suitcase. "I'll be back in a week or two."

"You're not leaving me with the honeymooners

from hell," Slade said. "I'm coming with you, love."

"It's a family thing, Slade. You'd be bored to tears."

"New Jersey hasn't been a veritable fountain of delights. I'll take my chances on Nevada."

"If you're thinking Las Vegas, you're going to be disappointed."

He aimed his Hasselblad in her direction and took a quick series of candid shots. "Nothing about you disappoints me, Christine love. Besides, I've always wanted to see you decked out in cowgirl gear. Might make a nice cover for *Vanity Fair*."

She laughed despite her foul mood. "I think you've seen a few too many Westerns."

"Yee-hah!" said Slade, twirling the Hasselblad over his head like a lariat.

He was an opportunist, Terri had said. *Be careful.* But she felt so alone, so empty, that the thought of returning home by herself made her feel like weeping.

"The party," she said after a moment. "You could take pictures."

His brow arched. "Loving portraits of family and friends?"

"It's that or New Jersey."

Slade peered through an imaginary camera. "Say cheese, love."

When Joe and Marina went off to the mall to buy the girl something decent to wear, Christine took the opportunity to escape. She tossed her suitcases into the trunk of the Buick, waited impatiently for Slade to get his act together, then left for Newark Airport. She'd rather spend a few hours watching jumbo jets take off and land than spend another minute in her ex-husband's company.

Slade amused himself for a few hours by staking out International Arrivals while Christine returned phone calls, one of which was to Terri.

"You're certifiable, girlfriend," Terri stated flatly. "Why don't you just throw yourself in front of an airbus while you're at it? You'll save time."

"That's what I love about you," said Christine. "You never blow things out of proportion."

"Trust me," said Terri. "You're courting disaster."

"Isn't that a bit of an overstatement, Ter?"

"We're talking blind ambition here. Slade's a throwback to the eighties. He doesn't play by the rules, Christine." Terri's laugh was harsh. "Slade doesn't even realize there *are* rules."

Her friend's words lingered with Christine despite her best efforts to banish them from her mind. Terri tended to view life with dead-eyed honesty, a trait that carried over from her professional life to her personal one.

You're wrong this time, Terri, Christine thought as she opened her laptop and got down to business. *I know exactly what I'm doing.*

Time passed swiftly. In truth it was probably the first full day's work she'd put in since she left Los Angeles, and it felt good to be reminded that there were still parts of her life that remained firmly under her control.

She treated Slade to a boozy dinner at one of the members-only clubs to which she belonged, and by the time they boarded the evening flight to Las Vegas, she was feeling relaxed and pleased with herself for turning a difficult situation into something relatively pleasant.

"Good evening, Ms. Cannon," said the smiling flight attendant. "Glad to have you with us. I'm looking forward to your new show this fall."

Christine smiled back at the man. Celebrity did have its benefits. "Good flying weather tonight?" she asked as he showed her and Slade to their seats.

"The best," said the attendant, casting a curious look at Slade, who had claimed the window seat.

"Champagne, my man," Slade ordered with an aristocratic wave of his hand. "And keep it flowing."

"He's harmless," said Christine as she tossed her makeup kit in the overhead compartment. "I'll keep him under control."

The flight attendant, ever polite, smiled even wider, then retreated.

"There's a movie, isn't there?" Slade demanded, thumbing through the in-flight magazine. "I missed *Groundhog Day* when it first came out."

"Count your blessings. If I were you I'd get some sleep. We have a long drive ahead of us when we reach Las Vegas."

In fact, why wait until they were airborne? Christine adjusted her seat belt, placed the tiny white pillow behind her head, and closed her eyes. She was vaguely aware of the bustle around her, the loud whispers from boarding passengers when they recognized her, but she let it all wash over her.

You're running away, Cannon.

That's right, she thought. That's exactly what she was doing.

What're you afraid of? It's not like you're in love with him, is it?

Absolutely not. Besides, he's married.

You don't believe that's a real marriage, do you?

"Shut up," she mumbled under her breath. The last thing she needed was a heated discussion between her head and her heart.

Running away from danger was the sensible thing to do. If you were lucky, that was the first thing you learned on the road to adulthood. She was a sensible woman. She saw danger and she did something about it.

She ran for her life.

The voice came to her from her dreams. "Fancy meeting you here."

A sizzle began deep inside her chest and radiated outward. She didn't want to feel this way, so painfully, completely alive. It was an impossible situation, one that could only lead to heartache.

"Tell me I'm dreaming," she said, forcing her voice to remain light and vaguely annoyed. "You're not really here."

"You didn't think you'd get away without me, did you?"

She opened her eyes and looked up at Joe, who stood blocking the aisle. "Very funny," she said. "You've had your fun. Now stop grinning like an idiot and get off this plane."

He waved his boarding pass at her. "Got me a ticket, Christie." The perfect parody of the western twang she'd had when they first met. The louse.

"You're not serious, are you?"

He glanced at his ticket. "Eleven hundred dollars sounds pretty serious to me."

"You're flying first class?"

His expression was one of utter innocence. The rat. "You wound me."

"This isn't your usual style, Joe."

His look of innocence sharpened, and she knew she was in for it. "You think you're the only one who can afford it?"

Her cheeks burned from the sudden rush of blood. "I didn't know saving the world paid so well these days."

". . . an unconscionable waste of money," came Marina's voice from somewhere behind Joe. "And the segregation of the lavatories according to wealth is an affront to humanity."

Christine gestured over Joe's shoulder. "You sure she won't hijack the plane and hold us for ransom? There might be some starving splinter group somewhere who needs our hard-earned money."

"Don't worry. They checked her out back at the gate."

Despite herself, Christine started to laugh. "She set off the metal detector?"

"Not only that, she got the matron in a headlock when the woman came at her with the wand."

"I wish I'd been there to see it." Marina was a feisty little thing. Christine had no doubt she gave as good as she got. "What set off the alarm?"

Joe shrugged. "Some coin she carries around for luck."

Christine must have looked unconvinced.

"Don't worry," said Joe. "I'll order her a Happy Meal and tuck her in for the night."

". . . a vile example of capitalism run rampant . . ." Amazing how well the girl's voice carried.

"As far as I'm concerned, she's the only one on this

plane with half a brain," Christine muttered. "Like I said before, since when do you travel first class, Joe? You were always smarter than that."

"You're not the only one making money these days." He sank down into the aisle seat opposite hers. "Figured it was time to see how the other half lives."

Suddenly the light dawned. "No empty seats in coach, huh?"

Joe grinned. "Can't put anything over on you investigative journalists, can I?"

She threw a copy of *Time* at him and told him to shut up.

Marina, glowering like a thunderhead, climbed over Joe's legs and slumped into her window seat. She wore a shapeless navy sweater and beige trousers. The clothes were obviously new, but they managed to uphold the girl's commitment to a lack of style. "I am here under duress," she announced to one and all.

"Great," said Joe, flipping open the magazine. "We'll keep that in mind."

Marina flashed him an evil look that made Christine smile. "You're my husband, not my father. I will not be patronized."

"The sound of anarchy," said a boozy Slade. "Music to my ears."

"The sound of Heineken," Joe observed. "Are we lucky or what?"

The door slammed shut, and Christine heard the clunk of apparatus as the ground crew prepared to separate the plane from the jetway. *It's not too late*, a voice whispered. *There's still time to get out.* As long as the plane was on the ground, there was a chance to escape.

"Why are you doing this?" Christine asked as the plane rolled slowly away from the terminal. "You're not part of the family any longer. What do you care about my parents' anniversary?" They were divorced, damn it. Didn't he understand the rules? Divorced people divided up the silverware and the bank accounts. They didn't fight for custody of the in-laws.

"If you have to ask, Christie, then you'll never understand the answer."

"Oh, what in hell is that supposed to mean?" she snapped. "I hate it when you talk in riddles." *And don't call me Christie.* Christie was another person, younger and more hopeful, a girl who believed she could bend the world to suit her will. The one who believed in happy endings.

"What about you?" he countered. "Yesterday you swore you wouldn't be caught dead on the ranch. Why the sudden change of heart?"

"None of your business."

"A sudden burst of filial affection?"

"I love my parents," she said, voice breaking. He of all people should understand. Why was he making her explain the obvious? "Don't you dare imply otherwise."

"If you love them so much, why were you staying away?"

"I don't owe you any explanations."

"Maybe not, but you owe them a few."

"That's their business . . . and mine."

He leaned across the aisle, focusing those clear blue eyes on her until she couldn't look away or breathe or even think. "Sooner or later even you have to stop running, Christine Cannon."

"Welcome aboard Continental flight one twenty-seven, nonstop from Newark to Las Vegas," said the smiling flight attendant. "Now, if you'll watch the screen we have some important safety information. . . ."

Do you know how to keep my heart from breaking? Christine wondered. Or was it already too late for that?

7

Slade fell asleep before they reached cruising altitude. Marina struggled to stay awake, but she nodded off as dinner was being served.

"Great champagne," said Joe, polishing off his second glass. "They're on bread and water back there in coach."

"How'd you like the shrimp cocktail?" Christine asked.

"Skimpy."

"You ate four of them," she pointed out. Slade's, Marina's, hers, and his. "The flight attendant thought you were going for the *Guinness Book of World Records*."

"You got any more of those peanuts? I'm down to my last two packets."

She shook her head and continued thumbing through the latest issue of *Newsweek*. "You realize you should be a very fat man. You eat enough for an army and don't gain a pound."

"Still bugs you, doesn't it?"

"It doesn't bug me at all."

"The hell it doesn't."

"Don't be ridiculous. Why would I care how much you eat?"

"You noticed."

"Natural phenomena are hard to ignore, Joe. Your appetite is legendary."

He bummed a few packets of peanuts from the flight attendant. "Remember what Sam used to say?" He deepened his voice to a ranch-style boom. "'Son, keep eatin' like that and one day you're gonna wake up with a big fat belly and the heartburn to match.'"

Christine laughed. "Your fortieth birthday," she said, remembering. It seemed a hundred light-years away.

"Think Sam's prediction's going to come true?"

"Fishing for compliments?"

"When in doubt, opt for the direct approach."

"Ask Marina," Christine said, an edge to her voice. "Never too soon to train a girl in the wifely art of tending the male ego."

He inclined his head in Slade's direction. "From what I saw, ol' Glade does his fair share of butt kissing."

"I'll have you know *Slade* is an equal opportunity butt kisser."

"You like him, don't you?"

She nodded. "Yeah, I do."

"He's not your type."

"I know that." She shot him a sidelong glance. "Neither were you."

"True," he said. "If memory serves, you liked the scrawny intellectual type."

She suppressed a grin. "In my experience, muscles and brain power were mutually exclusive."

He flexed his left bicep. "I have muscles."

"I rest my case."

"Following that line of reasoning, Flash over there must be Einstein's rival."

"You muscle-bound types have a nasty streak, don't you?"

"You never did tell me if you were sleeping with him."

She allowed herself a Mona Lisa smile. "And I never will."

"That means you're sleeping with him."

"No, it doesn't."

"So you're not sleeping with him."

"I didn't say that."

"You can do better than him."

"That assumes I'm doing something in the first place."

"You're celibate?"

"You're pushing, Joe. Back off."

"Don't worry," he said. "You're not going to find this on the front page of the *New York Post*."

Next to him Marina stirred. She looked painfully young when she slept, all angles and soft murmurs. Christine felt like a rat for kissing Joe the other morning in the kitchen, and she responded the only way she knew how. "She sleeps like a baby. Careful she doesn't suck her thumb. You wouldn't want her to ruin her smile."

"Not bad," Joe said. "Not terribly original, but still not bad."

"So when did you start cruising grade schools for your girlfriends?"

He tossed an empty peanut wrapper in her direction. "She's older than she looks."

"She'd have to be, or you'd be behind bars." She took a deep breath and pushed on. It was like some demon had taken possession of her sense of fair play.

She wanted all of the gruesome, sordid details and she wanted them now. "Where did you meet her?"

He took a moment to answer, and she thought her heart would thud through her chest. "We were introduced."

"While you were in Europe?"

"What difference does that make?"

He was being protective. Somehow that made her feel very sad and very, very old. "Who introduced you, her babysitter?"

Another moment. "Her father."

"Condoned cradle-robbing. They really are civilized on the other side of the pond, aren't they?" She cleared her throat. She'd gone this far; she might as well see it through to the bitter end. "Love at first sight?"

"I wouldn't say that."

"What would you say?"

"Give it a rest, Chris," he warned. "This isn't any of your business."

"Afraid it might tarnish your Boy Scout image?" He didn't respond. She didn't blame him. Bitchy, jealous comments from a lonely ex-wife didn't deserve a response. *You're losing it, Cannon,* she thought. *He might end up thinking you still care.*

Somewhere over Indiana the crew lowered the cabin lights and started the movie. Joe had no particular interest in watching Bill Murray struggle with a time-warped groundhog, so he declined the headphones. He also had no particular interest in sleep, but that seemed a safer bet than continuing the verbal skirmish Christine had initiated. Her comments had gotten under his skin, but not for the reason she thought. *I'd like to tell you the whole story, Christie,* he thought, glancing at her across the darkened aisle.

Despite the divorce, despite the anger, he'd always had the feeling that there was something of forever about the two of them, and judging by her reaction to his marriage to Marina, he suspected Christine had felt the same way.

None of which made sense considering the way she'd walked out on him. No explanations. No apologies. And, until now, he would've figured no regrets. Truth was, he was no longer so sure about that last one. She had everything she'd ever wanted back in their salad days. Fame, fortune, beauty— even if those damn turquoise contracts were pushing the edge of the envelope. He'd liked her blue-gray eyes the way they were.

But Christine had never been satisfied with anything the way it was. She was always striving for something bigger and better, a perfection that didn't exist anywhere except in her dreams. Was it any wonder when trouble knocked on their door she was the one who went packing?

"Can I get you anything, sir?" The flight attendant hovered over him, all paid solicitude. "Champagne?"

"Coffee," Joe said. "Black, one sugar."

The flight attendant disappeared back into the galley.

Joe leaned back in his seat and closed his eyes. He measured his progress in daily increments. In the past six years he'd drowned too many sorrows in too many bottles and never managed to come to grips with the basic problem: what he would do if he ever saw Christine again. For a long time murder had been at the top of the list of possibilities. The anger was still there and the pain, but there was something else, something he had neither wanted nor expected.

Desire.

Fierce. Hot. Undeniable.

Just thinking about her was enough to bring him to the brink. Those long thoroughbred legs. That telegenic face. The formidable intelligence that had kept him scrambling to keep up with her during their marriage. And all of it was combined with an astounding appetite for life that used to take his breath away.

Used to, he thought. Past tense. That was the key.

The flight attendant presented the coffee with a flourish, but Joe barely noticed. For the last two weeks he'd been trying to figure out what was different about Christine, and the answer had been right there in front of him the whole damn time.

The spark was gone. The flash of brilliant energy that had characterized the woman he'd married was hidden behind turquoise lenses and highlighted hair and a sense of vulnerability that was at odds with her glossy high profile. And the thing of it was, Christine was so damn good at playing the role that he might have missed it entirely if he hadn't watched her sleep.

Not even Christine could maintain a facade when her defenses were down. Her face was softer, the line of her jaw less stubborn. For a moment he saw the girl he'd fallen in love with a long time ago, the one he'd been willing to spend his life working to deserve. He could almost believe they were back at Columbia, arguing about ethics while they lay naked in bed under a pile of quilts Christine's mother had sent them for Christmas.

But not even Joe could maintain the fantasy for long. Christine had a new life, new friends, and a career that was taking her all the way to the top. No matter how hard he tried, he couldn't find a place in that scenario for an ex-husband. Especially one who still believed there were more important things in life than celebrity.

Christine had changed, but apparently he was the same horse's ass he'd been ten years ago, fighting a losing battle in his quest to save the world.

All things considered, maybe the avalanche should've won.

Despite the surge of excitement she'd felt at the sight of the neon lights glittering along the Strip as they made their approach, Christine was overwhelmed by the certainty that she was heading toward total disaster.

I should've told them, she thought as she gathered up her carry-on luggage. How hard would it have been to call her father and let him know that Joe was bringing a brand-new wife to the anniversary party? She'd heard the sound of hearts and flowers in her sister Nat's voice, and she could just imagine her parents' excitement at the thought of possible reconciliation between their youngest daughter and their favorite in-law.

"It's not going to happen," she muttered as she headed for the jetway. "Not in this lifetime."

"What's not going to happen?" Slade asked, moving into the aisle behind her.

"Don't ask," she said darkly. "My parents don't know about Marina. For all I know, they're planning a party for Joe and me."

"Should they be?"

"Get real. He has a wife, in case you haven't noticed."

"What if he hadn't? Would you be in the running?"

"Heaven forbid. The only thing I'm concerned about is my parents' reaction." She considered the wisdom of hitting him in the head with her cosmetics case. "My parents believe in happy endings. They were crushed when we broke up." Especially her father. You didn't make it to your fiftieth wedding anniversary by not believing in things like "for better and for worse" and "until death us do part."

"Nothing lasts," Slade said. "Why should your marriage be any different?"

Exactly what Christine had been asking herself since the day she walked out the door. But that didn't make the situation any easier. In a few hours she'd be pulling into the drive that led across the ranch's south property and up toward the main house where her entire family awaited their arrival. What on earth was she going to do when they all came running toward the car, eager to embrace the prodigal daughter and the triumphant ex-son-in-law?

"Christie!" her father would boom, arms open wide. "Let me hug you, girl." Her nose would be pressed up against his chambray shirt, and she'd smell the familiar blend of sun and soap and leather that belonged to her father and nobody else. "You're too damned thin," he'd continue. "Need some of your ma's good food to fatten you up."

And then it would happen. Her father would see Joe. He'd let out a whoop of delight and just before he had a chance to grab his ex-son-in-law in a bear hug, Marina would climb from the car and fix Sam with one of her solemn looks; Christine would wonder why on earth she'd ever thought it vital to leave New Jersey.

They met up with Marina and Joe near a bank of slot machines that were manned by a guy in a Kansas City baseball cap. Marina watched, obviously astonished, as the guy popped quarters in each of the four machines, then pulled the arms in quick succession.

"Welcome to Las Vegas," Christine said with a quick smile. "Check your inhibitions at the door."

"Yes!" roared the slot machine man as a one-armed bandit set off bells and whistles, followed by the distinctive sound of silver coins tumbling into the metal tray.

"Disgusting," said Marina, shaking her head. "An appalling waste of money."

"Anybody have a quarter?" Slade asked, searching his pockets for a twenty-five-cent piece.

Joe was already feeding change into a machine called Triple Cherry.

Christine, feeling more disgruntled by the second, dropped her bags at his feet. "Watch these. I'll go get the keys to the rental car." He grunted something, and she poked him in the ribs. "Joe! Did you hear me?"

"I will watch them," said Marina.

"Thank you," said Christine, wishing she didn't like the girl. "I think those two have lost what's left of their minds."

"I am disappointed in Joseph. I thought he was a man of higher ideals."

"Life's filled with disappointments," Christine said, turning away. "Get used to it."

*   *   *

Marina sat down atop Joseph's overnight bag, rested her chin in her hands, and watched as her husband and Slade argued over a slot machine called the Midas Touch. She hadn't meant to upset Christine with talk of Joseph. How deep the wounds must be for such a simple remark to evoke so cynical a response.

All signs pointed to the fact that the divorce *must* have been Joseph's fault. Why else would Christine's pain still be so close to the surface? He must have done something so terrible, so unforgivable, that his and Christine's marriage fell apart.

Turning that notion around in her mind, she examined it from every angle. Of course it was his fault. On more than one occasion Marina had caught Christine looking at Joe, and there had been no mistaking the look in her beautiful turquoise eyes. *She still loves him,* Marina thought as tears welled. Whatever it was that had happened between them, it had been enough to destroy their marriage, but it hadn't destroyed the love.

The idea made her shiver. It wasn't supposed to be that way. Love was supposed to transcend the worst trials fate could throw in its path. She and Zee were separated by distance and a forced marriage, and yet nothing about her feelings for him had changed. She loved him more now than she had before, and she would go on loving him until the day she died.

There was only one thing she could think of that could make her turn away from Zee. Another woman. Someone who would love him and listen to him and hold him in the heart of the night when the world was cold. Someone who would do all of the things she'd done for Zee and more. . . .

Had Joe found another woman? She tried to imagine a woman who could compete with Christine, but failed. Christine was blond and beautiful and rich and successful. She was all things Americans held dear—and certainly everything a man could possibly want in a woman.

Still the marriage had failed. What was it her mother used to say as she primped in front of the mirror? *Even champagne grows tiresome if you have it every day.* Was it possible to be too perfect? God knew that thought was comforting. . . .

"Marina?"

She stared at the sound of Christine's voice, surprised to find herself sitting on her husband's suitcase in the middle of the Las Vegas airport.

"Are you okay?"

"I am fine," she said, collecting herself once more.

Christine crouched down until her eyes were level with Marina's. "You were crying."

"I wasn't." The woman was too perceptive by half. "Why would you say that?"

Christine touched her forefinger to Marina's cheek but said nothing. Marina felt as if Christine could see inside her heart. She wanted to look away, but somehow she couldn't. The expression in Christine's eyes was so warm, so understanding, that Marina wished she could lay her head against the older woman's shoulder and tell her everything.

She's up to something, Joe thought as they climbed aboard the airport shuttle that would take them to the rental car. What the hell had Christine been doing, hugging his wife to her bosom as if they were sisters? He'd damn near had a stroke when he saw them with their heads pressed together, whispering the way women did when they thought they were putting something over on a man.

Maybe they were putting something over on him. Maybe Marina told her everything and Christine was busy planning the best way to break the story. He could see it now. Christine, all coiffed and made up and dressed in a Donna Karan or whatever the hell she wore these days, smiling into the big red eye of the camera. "Welcome to the premiere of "'The Christine Cannon Show,'" she'd say, batting her enhanced baby blues. "Royalty! Tragedy! Sex! We have it all for you tonight."

Jesus. The thought was enough to make him break out in hives. Look at the two of them, sitting together across the aisle. Marina was scowling at him as usual. Christine was looking right through him. He knew that expression. Whenever she had a particularly knotty puzzle to unravel, her brows drew together, her lids lowered to half-mast, and her chin visibly grew more stubborn than usual.

Oh, yeah. She knew something, all right. The question was: What exactly did she know? Asking her would tip his hand. Not asking her could be lethal. He glanced back toward his current wife, whose scowl had darkened into something downright murderous. Gimme a break.

"You got a problem?" he asked. The last time someone looked at him that way, they'd been fighting a to-the-death battle over a parking spot near the U.N.

Marina shook her head, but that rotten expression didn't waver.

"She doesn't like you, mate," Slade observed. "I wonder why that is."

"You married?" Joe asked.

Sledge feigned a shudder. "Not me."

"Never?"

"Never."

"Ask me that question again after you've tried it. Then we'll talk."

Facile but effective. With a little luck he'd be divorced next time the photographer asked.

It occurred to Slade that he could call the Boy Scout's bluff, but power was ten percent information and ninety percent how you used it. And this wasn't the time to use it.

"I'll drive," Joe said to Christine after they tossed the luggage into the trunk. "You get some sleep."

"Thanks, but no," she said. "I'll drive."

"You're beat. You'll fall asleep behind the wheel."

"I slept on the plane," she said through clenched teeth. "I rented the car. I'll drive it."

"Bloody hell," said Slade from his perch on the front fender. "Give me the keys, and I'll drive the bleedin' car."

Joe ignored him. Christine told him to shut up.

"It's none of your business," Marina said to him. They were sitting on the front fender. "This is between the two of them."

He looked at the girl and laughed. "They're bickering about who gets to drive. You sound as if you think it's a bloody lovers' quarrel."

"Don't be ridiculous."

There was something about her tone of voice that told him he was cutting close to the heart of it. "Shouldn't you be over there scratching Christine's eyes out or whatever it is you women like to do to each other?"

"They share a past," said Marina calmly. "It has nothing to do with me."

"He's your husband," Slade reminded her. Not that he believed that meant much to either one of them.

"I know who he is."

"You're not jealous?"

She shook her head. "Not in the slightest."

"You should be."

She considered him carefully. "Is there something you wish to tell me, Slade?" Where the hell had she acquired that air of self-possession? It was hard to believe she was only nineteen. There were times when he would swear she was the oldest of the four of them.

He supposed he could tell her about the kiss Christine and Joe had shared in the kitchen, but the time wasn't right for that, either. "I get carsick," he said instead. "You might want to sit up front."

"I get carsick, too," said Marina with a half smile. "Perhaps we belong together."

They looked at each other and started to laugh. From another woman that statement might have been wrapped around an invitation, but from Marina he knew it was nothing more than it seemed. Which was fine with him. What he wanted from her had nothing to do with the bedroom. Just her bedroom secrets.

I'm a nice guy, he thought as he climbed into the back seat with her. *You can tell me anything.* Dark pleasures. Wicked dreams. The truth about her marriage.

Christine slid behind the wheel. "Seat belts," she called over her shoulder, buckling hers with quick, sharp movements.

Marina obeyed like a dutiful child. So did her husband. Slade went through the motions but didn't buckle up. Bad enough his toes were pinched inside worn-out Nikes instead of Gucci loafers of buttery soft leather. He wasn't about to slice himself in two on the off chance Christine drove the car into a stanchion.

"I need a loo," Marina said as they entered the highway.

"I need an ATM," said the Boy Scout from the front seat.

Christine looked at him through the rearview mirror. "How about you, Slade? I suppose you'd like a visit to the casinos?"

"Nice of you to offer, love, but I wouldn't mind the chance to use a telephone."

He didn't have to see her face to know she was royally pissed. "One stop, and that's it. Once we leave Las Vegas, we won't see civilization until we get to the ranch."

"You're having us on, aren't you, love?"

"Five hours, no bathrooms," said Joe. "Think you can handle it, cowboy?"

If the guy hadn't been made of solid muscle, Slade would've gone for his throat. "Go to hell," he said instead. From the sound of things, the rest of them would follow soon enough.

Ten minutes later Christine pulled into the lot at

the Mirage Hotel. "Five minutes," she said. "If you're not back, I'm leaving without you."

"Western hospitality," said the Boy Scout with one of those smirking American grins Slade had come to hate. "Is it great or what?"

"Are you coming, Joseph?" asked Marina.

Everybody's favorite husband shook his head. "I'll stay here and watch the car."

"Not necessary," said Christine. "I'll watch the car."

You want him, love, and you don't have the foggiest how much. That fiery sparkle was back in her eyes, and Slade saw the cover of *Vanity Fair* dancing just out of reach. That's the picture he'd been waiting for, the perfect blend of beauty, brains, and molten lava guaranteed to send sales soaring.

And his career along with it.

"I don't know where the loos are," said Marina. She sounded like a petulant child instead of a happy new bride.

This was one opportunity he wasn't about to miss.

"Come on, love." He slipped an arm around her shoulders. "I'll help you find the loo, if you help me find the phones."

Christine and Joe stood together by the Ford and watched as Marina and Slade disappeared into the hotel.

"Do you think we'll ever see them again?" Joe asked.

Christine had a half dozen smart remarks ready to toss back at him when, to her dismay, she began to cry instead.

"What the hell—?" Joe stared down at her as if she'd sprouted a second head.

"Stop looking at me l-like that," she managed, covering her face with her hands. "You've seen me cry before."

"Not in a parking lot."

"I wish I'd never come," she sobbed. "I wish I'd stayed in New Jersey."

"And I wish I had that on tape," said Joe, patting her shoulder with an awkward gesture. "Bet that's the first time anyone ever said she wished she'd stayed in New Jersey."

"D-Don't make me laugh," she said, still crying. "I want to enjoy feeling miserable."

"Now that's the Christine Cannon I know. A woman who knows what she wants."

"Are you m-making fun of me?"

"No," he said, pulling her hands gently away from her face. "I'm not making fun of you, Christie."

She didn't want to meet his eyes, but his gaze was so intense, his power over her so strong, that she was helpless to do otherwise. "No one calls me Christie anymore," she managed, tears slowing. "Only my family."

"I was your family," he said. "Or don't you remember?"

"I remember," she whispered. She felt as if her heart was on the verge of breaking. In truth she doubted if a broken heart could hurt any more than her loneliness already did.

"Why did you do it, Christie? What the hell went so wrong that you'd walk out without saying good-bye?"

"I can't," she said, trying to pull away from him. "This is too hard, Joe. Don't ask it of me."

"For six goddamn years I've been wondering if there was something I could have said, something I should have done, but you've frozen me out cold."

"We can't change the past. Why don't we just put it aside and go on with our lives?"

"Because you owe me an answer." He grabbed her by the upper arms and forced her to meet his eyes again. "You're not the only one hurting." His voice was low, fiercely urgent. "And you're not the only one who lost something important."

Tears threatened again, but she bit the inside of her cheek to stem the flow. "They'll be back any minute. We can't let them see us like this." She brushed the tears away with her hands. "Joe, please, if you ever felt anything for me, don't do this in front of my family. I beg you—"

The sound of laughter, high and feminine, drifted toward them.

"Marina?" they asked in unison.

"I didn't know she laughed," said Christine.

"Neither did I," said Joe.

They turned to see the girl and the photographer strolling toward them. Each carried a towering ice cream cone, and they seemed to be in wonderful spirits.

"I don't like this," said Joe.

"Neither do I," said Christine.

"He's too old for her," Joe said.

"She's married to *you*," Christine reminded him.

He looked down at her, an odd smile on his face. "Thanks for reminding me."

"You're welcome," she said. Maybe they both needed to be reminded.

"Slade won mountains of money in the slot machine near the loos," Marina announced.

"I thought you said gambling was an indecent waste of money," Joe pointed out to his wife.

"It is," said Marina between attacks on her ice cream cone. "But there's really something quite amazing about the system."

"Another convert to capitalism," Joe muttered sotto voce.

"You didn't bring us any ice cream," Christine said, aggrieved.

"Didn't want to be late." Slade aimed an evil smile in her direction. "You'd hate that, wouldn't you, Chris love?"

"Ice cream would have been nice," she said, feeling terribly put upon.

"We'll watch the car," said Marina. "You two go get ice cream."

They looked at each other. She saw her past reflected in his beautiful blue eyes, and she saw the present, but it was a brief, shining glimpse of an unknown future that scared her yet gave her hope.

What's going on, Joe? Do you see it, too?

"I think we should hit the road," Joe said, not breaking the spell gathering around them. "It's after midnight as it is."

"Yes," she said softly. "We should get going."

They stood there, not moving, not speaking, scarcely breathing, until Slade poked her in the ribs and broke the spell.

Joe smiled at her the way he used to in the beginning.

She smiled back at him the way she used to when she thought the world was theirs for the asking.

I didn't imagine it, she thought as she climbed back into the car and started the engine. *You felt it, too.*

There was magic in the air and a sense of destiny that would have terrified her if she'd only been in her right mind. But she wasn't in her right mind. She was dazed and bewildered, overwhelmed by the sense that she was heading full speed toward something she couldn't possibly know how to handle . . . and that Joe was heading there, too.

God help them both when they collided.

8

"I thought you'd sit in the backseat with your wife," Christine said to Joe as they left the bright lights of Las Vegas behind.

"She's asleep. Besides, I figured you'd need a navigator."

"She's not asleep," Christine pointed out, glancing at the girl in her rearview mirror. "And I know how to get to my parents' ranch without your help."

"You sure of that? You haven't been there in a long time."

"Four years isn't that long." And it wasn't as if she hadn't seen them. Her parents had come to visit her in Los Angeles a number of times, as had a few of her siblings and their families.

"Couldn't keep me away from that ranch for four years."

"You didn't grow up there," she pointed out. "I doubt you'd feel so mellow about it if you were trapped there for eighteen years with only cows and horses for company."

"Better than some of my neighbors back in Brooklyn."

"You've always had a romanticized view of ranch life, Joe," she said, easing up on the gas as they passed a lone police car going in the opposite direction. "There's more to it than playing with a lariat and singing around the campfire."

"Two things I would pay big money to see you do."

"Not in this lifetime," she muttered, unable to suppress a smile. "I'm a city woman who just happened to be born in the country."

"And I'm a country boy at heart who just happened to be born in Brooklyn."

"One of life's little ironies," she said lightly.

The phrase lingered in the air long after the words faded away.

One of life's little ironies.

He looked over at Christine and felt a heaviness inside his chest. She looked like some kind of Viking princess with the moonlight illuminating the chiseled lines of her profile. He'd never been prone to flights of fancy, but Christine was the kind of woman whose existence reminded you why men fought wars to win the hand of a beautiful woman. The classical symmetry of her features was saved from perfection by the stubborn thrust of her chin and the indefinable sense that what you saw was only the beginning.

There'd been a time when he thought he'd spend the rest of his life discovering all of her secrets, watching as she moved through the years, going from beautiful to magnificent with the same fierce grace and intelligence that marked every single thing she did.

One of life's little ironies that they'd find themselves together driving down a lonely Nevada road on a night filled with stars while his child bride slept in the backseat.

"I know what you're thinking." Her voice was soft.

"That we've done this before?"

"There's that." She glanced in the rearview mirror. "But never quite like this."

He felt the deep tug of memory pulling him back through time. "We were alone in that old Chevy we bought from one of my father's gambling buddies, heading back to the ranch to tell—"

"Don't." Her voice caught, and she cleared her throat in a clumsy attempt to cover up. "Talk about anything, Joe, but please don't talk about that."

"It was a good time, Christie. For a while there it was about as good as it gets. We should be able to—"

"No!" Her voice rose, and he recognized the effort it took for her to bring it back under control. "We can't change things. We can't undo what happened."

"That's why you don't go home anymore, isn't it?" The truth had been staring him in the face the whole damn time, and he'd been too blind to see it. "It hurts too much."

"I don't go home as often as I'd like because of my schedule."

"Bullshit, Christine."

"I refuse to be drawn into this conversation."

"I admit this time you almost had me convinced. But it's not gonna work."

"I don't particularly give a damn if it works or not. This is between my family and me. You have nothing to do with it, Joe. Not one damn thing."

The rage and the fury were on him in a second. Six years of pent-up pain that came close to swallowing him whole. He leaned across the bench, seat belt straining across his chest, and he saw her fear, but he didn't give a damn. She was hurting, but so was he, and it was time she realized it.

"Don't look at me like that," she said, and he had to admire her bravado in the face of real danger. "You mind your own business, and we'll be fine."

"You're forgetting something, Christine," he said with deadly calm. "That baby you lost was mine."

Slade opened one eye and glanced at the microrecorder cradled in the palm of his right hand. It took a second to adapt to the darkness, but he managed to see that the tiny tape cassette was whirring away, exactly as it should be.

Yes.

He shifted slightly, careful to make no noise, and looked toward Marina, curled in the seat next to him. Her eyes were closed. Her breathing was deep and regular.

You missed it, love. I finally know the secret handshake.

He almost felt sorry for the girl. Even on a level playing field, competing with Christine was a losing battle. Christine had it all, and at first glance Marina had nothing. Except, of course, for one very important detail: Marina had the Boy Scout, and Christine didn't.

The bond between Christine and Joe was stronger than Slade would have figured. So there'd been a baby after all. He'd often wondered about that, but he'd chalked up her childlessness to a case of being dealt hormones that leaned toward ambition rather than maternity. People discarded marriages every day of the week, but there were some things you couldn't walk away from. The memory of a child was one of them.

Sex sold newspapers, but tragedy—that was the stuff of tax shelters. And Slade was going to be there with his hand out when it was time for the story to pay off.

They stopped twice so Marina could duck behind a Joshua tree and relieve herself with a great deal of grumbling. Christine couldn't blame her. There was something to be said for porcelain fixtures and hot and cold running water.

Marina stumbled back into the car after her second rest stop and was asleep before Christine and Joe climbed back into the car.

"You look beat," Joe observed as Christine stifled a yawn. "Let me drive."

She considered the wisdom of arguing, but her yawn proved Joe's point. "I'll navigate."

"It's a straight road, Christine." He slipped behind the wheel while she settled herself in the passenger seat. "I can manage without you."

"No," she said, yawning again. "I'd feel better if I navigated."

"Suit yourself."

"Thank you," she said tartly. "I will."

He gunned the engine, and the car leaped forward.

"Joe!"

"Just testing."

He settled into a nice even speed, and she found herself hypnotized by the unending road opening up before them. With only the moon for light, the world was a study in shadows. The dark shapes of Joshua trees and creosote bushes. The moonswept wash of rocky earth. The angular mountains reaching toward the sky. So beautiful. So unforgiving.

"Why is it I expect John Wayne to come riding toward us?" Even Joe's deep voice seemed part of the whole.

Christine chuckled. "Maybe it's because a thousand Westerns were filmed here."

He gestured toward a bluff in the distance. "Look fast and you'd swear there was an Indian on horseback watching us."

"Quite the imagination, Joe."

"Doesn't take much in a place like this. I grew up on "Gunsmoke" and "Rawhide" and would've sold my TV to live on a ranch."

She rested her head against the seat and closed her eyes. "Life is strange, isn't it? I grew up reading *Vogue* and *Glamour* and dreaming about an apartment on Fifth Avenue with a view of the park."

"So where's the new apartment, Christie?" His tone was light, but she caught the edge lurking beneath the surface.

She resisted the urge to look at him. "Central Park West."

"Great view?"

"Mm-hmm."

"You don't sound happy about it."

"I will be when it's ready."

"Be careful what you wish for?"

"Not at all. I couldn't be more pleased with my success."

"How about your choices?"

Her eyes opened. "I didn't have a choice in everything, Joe."

He looked straight ahead at the unvarying length

of dark road and made no comment. He didn't have to. She knew that he understood her meaning. She could see it in the set of his jaw, the way the index finger on his right hand tapped out an inner rhythm on the steering wheel. *Da-da dum. Da-da dum.* It wasn't something she could have added to a list of things she remembered about her ex-husband, but the second she heard it she was tumbled back ten years to when they were starting out together.

How many times had they made this same drive, gulping coffee to stay awake, eating jelly doughnuts and Hershey bars, and talking. God, how they'd loved to talk. Nothing had been off limits. They'd debated everything from abortion rights to Reaganomics and whether or not God was dead. Christine lectured, Joe yelled, and they both exhausted their vocabularies of four-letter words. When it was over, they ended up in each other's arms, making love with the same passion they brought to every other part of their relationship.

Maybe it wasn't fair to judge every experience, every man, by what she'd shared with Joe. She'd given her heart to her husband when they married, and it still belonged to him—even if that was the one thing she could never tell him.

Clouds drifted across the moon, and for a moment his face was obscured in shadow. Some nights she would lie awake, watching him sleep, struck by the wonder of it all. He wasn't like anyone she'd ever known. He was loud and aggressive, unabashedly ambitious and fiercely smart. He was as purely a product of the New York streets as she was a product of the ranch; yet when it came to the important things in life, they were like one entity.

She'd loved his body and she'd loved his mind and she'd loved the thought that fate might smile on them long enough to make one more miracle and give them a child to share their riches.

Too bad miracles that year had been in short supply.

"I think we could use a little music," Christine said, her voice husky with emotion. Anything to anchor her in the here and now and keep the memories at bay.

"Yeah," said Joe, reaching for the dial. "I think you're right."

Slade wasn't about to waste tape on Barry Manilow. He slipped the recorder into his pocket, where it bumped up against the coin he'd nipped from Marina when they were in the casino. She'd called it her lucky coin. He called it his lucky break. Unless he missed his guess, that coin would unlock the secret to Marina and the Boy Scout's implausible marriage. He already knew it wasn't a ruble or a kopek, but whatever it was, it would lead him closer to Marina's truth. Christine thought the kid was a Brit same as he was, but you didn't grow up on the London streets and not know a boarding school accent when you heard one. Marina hadn't been born in England. He was sure of that. There was the flavor of something else in her voice, something he couldn't quite identify. At least, not yet.

He did know exactly who sent their offspring to boarding schools, however.

Rich people with money to spare who wanted to make sure little Hamish or Pamela made the right social connections as soon as possible.

He scrunched his jacket behind his head and settled

back. They'd disappointed him with all that nattering on about ranches and reading *Vogue*. He'd hoped for a lot more juice out of Christine and Joe's waltz down memory lane.

"Are you awake?" Marina whispered. Not that anyone could hear her over Barry's nasal whine.

He feigned a yawn. "Wha's that, love?"

"Your eyes are open."

He turned toward her. Her cheek was creased from being pressed against the car door and her mousy brown hair stood up in spikes. The thought of her following in the footsteps of the beauteous Christine was laughable. "Barry Manilow wake you up, too?"

She tilted her head as Manilow segued from "Mandy" to "Copacabana." "I like it."

He unrolled the window a crack. "You need oxygen."

She leaned closer to him. "What were they talking about?"

"How much did you hear?" he countered.

"Tell me," she commanded. "Every last detail."

"They talked about ranches and magazines. You didn't miss much." He considered her more closely. "You jealous of the first Mrs. McMurphy?"

"Not at all," she said. Either the girl was a great actress or she was telling the dead-on truth. Strangely enough, he thought it was the latter. "Aren't you ever curious about people, what brings them together, why they grow apart?"

"Only if it gets me a picture credit," said Slade. "Otherwise I don't give a blody damn what they do or who they do it with."

Those brown eyes of hers grew all moist and dewy as if she was feeling sorry for him. Another dreamer, he thought, just like the Boy Scout. Maybe they weren't such a bad match after all.

"Do you think they're still in love?" Marina asked.

He could tell her about the baby, about the sparks that had been flying in the darkened car, but again this wasn't the time. At least that's what he told himself, but not even Slade had the heart to tell the little bride the truth.

"They don't like each other very much," he said after a moment and hoped she was too young to know that really didn't answer her question at all.

"We're almost there," Christine said as the sun rose over the mountains to the east. "Maybe an hour until we're at the house."

"How can you tell, love?" Slade asked. "Everything looks the same."

Joe was in the passenger seat once again, and he unrolled his window. "See that outcropping of rock over there?" He pointed to some indeterminate area in the distance. "That's where Sam's grandfather first thought about building the ranch house. He'd placed a marker there the day he married Grace, but there was a problem with water rights so he ended up farther north."

"Who is Sam?" asked Marina.

Christine, whose stomach had been tying itself into knots for the last hundred miles, looked at the girl in the rearview mirror. "Sam's my dad."

"Last of a dying breed," said Joe. "The only time he left the ranch was to fight in World War II. It's his lifeblood."

"It's also a losing proposition," said Christine.

"They haven't turned a profit in my lifetime. Why do you think they've gone the *City Slickers* route?"

Joe looked appalled. "They're taking in guests?"

"Spring and fall, to help with the cattle drives. They've been able to cut back on the hired help and pay off a few bills." She'd tried numerous times to give her father some help, but he was a hardheaded cowboy who wouldn't take help from anyone, not even his own flesh and blood.

"Cut back?" Joe asked, clearly agitated. "Sam didn't fire Zeke, and that bastard was skimming money off the top. Half of your dad's crew is in their sixties. No way is Sam going to give them pink slips."

Joe knew her father almost as well as she did. "Early retirement," she said with a rueful grin. "Complete with a pension, plus room and board in the bunkhouse."

"My old man would've lost their pensions in a crap game and put them out on the street."

"Have you called him since you've been back?"

"Yeah," said Joe. "We had a great three-minute conversation that ended with him telling me to say hi to the little woman."

"Marina?"

"You," Joe said. "He didn't listen to a goddamn thing I had to say." He dragged a hand through his thick, dark-brown hair. "Beats me why I'm so surprised. I was in high school before he remembered my name."

Christine didn't know what to say. John McMurphy was a bitter, difficult man who'd never had a kind word to say for his son. She couldn't count the number of times she'd invited Joe's father to dinner, only to receive the same response, "Busy. Maybe some other time." Joe had told her to forget about him, that John McMurphy didn't give a rat's ass about them, and the feeling was mutual, but Christine couldn't let go.

Family was important to Joe. The way he let himself be embraced by her own ebullient, expansive clan told her all she needed to know about the way he felt. And she wasn't immune to that need to belong. She'd had his aunts over for Christmas and Thanksgiving, but more than anything she'd wanted to win over his father—as much for herself as for Joe. But there'd been no convincing her father-in-law that anything mattered beyond the two-dollar window at OTB and the second stool from the right at McTiernan's Bar and Grille.

Marina leaned forward. "This isn't at all the way I'd imagined things," she said to Christine. "I thought you'd grown up in a mansion with servants and fancy cars."

"You have the strangest opinion of me, Marina. I wasn't born a princess, you know."

Joe and Marina exchanged looks.

"What?" asked Christine. "Did I miss something?"

"I wish to hear more about being a cowgirl," said Marina.

"I was never much of a cowgirl," Christine said with a shake of her head. "I'm the only one in the family who'd rather stay inside and read than commune with nature."

"Still it is difficult to think of you living a common existence," Marina continued. "You're not like anyone I've ever known before."

"It's the contact lenses," Joe said.

Marina looked at him. "What?"

"Forget it," said Joe. "Private joke."

Christine made a face. "I wear contact lenses," she told Marina. "They're bluer than my natural color because that looks better on camera."

"Bullshit," said Joe.

"Mind your own business," Christine snapped. "If I feel like wearing chartreuse lenses, that's no concern of yours."

"There was nothing wrong with your old color eyes," Joe said.

"Pop those babies out, love," Slade piped up. "Give us a look at the real thing."

"I would like color lenses one day," Marina said to everyone's surprise. "Emerald green."

Joe shot her a look that was anything but husbandly. "Wouldn't that feed eight families for a week?"

"There's nothing wrong with a woman wanting to look her best," Christine said with a smile for Marina. "The world judges a woman's appearance much more harshly than it judges a man's. If it takes a pair of contact lenses to give you a boost, so be it."

"Women are pawns in a man's world," Marina said hotly, "and we must use whatever weapons we have at our command, no matter how distasteful." Of course, the wistful look on her face spoke volumes. The desire to be beautiful cut across age, social status, and political persuasion, and for an instant Christine wondered how her own life would have been had she not been blessed with beauty.

"You disappoint me, kid," Joe said to Marina. "I thought you weren't swayed by the pleasures of the flesh."

"Leave her alone," Christine said to Joe while

Slade listened raptly. "You can wear tinted contact lenses and still have a social conscience."

"And you probably think eye lifts should be tax deductible," Joe shot back.

"Damn right I do," Christine retorted. "In television a woman's career would be over before her thirty-fifth birthday if she didn't get a little help from her friends."

"You're thirty-five," Joe pointed out. "How many eye lifts have you had done?"

"I'm thirty-four," she corrected him, "and I haven't had any yet, but the second I need one, I'll be first on line for the plastic surgeon."

"That's pathetic," said Joe.

"That's reality," said Christine.

"You're a beautiful woman. You don't need all that crap."

"I'm a professional woman. I need to stay on the cutting edge."

He looked at her.

She glanced over at him.

They burst into laughter.

"I can't believe I said that." Christine wiped away tears with the back of her hand. "Of all the stupid—"

He leaned over and pushed a strand of hair back from her cheek. "Don't change, Christine. Don't let them turn you into someone you're not."

Kiss her, Marina thought as Joe reluctantly moved his hand away from Christine's cheek. *Can't you see she wants you to?*

What was the matter with Joseph? Was he blind or didn't he recognize an invitation when he saw it?

Christine's face had gone all soft and womanly. And Joe had that dazed look that Marina had seen on Zee when he was feeling particularly loving.

The night before they left for Nevada, she'd stayed up late to watch a movie on the telly, and she'd been reminded of Christine and Joe. A beautiful but starchy New England woman and a gruff, tough-talking New York man engaged in a glorious battle of the sexes that had been very reminiscent of the battles Marina had seen and heard right there in New Jersey. "Hepburn and Tracy," Slade had said, sitting on the edge of the couch while he nursed a bottle of beer. "Shove over, love, and let them show you how it's done."

Truth was, she'd put her money on Christine and Joseph any day. When they were together, the very air they breathed seemed to sizzle with possibilities. They argued, they laughed when you least expected it, and they stole glances at each other when they thought no one was looking.

Joseph was certainly not Marina's particular cup of tea, but there was no denying the fact that he made Christine's entire being light up just by entering the room. It didn't matter if she was yelling at him or aiming a magazine at his head. All that seemed to matter was that life was a little brighter, a little more exciting, with him in it.

"You've got a problem," Slade said softly so only she could hear.

"I know." Joe wasn't half good enough for Christine, but if he made her that happy, maybe there was more to her husband than met the eye. She narrowed her eyes and looked at Slade. "You look dreadful."

"I feel green."

"You are green," said Marina, fearing the worst.

"Pull over," Slade said, tapping Christine on the shoulder.

"We're almost there," she said over her shoulder. "Can't you wait a little?" If she stopped the car, there was a chance she'd jump out and start running all the way back to New Jersey.

"Stop the bleedin' car!"

Christine pulled over in a cloud of dust, and Slade leaped out.

"He's carsick," Marina said. "He had too much pride to tell you."

"My heart's breaking," Joe muttered.

"I need a loo," Marina said.

"So do I," said Christine.

"There's a Joshua tree over there." Joe pointed to a spot some fifty yards away from the car.

"I'd rather die," said Marina.

"Well put," said Christine.

"You went behind a Joshua tree last night," Joe pointed out to his wife.

"Last night it was dark," said Marina.

"A perfectly logical explanation," said Christine.

"I won't peek," said Joe, grinning.

"And I won't go," said Christine. "At least, not here."

"How you doing?" Joe called out to Slade, who was doubled over behind the car.

"Naff off," came a strangled voice.

Christine and Marina looked at each other. One husband between the two of them. One carsick photographer. Two women in search of a loo.

"Drive fast," said Marina.

"At the speed of light," said Christine.

9

Samuel Clemens Cannon usually greeted the dawn on horseback. To him there was no sight in this world more beautiful than the sun rising over the eastern ridge, signaling a new day in the most beautiful place on earth.

He supposed every man felt that way about his home, but Sam knew he had more cause than most for pride. The Cannon Ranch wasn't the biggest in Nevada or, God knew, the most profitable, but every square inch of it was steeped in family history. He knew the spot where his daddy Will had proposed marriage to his ma Vi. And there was the gully down past the stables where he'd been sitting when Nonie told him they were expecting their first. Everywhere you looked, every thing you touched—it was all part and parcel of his life, and he wouldn't have it any other way.

No telling where he might be if he hadn't been lucky enough to be born into the most beautiful place on earth. He felt sorry for city people. What the hell kind of life was it for a man, wedged between concrete and steel, breathing smoke and fumes, unable to see the stars in the night sky the way the good Lord meant him to?

City living didn't hold anything for Sam, and he

considered himself damn fortunate that his wife and children felt the same way. A man was meant to live on his own piece of land, the same land his daddy and his daddy's daddy had loved. Right there in the bosom of his own family he'd got himself a lawyer, a veterinarian, a top-notch foreman, and the best ranch hands either love or money could buy. There was no denying the pride swelling up inside his chest that his and Nonie's children felt the same way about the ranch as he did.

At least, all of them but one. Christie, child of his heart, apple of his eye, had been looking for a way out since the day she was born. She'd come into the world with a restless heart and a need to be somewhere Sam had never wanted to go. He'd known from the very start that she'd been touched with stardust, and he and Nonie had watched, with a mixture of awe and admiration, as she began to sparkle.

They had themselves a pile of scrapbooks, a shelf stacked with videotapes of her shows, and more glossy photographs than you'd find in some fancy museum. Seeing his baby girl on the cover of *Time* had made him real proud, but not even that could hold a candle to the way he'd felt the day she married Joe.

He remembered it like it was yesterday. The sun was shining, the lupine was in bloom, and he'd had family and friends gathered round and two very special young people about to embark on the most exciting journey this side of the moon. His eyes had misted over with tears, and Nonie'd pulled a handkerchief from his back pocket.

"I ain't the kind to be ashamed of honest emotion," he'd said. "Hell, it's honest emotion that's kept us married all these years, Nonie, and it's that kind of feelin' that'll keep our Christie and Joe together when the times get tough."

Everyone had smiled because they knew that Samuel Clemens Cannon was a man of few words, and not one of those words was sentimental. But this was a special occasion, the wedding of his pride and joy, his baby daughter, to her college sweetheart, and not even Sam could stem the flow of happiness and pride.

"You're going to have a long and happy life together," he said, his voice breaking with emotion. "It may not always be easy, but none of what's good in this world comes without a struggle.

"It's up to the Almighty if He sees fit to bless you with children, but I can't imagine two people better suited to showin' young ones how to make their way through this world.

"And so I give you Mr. and Mrs. McMurphy. May the good Lord bless you and keep you in the palm of His hand. May you be as happy next year and all the years after as you are at this moment . . . and may we always be here for you whenever you need family by your side." The tears ran freely down his weathered cheeks, but he still made no move to brush them away. He clicked glasses with his wife. "To Christie and Joe!"

The room echoed with cheers, everything from wolf whistles to rebel yells to elegant hurrahs. Christie was their girl, the one who was destined to break out of their small town and see the world, make her mark on it. She'd never quite fit in with the rest of them, but somehow it hadn't mattered.

She was different, always had been, right from the start. She had a different way of thinking, a different way of looking at things, and who could blame her. Growing up hadn't been easy for her. Not even money and good looks had been enough to shield her from life's hard knocks.

That's why Joe was so good for her. He was from New York City, but they didn't hold that against him. He shot from the hip, same as they did, and when it came to loving Christie there wasn't anyone anywhere who could measure up quite the way he did.

He closed his eyes and saw in his mind the way Christine and Joe had looked at each other, then at the champagne, at the glittering gold rings on their fingers, and he heard them laugh, softly at first, then louder, until everyone in the room was laughing with them. There was so much joy in them you felt good just being around them, as though you had champagne and sunshine and someone to love all wrapped up in one sweet package.

The bandleader had gestured to Sam. He pushed back his chair, hiked up the fancy pants Nonie said he had to wear for the occasion, then made his way over to the daughter he loved more than life itself.

Christie stood up, adjusted her veil, then flashed him a smile so pure and radiant that Sam could've sworn he'd just seen a glimpse of heaven. He was surprised pride didn't pop the buttons on his tuxedo jacket right off. Joe rose when Sam approached. It was the kind of thing that made a man look kindly on his son-in-law. Sam patted the kid on the shoulder. "I think I have the next dance with . . . your wife."

The words didn't come easy to Sam, but they felt right.

Christie took his arm, and they swept out onto the dance floor in a flurry of white veil and lace.

The pride he felt as she stepped into his arms surpassed anything he'd imagined.

"The last time I felt this good was the day you were born."

Her smile was dazzling. "Oh, come on, Pop. You've said the same thing to all seven of us."

"You always were special, Christie. The one who was going to make me proud."

Her eyes, blue-grey like the Nevada sky when a storm was gathering, glittered with happy tears. "I only wish I could give you grandchildren, Pop. The easiest thing in the world, and I doubt—"

"You're a blessing to us, Christie, you and that fine young man you just married. We got more than enough grandkids to go around."

He meant every word even if his heart ached for her and Joe. Sam knew bloodlines, and one look at his beautiful girl and her handsome husband had been enough to tell him that their children would be something special. Tall and strong, bright but not without compassion for the have-nots of the world.

The world was theirs for the asking, a different world than the one he'd faced forty years ago. His girl could be anything she wanted to be. He only wished she could follow her dreams right there on the ranch.

"I love you, Pop," she'd whispered. "Have I told you that lately?"

The music swelled, and they began to dance to "Daddy's Little Girl." His heart did a quick two-step inside his chest. He wanted so much for her. A good marriage. A job that mattered. Kids. He knew the odds were against his Christie, that they'd been against her from the start, but Sam Cannon and his family believed in miracles. Why else would he have given his heart and soul to ten thousand acres of harsh land and a handful of dreams?

He looked at his baby girl and the man she loved. *What are your dreams?* Sam wondered. *How are you gonna feel if they don't all come true?*

But that was a long time ago.

He opened his eyes and looked out toward the distance. The sun was beginning to rise over the low mountains, washing the land with light. You could do every damn thing right, dot all your i's, cross all your t's, and still come up wanting. In the end it always came down to what a man and a woman felt for each other. Life didn't come with guarantees, not for anybody. Not even for his Christie and Joe.

He heard the sound of his wife's footsteps moving up behind him. "Samuel?" She moved closer on a cloud of shampoo and rosewater. "I thought you'd be out on Smoky."

He grinned. "Not today, Nonie."

"You know, don't you?" she asked, resting her head against his shoulder. "Fifty years I've been tryin' to keep a secret from you, you old buzzard, and I still can't do it." She poked a finger in his ribs. "How did you find out Christine was coming out for the party?"

"You don't live as long as I have without learning a few things along the way."

"Natalie told you, didn't she?" asked Nonie with

fire in her eyes. "That darn gal hasn't the sense she was born with."

"Natalie didn't tell me, woman. I figured it out. All that whisperin' going on—I'd be a dadblamed fool if I didn't know what you were up to."

"Now, don't you go readin' anything into it."

"Talk English, woman," he barked. "What in hell am I goin' to read into my gal comin' home for our anniversary party?"

"I'm talkin' about Joe."

His jaw dropped. He'd read about things like that, but this time he actually felt it hit his chest. "Joe's comin'?"

"Hah!" Nonie threw back her head and laughed. He'd always thought she had the prettiest laugh in four counties, but this time it was a shade too darn pleased for his taste. "So you don't know everything!"

He lifted her up and spun her around. A little bit slower, maybe, than when he was in his prime, but not bad for a man pushing seventy. "Christie's a sly fox," he said as he and Nonie regained their balance. "Bet they've been courtin' these last couple of years." That would go a long way toward explaining why she'd been staying away.

Nonie's brow furrowed, and she placed a hand on his forearm. "Don't you go gettin' your hopes up, Samuel. I think he's just coming out here to pay his respects."

"You can pay your respects on the telephone," said Sam. "If he's comin' out here with Christie, that means somethin' big is brewing."

"They have to find their own way. We can't go stickin' our noses in where they ain't wanted."

"I know," said Sam, putting his arm around his wife. But he couldn't help believing in miracles.

The monument marking the start of Cannon property was situated two miles from the main house on the west side of the road to the left of a venerable old Joshua tree that had survived mother nature and the seven rowdy Cannon siblings.

"You finally slowed down," Joe said to Christine. She looked at him. "I did not."

"Yes, you did, love," said Slade. "Appreciably."

"I'm savoring the trip," she said grimly. "You all have been such a joy that I hate to see it end."

She heard a muffled laugh from Marina in the backseat, and she grinned despite herself. Truth was, she'd run out of delaying tactics. She considered throwing the car into reverse, but decided that was the coward's way out. What on earth was the big deal anyway?

She loved her family.

She'd missed her family.

She was about to see her family.

So why the knot in her stomach?

The ranch, she thought. That's what it was. Every place she looked she saw herself and Joe. It was like being forced into a time machine that let you relive all of your mistakes but refused to let you do one damn thing about them.

Behind her Marina unbuckled her seat belt and knelt on the back seat to look out the window.

"Marina! Buckle up."

"Someone is following us," Marina said, sounding uncharacteristically nervous. "He's on a horse."

"Get down!" Joe snapped. "On the floor! Now!"

Christine looked in the rearview mirror in time to see Marina disappear. "Very funny, you two. Get back up on the seat, Marina." It was like having two kids in the car, except the kids were her ex-husband and his new wife.

"Shut up and drive," said Joe, looking like Clint Eastwood in a Dirty Harry movie.

"Shut up and drive?" She started to laugh. "I can't believe you said that."

"As much as it pains me to say this, you'd better listen to him, love," said Slade. "I believe the Lone Ranger back there has a gun."

The hoofbeats were getting closer. She looked out the side mirror and saw a huge black horse with an equally huge rider galloping her way. The rider wore head to toe denim, except for a black Stetson and snakeskin boots that glistened in the morning sun.

She slammed on the brakes, sending Joe into the dashboard.

"Son of a bitch!" Joe roared. "What the hell are you doing?"

If she didn't know better she'd think Joe was really worried. "It's Franklin."

Joe craned his neck to look at the approaching rider. "In snakeskin boots? No way. Get this heap moving, will you?"

"What's your problem? We're on Cannon property. Anybody we run into is bound to be related to me."

"You can't be sure that's Franklin yet," he pointed out.

"So what? If he isn't a Cannon, he's probably employed by a Cannon."

"I don't like this," Joe muttered.

"Neither do I," Christine retorted. "What on earth is the matter with you, Joe?" A terrible thought struck her. "Good God! You're not wanted by the police, are you?"

"Where the hell did you get an idea like that?"

Her laugh held the edge of hysteria. "Look at you!" she said, turning the rearview mirror in his direction. "You look like a wild man, and your wife is hiding on the floor. I may not be a deductive genius, but those are pretty substantial clues, Joe."

"I say we call the authorities," Slade offered from the backseat.

"Shut up!" said Christine and Joe.

"The carpet smells dreadful." Marina's voice was muffled. "How long must I—"

Christine opened the car door and leaped out. "That's it!" she roared. "You people are driving me crazy. I'm walking the rest of the way." Or at least she'd walk until Franklin caught up with her and she could hitch a ride on his horse. If Joe and Marina were running from the authorities, that was their problem. Maybe Slade would take their picture, send it to the FBI, and they'd be carted off in leg irons, a fate Joe, if not Marina, richly deserved.

She stormed off down the road, scarcely registering the cool, sweet air or the morning sun or the fact that her brother was about to trample her with his horse.

"Christie!" Franklin's deep voice boomed. "Get ready!"

She grinned and stopped dead in her tracks.

When they were kids she used to pretend she was the Hollywood heroine of a big-budget Cinemascope Western complete with handsome cowboy heroes and exciting villains. Now and then she'd been able to convince her oldest brother to enter into the spirit of things and practice chase scenes and kidnappings.

A kidnapping, she thought, standing perfectly still as he galloped toward her. Such a silly little thing— and so long ago—and yet he remembered. She experienced a definite tug at her familial heartstrings as she waited for her big brother to sweep her off her feet.

"He kidnapped her!" Marina screamed as Christine, the man, and the horse, galloped off in a cloud of dust. She pounded on Joe's shoulders. "Follow her, Joseph!"

He unrolled the car window and leaned out, watching until Christine disappeared from view.

"Are you insane?" Marina pounded even harder. "Something terrible is going to happen to her." She tried to scramble into the front seat and climb behind the wheel. "We have to—"

"Don't sweat it, kid," Joe said with an unpardonable lack of concern. "She's not in any danger."

"She's been captured by a madman!" She stopped, gasping for breath, as the seat belt tugged her back. "Oh damn!" She popped the buckle and tried again, but Joe blocked her by sliding behind the wheel himself. "You're despicable," she raged. "Both of you. That man came out of nowhere and picked Christine up like she was a rag doll, and all you . . . you *monsters* can do is sit there!"

"That was her brother," Joe said with maddening calm.

"I don't believe you."

"This is the Wild West, gal," said Slade. "They don't play by normal rules."

"Your American accent is dreadful," said Marina with a shudder. She turned to Joe. "Was that *really* her brother?"

"Franklin Cannon," Joe acknowledged. "First child, ranch foreman."

"Snakeskin boots?" Slade said with a grimace. "God."

"Took me by surprise, too," said Joe. "Frank was always partial to plain old cowhide."

"But did you see the way he lifted her up off the ground?" Marina asked, fascinated now that the threat of danger had passed. "That's was like something out of a movie!"

"Stick around," said her husband. "You ain't seen nothin' yet."

It was everything he remembered and more. The wild beauty of the land. The tumultuous sky overhead. The easy grace of man on horseback.

And that almost-forgotten feeling that anything was possible if you worked hard enough and wanted it badly enough.

"You missed a great shot," he tossed over his shoulder to Slade as he gunned the engine. "How much do you think they'd have paid you for a shot of Christine being kidnapped by a renegade cowboy?"

"A hell of a lot," Slade said. "Especially if they didn't know he was her brother."

"Truth in advertising?" Joe laughed. "Since when does that stop you guys?"

He was glad the photographer had missed the shot. Not just because he hated everything the Brit stood for, but because there was something so special about the moment that he'd hated the fact that anyone else had been there to see it.

When she first got out of the car, the sight of her stomping down the road in her high heels and pale linen trousers was laughable. The city girl trying to fit in with the country folk. And the next instant she was being swept up onto horseback, hair whipping about her face, her laughter ringing out, and Joe found himself falling in love again.

Something he intended to get over by the time he pulled up in front of the ranch house.

"You always did know how to make an entrance," Franklin said as they raced toward the house. "This is gonna make Pa's day."

"Is everybody home?" Christine asked, hanging on to the pommel. "I don't want to waste all of these theatrics for nothing."

"Hell, yes, they're home. They've been countin' the minutes until you all showed up."

"They're happy to see Joe again?"

"Can't speak for none of them, but I'm a damn site happier to see him than you, little sister."

She elbowed him in the gut. "Stinker," she said. "Your stomach is still flat as a washboard." No treadmill or step aerobics for Franklin. Real life kept him in shape.

"You're blonder than last time," he said. "Saw that magazine cover. Since when are your eyes so blue?"

What was the fascination with her eye color anyway? "Contacts."

"Nothing wrong with your old color."

"Better for television," she said, wondering why the explanation sounded dumber each time she gave it.

They reached the top of the ridge, and Christine's

heart did a funny little dance inside her chest at the sight of the ranch house. Last year she'd interviewed a score of the hottest-and-brightest for a homecoming special to run the night before Thanksgiving. The stories were as varied as the subjects, but they all had one thing in common: the old homestead grew smaller on every return trip.

But not the Cannon house.

Christine knew it was only a trick of memory and emotion, but to her eyes the house seemed to expand with the family, growing larger and more welcoming with every year that passed. And despite it all, she felt as if there wasn't room enough for her.

I'm not going to cry, she told herself, blinking madly. *This time I'm going to get through a visit without falling apart.*

"Hang on, sister! We're goin' for a ride!" Franklin nudged the horse forward, and they galloped full speed down the slope toward the house.

Sam was the first one to pop out. His speed and agility belied his seventy years, and her dad raced across the porch and down the steps before her mom Nonie had a chance to get out the door. Christine heard a whoop of excitement from the barn, and a stream of little kids, followed by her sister Nat, ran toward the house.

I'm connected to every single one of you by blood, so why is it I feel so damn alone?

They seemed to come from everywhere, spilling out of the house and barn and stable, laughing, shouting, being their rowdy, enthusiastic selves. She saw herself as a little girl—too small to play with the older kids, too grown up to be bothered with her little brothers—looking for a secret hiding place where she could dream of the day when she was rich and famous and everyone would know her name.

Be careful what you wish for . . .

Moments later she found herself enveloped in one of her dad's big bear hugs.

"You're too thin, gal!" he said, pushing her away so he could take a good look at her. "You on one of those damn diets?"

"Camera adds pounds, Daddy," she said, hugging him back. "Television's unforgiving."

"Come here, baby!" Her mother Nonie opened her arms wide. "You're home now, and I'll see to it you get some good food in you."

Her mother smelled, as she always had, of Breck shampoo and rosewater, a comforting scent that made Christine smile. The two women hugged. "New hairstyle, Mom?"

Nonie patted her hair and performed a pirouette. "Natalie said it was about time."

"*I've* been telling you that for the past five years," Christine said, feeling a tad put out. "You know I would have taken you to my salon when you were in L.A. last year."

Nonie wrinkled her nose. "Now, you know I wouldn't have felt comfortable in one of those fancy beauty parlors you go to, Christie. Natalie took me to her gal in Branchwater, and she did me up just fine."

Knowing Natalie, the gal in Branchwater probably coiffed more poodles than people. "You look beautiful, Mom," she said, meaning it, "but it would have been nice if just once you let me do something extravagant for you."

Nonie patted her on the cheek, same as she used to when Christine was a little girl and her feelings were hurt. "You work hard for your money, baby. I don't want you spendin' it on your old mother."

"Nat works hard, too, but you let her spend it on you."

"That's different?"

"How is it different?"

"Natalie has a husband."

"Mother!" Christine's voice rose a full octave. "That is absolutely the most ridiculous thing I've ever heard you say. What possible difference can a husband make?"

"More laundry, for one thing."

Christine spun around to see Nat, loping toward them, her lanky body a study in rangy grace. The two sisters hugged with affection. "So how's that Abyssinian you neutered?" Christine said after she admired Natalie's new hairstyle.

"Cranky," said Nat with a grin much like their father's. "He may hold a grudge for quite a while."

"Where's Karl?"

"Holding down the fort. Two of the bitches are whelping today. The twins'll be here by lunchtime, but Mark's girls are here and little Bree."

Christine glanced toward the knot of kids playing near the rosebushes. "I'm not related to all of them, am I?"

"Ellen's doing some babysitting. She figures she's home all the time with Bree, and the extra money wouldn't hurt."

Christine tried to ignore the sound of a car bumping its way up the drive. "So," she said brightly, "where are the twins? I haven't seen them since—"

"Who cares about them?" Nat said, cutting Christine off. "The question is, where's Joe?"

"He's coming along," said Christine, gesturing toward the Ford.

Sam shaded his eyes and peered into the sunshine. "Looks to me like you've got a full house, Christie."

"It happened so fast I didn't have time to tell you about it, Daddy. Slade's my photographer and—"

Damn. Joe chose that moment to blare the car horn, sending her family into whoops of delight. Good grief, didn't any of the Cannons do anything at less than full volume?

Joe stopped the car a few yards away from Franklin's horse, then jumped out.

She watched from the porch as he was surrounded by Cannons of all ages, shapes, and sizes. The noise brought Trace from the stable, and when he saw Joe he let out a holler and charged his former brother-in-law, nearly knocking him over.

Their voices melded into one solid mass.

"Man, is it ever good to see you, Joe . . . how you been doin' . . . you're too thin, son . . . I'll have to fatten you up some . . . so where are the twins—"

The back doors of the Ford swung open, and Slade climbed out, looking out of place and very English. Christine snapped out of her fog and dashed down the steps.

"This is Slade," she said, dragging the reluctant photographer over to meet her father. "Slade, this is Sam Clemens. My dad."

Sam extended a weathered hand. "Pleased to meet you." The two men shook hands. "You got yourself a last name?"

Slade's eyes widened, and Christine jumped in.

"Slade goes by the one name, Daddy."

"You must've been born with two names," Sam went on in his blunt American fashion. "Don't know much about England, but it seems to me everyone over there has a last name."

"The Queen doesn't," said Slade.

Sam's eyes narrowed. Joe grinned at her from across a knot of relatives.

"Slade is teasing, Daddy," she said, ever the peacemaker. She shot the photographer a quelling look. *I don't care if you tell him your last name is Smith,* the look said.

"Ainsley," said Slade at last.

Christine breathed a sigh of relief. The last hurdle was climbing out of the car.

Slade, a wicked grin on his lean face, strolled over to Marina's side. "This is Marina," he said, obviously waiting for Sam to demand a last name from the girl.

Sam, however, surprised him. "Ain't you a sweet little thing," he said, pumping the girl's tiny hand. "Puts me in mind of one of the grandkids, don't she, Nonie?"

Nonie was beside herself with joy. "Doesn't anybody eat anymore?" she fretted. "A strong wind would blow you all away."

I'm going crazy, Christine thought. She could almost feel the pounds adhering to her hips and thighs. If her mother had her way, the hollow in her cheeks would become nice soft cushions of fat that would photograph like tubs of butter.

And what on earth was Slade thinking of, acting as though he and Marina were a couple? Even worse, Joe was over there by the rosebushes, lapping up attention like a starving dog and totally ignoring his bride.

One day you'll look back on this and laugh. Her mother led the way into the house.

"You take your old room, Christie," she said, the domestic general in her element. "Joe, you can bunk in the twins' room." Nonie turned her benevolent gaze on Slade and Marina. "And you two nice children can have the guest room."

Christine looked at Joe. Joe looked at Marina. Marina looked at Slade. Slade looked straight ahead.

"Well, let's get crackin'!" Sam ordered. "Nonie's got a real ranch breakfast ready to go soon as you all get your fannies in the seats."

"Uh . . . Sam," Joe looked as miserably uncomfortable as Christine felt. "We've got a small problem with the sleeping arrangements."

"Hell, boy, you don't have to bunk in the twins' old room. If you got your heart set on someplace else, don't be shy. This is your home, same as Christie's. Just speak your mind."

The photographer stepped forward.

"Don't even think about it," said Christine.

Slade shrugged and stepped back. Marina took three steps to her right until she stood next to Joe. Joe, a look of utter misery on his face, draped an arm across the girl's shoulders.

The room fell silent. All eyes were on Christine and Joe. It took all of Christine's self-control to keep from bolting for the door.

Finally Nat spoke up. "So what does this mean, Joe?" she asked in her no-nonsense way. "It's not you and Christie, it's you and—"

"Marina," Joe said quietly. "We're married."

10

"We're real sorry, Marina," Sam said. "No harm intended."

Marina managed a weak smile. "I understand."

Joe couldn't help but notice that she looked like anything but the happy new bride, and he had the feeling so did everyone else.

"Well, congratulations, Joe!" Natalie gave him a warm hug, but he could see the question in her eyes. She turned toward the kid. "You, too, Marina honey."

Nat's action prodded everyone else into motion, and Joe endured a round of congratulations that, despite their sincerity, were laced with the Cannons' disappointment.

He glanced over toward Christine, who was leaning against the door to the kitchen, and felt the full weight of their shared history. *You're right,* he thought, wishing she could read his mind. *I had no business coming here. I didn't mean to hurt Sam and Nonie.*

Joe had to hand it to the Cannons. They were dealing with the situation a hell of a lot better than he was. He felt like a bastard all around, and there wasn't a damn thing he could do about it. It was obvious they'd been expecting an announcement from Christine and him. He wouldn't be surprised if there was champagne chilling somewhere in anticipation. The last thing they'd expected was that he'd have the nerve to show up on their doorstep with his new wife in tow.

"Well," said Nonie brightly after the last round of congratulations faded away. "I'm sure you all want to freshen up before breakfast."

Yeah, he thought, he wanted to freshen up all right. All the way back to New Jersey, if possible.

"Don't worry about us, Mom," said Christine in her best television voice. "We'll see ourselves to our rooms."

"Notice the way they fought you for the privilege," Joe muttered as the four of them walked in lockstep toward the opposite end of the ranch house.

"Whose fault is that?" Christine snapped. "I told you to stay in New Jersey."

"I wish I had."

"So do I."

Marina and Slade were listening to every word. Let them, thought Joe. Maybe they'd learn something. He sure as hell had.

"This is yours, Slade." She gestured toward the first door after the guest bathroom.

He nodded and stepped inside without a word.

"This is worse than I thought, isn't it?" Joe asked. "Even Flash isn't saying anything."

Christine scowled at him. "You know which room is yours," she said, "and you know how to get back to the kitchen."

With that she stormed down the hall, jogged left, and headed for her old room.

"What're you waiting for?" he grumbled to Marina. "Get inside."

"How dare you," she said, lifting her chin. "Nobody orders me about."

"Get inside," he repeated through gritted teeth.

She dropped her bags to the floor with a thud. "No."

"Not today, Marina."

"Not today, Marina," she mimicked in wicked imitation.

"You asked for it." He swung her over his shoulder, stormed into the guest room, and tossed her across the bed. "Do what you want," he snapped. "I'm going to eat breakfast."

Thin walls, Slade thought as he tossed his gear into the closet. Maybe this wasn't going to be as bad as he'd first thought.

He heard the Boy Scout storm out of the adjoining bedroom, followed by the sound of Marina crying.

Opportunity never had to knock twice when he was around.

He stumbled over her bags in the hallway, mumbled a pungent epithet, and was about to walk into her room when it occurred to him that a touch of the Boy Scout might not be a bad idea.

"Delivery!" He pushed open the door and strolled inside with the bags. "Where do you want them, love?"

Marina sat cross-legged in the middle of the bed, crying. "In New Jersey."

He dropped the bags at the foot of the bed and sat down on the edge. "Dismal, isn't it?"

She nodded vigorously. "I feel trapped."

He grinned. "Are you talking about your marriage or the location?"

She looked down, red patches of color spreading across her cheeks. "I cannot discuss that with you."

He leaned back on his elbows and summoned up his most disingenuous look. "Think of me as a priest," he said. "Nothing you tell me will go beyond these four walls."

She looked very young sitting there. If he wasn't such a hardcore bastard, he might have felt sorry for her. "I can't," she said after a long moment.

"It might make you feel better."

"Or perhaps it might make *you* feel better."

She was young but not unsophisticated. He'd have to remember that. "That's fine," he said with a wide, friendly smile. "Tell me to naff off if I push too hard."

To his relief, she smiled back. "Naff off," she said.

"Boarding school, right?"

She nodded.

"North of London?"

She nodded again.

"But you were born somewhere else."

She said nothing at all. But then again she didn't have to explain. Sooner or later he'd find out everything he needed to know.

Christine finished putting her lingerie in the drawer, then set to work hanging up the rest of her clothes. When she finished that, she might line up her shoes in neat rows on the floor of the closet, then lock herself in the room until it was time to go back to New Jersey.

She'd seen the look on her father's face when Joe introduced Marina as his wife. Sam's disappointment had been plain as day, but he loved Joe too much to do anything but wish him the very best and mean it.

That was the difference between her father and herself, Christine thought, sitting on the window ledge and looking out toward the bunkhouse. Sam wanted Joe to be happy. Christine wanted Joe to be as miserably unhappy as possible.

And she wasn't about to ask herself why.

"Now, don't take on so, Nonie," said Sam to his wife as she flipped the fried eggs. "The boy's got a right to go get married."

"'Course I know that." Nonie clipped some parsley from her window garden.

"Couldn't expect him to wait forever for Christie to come to her senses."

"Never thought he should after what she did to him."

"Some people handle heartache better than others," Sam said, filching bacon from the serving platter. "You know why she left him, Nonie." Anyone who knew the situation would understand that Christie'd believed she was doing the best thing for Joe.

Except Nonie who turned toward him, eyes blazing. "Marriage doesn't come with guarantees, you old fool." She waved her spatula too close to Sam's nose for his liking, but no self-respecting husband backed down from kitchen implements. "For better, for worse. That's what you promise, that's what you do."

"She loved him enough to let him go." Enough so Joe could build himself a life—and one day a family—with another woman.

"And now she's lost him for good." Nonie attacked the fried eggs with a vengeance. "She's almost thirty-five and she's all alone. If you can find something to be happy about in that, then you're not as smart as you think you are, Samuel Clemens Cannon."

Sam opened his mouth to argue his point, but to his surprise, he couldn't find the words. In his heart of hearts, he'd never accepted his baby girl's divorce. He couldn't have said how, but he'd believed Christie and Joe would find their way back to each other.

And for some reason he still believed it. He wasn't the kind of man who took the marriage vows lightly. Fifty years with his hardheaded, beautiful Nonie was proof of that. You'd think he'd be feeling a mite strange thinking there was a chance for Christie and Joe, what with Joe being married to the little brown-haired girl they called Marina. Oh, they liked to tease Sam that he understood horses better than he understood people, and most times he just grinned and let them think any damn fool thing they wanted to.

"Sam!" Nonie's voice poked him in the ribs. "Get the blue flowered platter for the eggs."

He pulled it down from its keeping place over the icebox. Nonie slid the fried eggs onto it. One skidded across the ironstone like a hockey puck, and he stopped it from plopping to the floor with the base of his thumb.

"Don't let them get cold," she said in her no-nonsense way. "I'll be bringin' the rest directly."

He made his way into the dining room. He and Nonie liked to eat in the kitchen, but when the whole family was around, they needed more elbow room.

"Breakfast," he announced with a flourish. They all looked over at him and smiled. Seven sons and daughters, in-laws, grandbabies . . . but all he saw was Christie's ex and his new bride.

And what he saw on their faces made his old rancher's heart bust with hope. *They don't love each other,* he thought as he put the platter of fried eggs down in the middle of the table. *Never have and probably never will.*

"Pop?" Christie was standing at his elbow. "Where should I sit?"

He put his arm around his youngest daughter. "Next to me," he said, kissing her cheek. "We got us a lot of catchin' up to do."

He looked down at her. She was looking across the room at Joe, who was looking right back at her.

It was enough to make a man believe in miracles.

Christine spent her tenth summer convinced she was about to become famous. Her family had blamed it on an overdose of television and an overactive imagination, but nothing they said had been able to convince their daughter that fame was unlikely to visit itself upon the Cannon ranch anytime soon. "Not the ranch," she'd protested. "Me!"

She'd hide up in the hayloft with an apple and a glass of lemonade and devour novels about rich and famous people who led lives of unimaginable glamour and excitement. And she would dream about the day when all eyes would be upon her.

From the looks of things in that dining room, she'd just been granted her wish.

"The eggs look wonderful!" She smiled and took her seat. "Where's Mom?"

"Everybody get started," ordered Nonie as she bustled into the room bearing a platter piled high with sausage and bacon. "Nothin' worse than cold fried eggs. May as well eat a rubber chicken, if you ask me." Marina giggled. Nonie looked over at her and smiled. "You're a little bit of a thing. Joseph, make sure she eats."

Joe lifted his fork in salute. "Will do."

Slade met Christine's eyes and lifted his cup of black coffee in mock salute, and she felt the strong urge to punch him in the nose. He'd followed her to Nevada expecting to go celebrity-shopping at the great tabloid supermarket called Las Vegas. His disappointment rolled across the long pine table and dropped in her lap.

She'd told him to stay in New Jersey. There was nothing here that was going to put his name in lights.

The last time Joe had felt this happy was the last time he'd visited the ranch. Christine had just found out she was pregnant, and they'd flown west on a cloud of wonder and excitement. "How are you?" he'd asked each time she came back from the lavatory. "Morning sickness?"

"Morning, afternoon, and night," she'd said. "Isn't it wonderful?"

She'd spent much of the trip to her parents' ranch nursing a queasy stomach and searching for a bathroom, but not once did she complain.

"They're just going to go crazy," she said as they came over the ridge and saw the house below. "Who would've imagined this?"

"Miracles happen," Joe said, ruffling her hair. "Isn't that what Sam always says?"

His father-in-law's steadfast belief in the impossible had always puzzled Joe. Sam was a pragmatic man.

You couldn't run a ranch and not understand that life doesn't always play fair. Yet somehow Sam managed to hang on to an infectious optimism that Joe and Christine were about to prove right.

They'd gathered the entire Cannon clan in the dining room and told them the news. He remembered whoops of excitement, a lot of bear hugs, and the fact that Sam was nowhere to be seen. Joe stepped outside onto the back porch and found the tough old rancher leaning against the railing. "Sam?" No answer. Joe approached his father-in-law. "Are you okay, Sam?"

The older man turned toward him, and Joe saw tears of joy running down his leathery cheeks. This from the same man who'd let the doctor set his broken leg without anaesthesia because a little pain was good for building character. Sam Cannon was as tough as they came . . . and as soft. The two men had embraced awkwardly while Joe choked back a few happy tears of his own.

They never talked about it afterward, but it was that moment that defined fatherhood for Joe. And it was that moment he thought about most often in the months that followed when his marriage began to fall apart.

"Joseph." Marina tapped her fork against the side of her plate. "Pay attention."

He looked up to find all eyes on him. "Getting old," he said with a shrug. "Can't stop daydreaming."

Nat laughed, the kind of full-bodied laugh you never heard east of the Mississippi. "I just asked if you wanted to come back to the hospital with me. I've got a new litter of pups that need attention and I could use an extra pair of hands."

He turned toward Marina, but her expression gave nothing away. She hadn't tried to run away for at least a week. He'd actually found himself letting down his guard, but after that outburst in their room, he wasn't entirely sure how he felt about leaving his wife alone with a houseful of curious Cannons.

"Puppies, huh?"

Nat grinned. "Three weeks old."

"Don't worry, Joe." Christine offered a brilliant smile. "I'm sure Marina will be just fine with us."

Next to him Marina yawned. "Go play with the puppies, Joseph. I am going to sleep."

It was Slade's turn to yawn. "Sounds good to me."

Joe glared at him. The guy had a way of making the most innocent remark sound fraught with innuendo.

"See?" said Christine. "We'll all be tucked away in our respective rooms. You needn't worry about a thing."

Her father threw back his head and laughed. "What in tarnation would he be worried about here? Ain't a neighbor for miles, and the ones we got are salt of the earth."

Talk about being between a rock and a hard place. *Let's face it, pal. You can't watch her twenty-four hours a day.* If she wanted to shoot her mouth off, there was nothing he could do to stop her. Sooner or later she'd find a way. The good thing was they were too far from civilization for her to pull another disappearing act.

He pushed back his chair and tossed his napkin on the table. "Come on, Nat. Let's go to the dogs."

The puppies were nursing when Joe and Nat reached the animal hospital.

"I thought the mother was sick," Joe said, looking down at the family scene before him.

Nat's smile was a lot like her father's. "Another miracle for Dr. Cannon."

"Enough small talk." He leaned against the file cabinet. "Let's get down to business."

"No preliminaries?"

He chuckled. "Between us? Seems a waste of time to me."

"She's a little young for you, isn't she, Joe?"

"Didn't know you were hung up on age."

"She could be your daughter."

"Only if I married young."

"You know what I'm talking about."

"She's over eighteen, if that's what you mean."

"That's part of it." He watched as she drew a deep breath and regrouped. "What are you doing here, Joe?"

"You have a problem with it, Nat?" he countered.

"I'm not sure," she said with disarming honesty. "I guess I'm wondering if it's fair to Christie."

"You invited me."

"True," said Nat, "but I didn't know I was inviting your wife. You should've told me, Joe."

"You're right," he said. "I'm sorry."

"I'm worried about Daddy. He had his heart set on you and Christie getting back together again."

"I'll talk to him."

"He's not as young as he used to be," she went on. "This is the kind of thing that takes its toll on a man."

"I got married, Nat. I didn't steal one of your horses."

"You know what I'm talking about," she persisted.

"There was always something special between you and Christie. Nobody expected this."

"Yeah, well, I didn't expect it, either."

"What?"

"Let's just say it was an impulsive wedding."

"When did you get married?"

He glanced at his watch.

"Joe!" Nat started to laugh. "Be serious."

"He *is* being serious." They both turned to see Christine standing in the entranceway. "What is it, Joe? Two weeks? Maybe three?"

"Now I know how you get all those big stories," he said. "Eavesdropping."

Nat looked from Joe to Christine, then cleared her throat. "Didn't hear you drive up, Christie." She looked out the window. "Where's the car?"

Christine gestured toward the rear of the building, but her eyes never left him. "Part of my journalistic training," she said in a deceptively calm tone of voice. "Shady ethics, undercover work, and eavesdropping. I think Joe took a pass on that course."

"I think my pager just buzzed," said Nat.

"I didn't hear anything," Joe said.

"There it goes again." Nat hurried toward the door. "There's iced tea in the office fridge. I'll be back as soon as I can."

"Fast on her feet, isn't she?" Christie remarked as her sister disappeared.

"Must be a family trait," said Joe.

Christine ignored his comment and crouched down near the puppies. He heard her soft murmurs as she gently stroked the mother's muzzle. "I could use an iced tea."

Joe considered telling her to get it herself but ended

up pouring them each a glass. He crouched down next to her. "Salud," he said, handing her the cold drink. "So what are you doing here?"

"Same as you." She took a sip. He watched the movement of her mouth, the arch of her throat. "I came to see the puppies."

"Bullshit."

"Such language." She winced and pretended to shield the dogs. "Not in front of the children."

"You wanted to know what was going on."

"And what if I did?" He observed the dangerous thrust of her chin. "She's my sister."

"She asked me to see the puppies."

"Right," said Christine, "and you were out of there so fast nobody else had a chance to tag along."

"Didn't stop you, did it?"

"No, it didn't." She took another sip of iced tea. "Did Nat threaten to call the child welfare bureau on you?"

He gulped down the rest of his drink. "The jokes are getting a little old, Christine."

"Of course," she said with a brittle smile. "The jokes are old, but your wife is younger than spring-time."

"Knock it off," he warned.

"Feeling sensitive, are we? Poor baby. Maybe you should have thought about that before you married Lolita."

"You don't know what you're talking about."

"Explain it to me, then."

Great going, McMurphy. Let's see you get out of this one. "Forget it." He stood up and placed the empty glass in the sink. "I'm going back to the house."

"The keys are in the car," Christine said. "I'll hitch a ride back with Nat."

He nodded. It occurred to him that he should have been down the stairs and halfway to the car by now, instead of standing there looking at Christine.

"Don't let me keep you," Christine said. "I know you have things to do, a wife to diaper."

"Damn it!" The words exploded from deep in his gut. "This shit has to stop, Chris. We're knocking around one-liners like we're trapped in a bad sitcom."

"Soap opera," she said, her bland television expression in place. "Sitcoms are funny. There's nothing funny about this."

"You're right," he said. "This isn't funny at all. I shouldn't have come here."

"No," Christine said, her voice breaking unexpectedly. "I'm the one who should have stayed away. I knew this was the wrong thing to do."

"I pushed."

She looked at him. "I didn't have to listen."

"I backed you into a corner."

"You wouldn't have been able to if I hadn't let you do it."

"I should've told Nat about Marina."

"Damn right you should have." She paused. "I wish I'd told Mom and Daddy before we arrived."

"Why didn't you?"

Her sigh filled the room. "You," she said. "I wanted to hurt you."

"Jesus, Christ," he muttered. "How the hell did we come to this?"

"Timing and luck," she said. "Isn't that what you said about my career?"

"I was bent out of shape when I said that, Christine. The marriage was breaking apart, you were pulling away from me, and I wasn't a boy wonder anymore."

She nodded. "But there's an element of truth in it, isn't there?"

He couldn't deny it. "Can't blame me for wanting my fifteen minutes."

"But I can blame you for throwing my fifteen minutes in my face."

"Is that what you think I did?"

The silence seemed to last an eternity. "Yes," she said. "That's what I think you did."

"Would you have stayed if I'd played it differently?"

"No," she whispered. "I wouldn't."

"That's what I thought."

"Maybe you don't remember the way it was back then, Joe, but I do. We never saw each other. I was working late hours, you were drinking hard—weeks went by when we didn't touch each other, much less make love."

His gut twisted. "So you found someone who would."

Her cheeks reddened.

"Come on, Chris. It was a long time ago. What difference does it make?" He wasn't a fool. He knew when she left him that there was another man, but that didn't mean he wanted to talk about it.

"There was no one else, Joe." Her words were so soft he thought he'd imagined them.

He met her eyes. "What was that?"

"I didn't say anything." She crossed the room to the refrigerator and took out the pitcher of iced tea.

He watched as she rinsed out her glass, then refilled it. He watched as she opened the refrigerator again and put the pitcher back inside. She looked at him. "I thought you were going back to the house."

"You said something before. What was it?"

"Nothing."

"I heard you."

"Must be your imagination."

Must be, he thought as he drove back to Sam and Nonie's, because those words would have changed everything.

11

"I thought you'd left," said Nat an hour later as she rejoined Christine in the office. She peered out the window. "Didn't I hear a car backing down the drive?"

"That was Joe." Christine was sitting on the floor with the puppies. "He went back to the house."

"Guess he misses the little woman."

Christine looked up at her older sister. Only Nat could get away with such an archaic term. "That phrase takes on new meaning now, doesn't it?"

Nat sat down next to Christine and chuckled as a puppy scrambled onto her lap. "So what do you know about it?"

"Not much. I was hoping you'd found out something."

"Don't think it's much of a love match, if that's what you mean."

"Yes," said Christine. "That's what I mean."

"Never knew Joe to be so secretive. Almost as if he was hidin' something. Got downright touchy, if you ask me."

Christine knew exactly what Nat meant. All along she'd had the feeling there was much more to Joe's marriage than what little met the eye. She forced a smile. "Did you tease him about robbing the cradle?"

Nat looked a tad sheepish. "Couldn't resist."

"She doesn't look much happier than he does, does she?"

"Gotta admit I haven't paid her much attention. She has a way of blendin' into the woodwork."

"Not really. Marina has a mind of her own, and she doesn't hesitate to use it."

"Not exactly the type of girl I'd expect Joe to marry."

"Because she isn't pretty?"

"There's that. You're a tough act to follow, Christie. I kinda figured the next step was a hotshot New York model with big hair."

"Maybe he was looking for something else."

"Call me crazy, but I don't think he's found it yet."

"Well, I know he didn't find it with me."

"Maybe he would've if you hadn't walked out."

Christine cradled one of the puppies against her cheek. "No," she said softly, "what he was looking for was the one thing I could never give him."

Marina was sitting on the front porch with Slade and a half dozen people whose names she couldn't remember when Joe roared into the driveway. He didn't seem to notice her or anybody else, just climbed from the car, then kicked up a storm of dust as he headed toward the stables.

"What's his bleedin' problem?" Slade muttered as they watched her husband.

"I wouldn't know," Marina said. "I am only his wife."

"Wish you wouldn't say things like that, love. Makes my imagination do dangerous things."

At that moment Marina didn't particularly care.

She was bored unto death sitting there in the middle of nowhere, a virtual prisoner of circumstances over which she had no control. The very least she could gain from this dismal situation was some insight into her captors.

"Did you know Christine when she was married to Joseph?"

He leaned back on his bony elbows and stretched his jean-clad legs out in front of him. "Wish I had. Don't know about you, love, but I have a bloody awful time trying to imagine those two together."

"I know exactly what you mean! They are different in every way, yet I have the feeling they were very much in love."

Slade studied his feet in their ubiquitous running shoes. "Nice soft leather in a rich cognac brown."

"Slade," she said sharply, "what are you talking about?"

"A pair of shoes I've had my eye on."

"Why on earth would you talk about shoes?"

"Mention Christine and the Boy Scout, and my mind automatically turns to shoes."

"You're a very odd man."

He started to laugh. "At least I don't hide trinkets in the attic, love."

Her body jerked with surprise. "I—I don't know what you're talking about."

"Just a comment from one larcenous soul to another."

"You must be mistaken."

"I don't think so." He patted the camera hanging around his neck. "What is it they say? A picture's worth a thousand words."

He had to be lying. There was no way on earth he

could have taken a picture of her stashing things away in the closet. She couldn't allow herself to think otherwise. "Sleep deprivation is doing terrible things to your imagination."

"A camera lens, the Boy Scout's watch, and a handful of Christine's diamonds. And that's just for starters. Need I go on?"

"No," said Marina. "That is quite enough."

"I admire resourcefulness in a woman. You saw an opportunity and you capitalized on it."

"That isn't exactly the way it was."

"Poor Mrs. Cusumano. No wonder you brought back one of my lenses."

"I found it," she said primly. "You should thank me, not accuse me of wrongdoing."

"You should try telling the truth."

Her heart hammered against her rib cage. "You wouldn't understand."

"Bloody hell I wouldn't. We're cut from the same cloth, Marina. Neither one of us has half as much as we'd like." He offered her a knowing smile. "But we're accumulating, aren't we?"

She could deny it vigorously, call the man a liar and a monster and any other dreadful thing she could come up with. She could slap his face and demand that he leave the premises at once. But the truth was she was growing tired of pretending to be a little cipher, the wife of a man who didn't love her, and it felt good to exercise both her wit and her will.

"Yes," she said with an answering smile. "We're accumulating."

"The question is, *why* are we accumulating?" She motioned for him to continue. "I've been poor, Marina, and I bloody well didn't like it. But I have the notion that you really don't have the foggiest what I'm talking about."

"Look at me," she offered, gesturing toward her simple clothing. "Obviously I am not rich."

He considered her thoughtfully. "Good try, love, but I'm too quick for you. Your lack of style is a political statement, not an economic necessity."

"How could you possibly know that?"

"You're a type that I've met before. The plain young thing with a social conscience."

"That's a terrible thing to say!"

"You choose to be plain. A new bob, some paint—"

She waved her hand impatiently. "That isn't what I mean. You make having a social conscience sound like something dreadful."

"A cliché, love, that's what it is. A social conscience is a drag on the bank account."

"How cynical."

"How bloody accurate. Poor people understand that." His smile was triumphant. "And that's how I know you were born to money."

"Privilege," she amended, enjoying the verbal fencing despite the danger. "There is a difference."

"Not to me."

"Are you going to tell my husband?" she asked. Or, much worse, Christine.

"Should I tell your husband?"

She simply smiled. "That is your choice, isn't it?" Joe's opinion of her was of no consequence. Christine's opinion, however, was. Thank God Slade didn't know that.

"I might be persuaded to keep your secret."

"I will not sleep with you, if that is what you are suggesting." He started to laugh, and her brows slid into a scowl. "You rude, insufferable beast. As if you're every woman's fantasy."

"That's not why I'm laughing, love. It's going to take a great deal more than that to buy my silence." He leaned closer and pinched her cheek. "I don't want your body, Marina. I want your story. You don't love that superannuated Boy Scout you're married to, so that tells me there has to be a bloody good reason why you're together."

"How dare you! I—"

"Lie to the rest of them, but don't lie to me. We're two of a kind."

She shuddered. "What an abysmal thought."

He crossed his legs at the ankle and considered his tatty running shoes. "What do you think about slip-ons in a rich cognac leather?"

"What *is* this fascination with your feet?"

"You tell me your story, love, and I'll tell you mine. Might be a nice way to pass the time. The days can be long and boring this far from civilization."

"Never!"

"Ah, youth," said Slade, who couldn't be much more than twenty-five himself. "Don't you know that you never say never?"

"Are you blackmailing me?"

"What an ugly word." He rose to his feet. "Just think about what I said, Marina. Once we get back to New York, all bets are off."

The first time Joe met Christine's family, Sam gave him the once-over, obviously sizing up the city slicker come to court his daughter, then extended his hand. Joe had never felt awed by anyone in his life, but the lean and lanky rancher had somehow managed to put the fear of God in him with a glance. "How do you feel about horses?" Sam had asked, his blue eyes twinkling with amusement.

"Depends how they feel about me," Joe had answered, with all the city wiseass bravado he could muster.

He'd learned something that day about humility. It was hard to maintain that wiseass bravado on the back of a horse hell-bent on sending you to your doom. And it was hard to hang on to your dignity when you were shoveling shit in the stables and poking under a hen's ass looking for eggs.

But what he'd really learned that week was how to be part of a family. After all, it wasn't as if he had any experience at it. Watching the Cannons at dinner, listening to their good-natured banter, Joe felt like a child sitting at the grown-up table for the first time. He didn't understand all the words, but he got the message: This was what life was about.

He'd had a glimpse of what family life might be like before his mother died, but that glimpse had only lasted a few short years. His father was an angry, bitter man who knew as much about raising a kid as he did about being happy. Joe was left to his own devices and spent most of his early teens on the street with his pals. He was headed down a dead-end road, same as the rest of them.

When his best friend was sent to a corrections center during their sophomore year in high school, Joe finally realized he'd be stuck there in Brooklyn for the rest of his life unless he knuckled down to work. His maternal grandfather had left him some money for college and, fueled by fear, he got serious, did well on his SATs, then was admitted to NYU on partial scholarship.

That was where he met Christine. She had a kind of confidence he'd never seen before. His confidence came from anger, but hers came from security. She talked about not fitting in with her family, but she loved them—and knew that they loved her—and that made all the difference.

That first trip to the ranch had been like coming home . . . for the very first time. He didn't know his ass from a pickax but he was game to learn. They treated him like one of the family: irreverently, off-handedly, fairly—and, most important, with real affection.

There was gruff Sam, patriarch of the Cannon family, who'd been born on the ranch and intended to die there. And his wife Nonie was as much a part of the land as Sam was. She had been orphaned as a child of five and taken in by the widow of the Cannons' old trail boss. Family meant everything to her. With a husband and seven kids to care for, she had little time for anything else—and wanted for nothing more.

Losing the Cannons hurt as much as losing Christine. After the divorce he'd missed them almost as much as he'd missed Christine. You lost a hell of a lot more than a spouse when you split up. He wondered why nobody ever talked about that on Oprah or Phil. Joe had lost an entire family, people who couldn't have meant more to him if they shared the same blood, the same history.

But here he was, back at the same table, with the same people around him—six years and one divorce later—and he felt as if he'd never left.

"Pot roast, mashed potatoes, and gravy," Nonie said, handing him a platter piled high. "All your favorites, Joe."

Trace's wife Suzanne started to utter the standard nineties warning about cholesterol, but a look from Sam stopped her midsentence.

Christine smiled into her own plate. He knew damn well she wouldn't touch the gravy, and maybe two forkfuls of beef would pass those lips. Later on he'd probably catch her at the fridge, munching carrots and eyeing broccoli as if it actually tasted good. Nice to know some things never changed.

"This is great, Nonie," Joe said, devouring some pot roast dripping with gravy.

"Bet you don't get anything like this in one of your fancy restaurants, Christie." Franklin was the eldest of the seven Cannon children and the one least able to understand why his sister had left the ranch.

"No one cooks like Mom," said Christine. "She could put Spago out of business if she had a mind to."

Joe saw the smirk flicker across Slade's face, and he resisted the urge to knock the photographer's teeth down his scrawny throat. *You don't get it, do you, you son of a bitch. She means every word.* Christine wasn't being flip. The love and respect she had for her parents were a large part of the woman she was. But he didn't expect an opportunistic bastard like Slade to understand.

He ate some more, then washed it down with some cold water while he listened to the bits and pieces of conversations arcing and diving across the huge pine trestle table.

"So what's this I hear about taking in guests?" he

asked Sam after an especially spirited exchange about profit margins.

"Sorry to say it came to that." Sam passed the buttermilk rolls to his right. "Started two years ago when the last of our old crew retired. We still needed to move the stock up to the pasture for the summer, but there wasn't enough of us to get the job done."

Marta, third child and resident attorney, put down her fork. "There are a number of precedents for this course of action," she said while her husband David, also an attorney, nodded solemnly, "but it's primarily a last resort."

"Things are that bad?" Joe asked.

Sam grunted and took a gulp of water. "Worse than bad. Once the damn government started messing with grazing rights, we found ourselves with big trouble."

Grazing rights were just the tip of the iceberg. Joe listened quietly while Sam, Franklin, and Marta laid out a story sad enough to break a man's heart. A way of life was dying west of the Mississippi, and so far nobody'd been able to do a goddamn thing about it.

"We're being blamed for everything from the hole in the ozone layer to water run-off problems," Sam bellowed.

"Sam." Nonie placed a hand on his forearm. "Remember your pressure."

"Hang my pressure. A man's gotta die of somethin', and I'd rather die speaking my mind than plowed under by a pile of regrets."

Hard to argue with that logic. Too few people stood for anything in this world. Sam Cannon was part of a dying breed, and Joe, for one, would be sorry to see his kind of man vanish into the history books.

"And what about the tree-huggers?" Christine's younger brother Mark asked. "They're stickin' their noses in where they don't belong."

"They got a right to worry about the land," Sam said to Joe's surprise. "Cattlemen have done a lot of damage. It's time we did our share to help."

"Damn sons of bitches," R.J., Mark's twin exploded. "They've cut our fences, fouled our water supply. Some SOB even wrecked the windmills on the Bar W ranch near Elko."

"Eco-terrorists," Joe said. The ranch equivalent of red paint splashed on a fur coat. He put down his fork, Nonie's pot roast all but forgotten. "Who's your advocate?"

"What do you mean?" Marta asked. "Congressman? Lobbyist?"

"Both," said Joe, "and whoever's covering the story nationwide."

"Don't really have nobody covering the story," said Sam, "but our congressman is . . ."

Christine watched her ex-husband scribble names and telephone numbers along the edge of a dollar bill. His eyes looked glazed, feverish. His voice was low, urgent. His movements had the quick, choppy quality of a tape on fast forward.

Ah, yes, she thought, sipping her iced tea. Joe had a new underdog to champion. She could almost see him beating back the flames of injustice with his bare hands. This was exactly the type of thing Joe lived for, that mythic battle between good guys and bad guys, right and wrong, the independent man and the soulless corporate entity.

How did he do it? Most people grew old and jaded. The edge of excitement that came naturally to Joe vanished somewhere along the way up the ladder of success for most people. Of course, there were those who might say Joe hadn't climbed very high up that mythical ladder, which made it easy for him to hang on to his ideals.

The conversation ebbed and flowed around her, but Christine found it impossible to keep her mind on any of it. She'd spent the morning watching Laramie's eight plump and healthy puppies nurse while Laramie napped. Scout and Blackfoot were due to have their litters any day now. Two of the horses had foaled that spring, and the colts were at the stage where they were all legs and spirit. Her little brother Trace's new bride was heavily pregnant with their first child while Mark's wife had apparently announced her third pregnancy during the Cannon Fourth of July barbecue. And there were Bobby's two and Marta's little Charlotte, Natalie's strapping twins who were home from Texas A & M. And who could forget Franklin's four, one of whom was pregnant with her second child.

Pregnant dogs, pregnant sisters-in-law, she wouldn't be surprised if her almost seventy-year-old mother was pregnant.

To hell with the Fertile Crescent, she thought bleakly, gulping down some iced tea. They should just name the Cannon Ranch "Fertility Acres" and be done with it. Was it any wonder she'd moved away as soon as possible? They made it all seem so damned easy, as if having a baby was as natural a thing to do as brushing your teeth. She stifled a bitter laugh. Sometimes it took a dash of black humor to get through times like this when the reality of her situation was staring her right in the face.

She could pick up the phone right now and have the President chatting with her a moment later. If she decided to throw a party, you could be sure that at least eight Oscar winners, four senators, and a Supreme Court nominee would all be vying for invitations.

Damn it, she thought. Wouldn't you think that would be enough to make any sane woman happy? She had four local Emmys to her credit, the cover of *Time*, and a future that would take her as high as she wanted to climb.

But there was one thing she couldn't do, one elemental, primal thing that was beyond her—and this was the one place on earth where she couldn't avoid the truth. The truth about her marriage, about her infertility, about the deep and aching loneliness in her heart that no amount of success had been able to fill.

She'd grown up with talk of bloodlines and gestation periods. The cycle of fertility and renewal had been the rhythm of life on the ranch, but she'd known from the start that her own life would never revolve around that same rhythm. The problems had started right after puberty, and two minor surgical procedures had gone a long way toward getting her back on track. "Many young women in your situation go on to successful pregnancies," the doctor had said with a reassuring smile. "DES exposure in utero may slow you down, but it won't stop you, Christine. One day you'll have your baby."

And for a while she'd really believed all of her dreams—every single one of them, fame and fortune and a family of her own—might come true.

Her father's booming laugh filled the room. Christine looked up and found Marina's grave, dark-eyed glance resting on her. *Are you going to do it?* she wondered, meeting the girl's eyes. *Are you going to give him the one thing I never could?*

"Hey, Joe!" Trace, her youngest brother, hollered down to the other end of the table. "Suzanne doesn't believe you survived an avalanche. Tell her I ain't lying."

Marina's eyes darted to meet Joe's. Apparently the second Mrs. McMurphy had yet to hear the infamous story about the boy king and the kid from Brooklyn.

"You guys have heard it a thousand times," Joe said.

"Since when are you shy, boy?" Sam thundered. "Damn exciting story."

"It's true?" Suzanne whispered, clasping her hands across her very pregnant belly.

Marina busied herself with her glass of water. Christine couldn't help but feel sorry for the girl. Marina's cheeks were red with embarrassment. It must feel rotten to learn things about your new husband from his ex-wife's family.

Joe told an admirably truncated version, but Suzanne was still duly impressed. Marina seemed downright uncomfortable.

Joe glanced toward the girl and whispered something in her ear. She shook her head. He said something more, and she nodded, a faint smile crossing her face.

"What about you, Christie?" Sam smiled at her

from the other end of the table. "We've all been runnin' off at the mouth about ranchin' and avalanches and such. You still planning to have the President and First Lady on your openin' show?"

She opened her mouth, but the words wouldn't come. Her show, the President, Q-ratings, none of it mattered. All that mattered was that the man she loved was sitting next to his brand-new bride, and Christine had never felt so lost and so alone in her life.

12

Christine pushed back her chair, rose to her feet, then fled the room as if the hounds of hell were at her heels. If Joe didn't know better, he'd think she was on the verge of tears.

Sam turned to Nonie. "Did I say something wrong?"

Nonie patted her husband's arm. "It wasn't you."

"She never did like ranch talk," Franklin said, looking at his wife, Annie.

"Maybe she's jet-lagged," Annie offered.

"Or nauseated," said their youngest, eighteen-year-old Hallie.

Joe heard Slade mutter, "Maybe she's bored," and he shot the wiseass photographer a murderous look. The urge to separate the guy's head from his torso was growing stronger by the minute.

Slade pushed back his own chair, muttered something, then lurched for the door. The SOB had youth on his side, but Joe had speed.

"Where the hell do you think you're going?" he asked, blocking the photographer's progress down the hall.

"The lady needs a friend."

"Maybe the lady needs to be left alone."

Slade ducked under Joe's arm and made it another few feet before Joe blocked him again.

"You're not married to her anymore, Boy Scout."

The warning was clear, and so was the reminder. Marina was back there in the dining room, surrounded by strangers who happened to be her current husband's former in-laws, a soap-opera situation if ever there was one. It should have been enough to stop Joe.

It wasn't.

"Slade." Both men turned to see Nonie standing in the archway. "Marina says you can answer Suzanne's questions about Princess Di."

"Do it," Joe said, in a low and deadly tone of voice.

He was out the back door before Slade's butt hit the dining room chair. The Nevada night sky had always dazzled him, but its wonder was lost on him tonight. He knew where he'd find her, the only place she could possibly be. He rounded the stable, then headed down the slope toward the stream. It wasn't much as streams went, but there was a hiding spot between the cottonwoods—a place that couldn't be seen unless you were right on top of it—and that was where he found Christine.

She sat with her back against a tree, knees drawn up to her chest, chin resting on her knees. Her sweep of blond hair drifted across her face. He couldn't make out her expression, but he had the feeling she'd been crying. Or was about to start.

"Some exit," he said, crouching down near her.

"Go away," she mumbled, keeping her face averted.

"Our friend Glade was on his way to the rescue, but I sent him packing."

"I can't do this, Joe." Her voice was filled with a pain so deep that he felt it in his gut. "It hurts too much to be here. Every place I look, everything I touch—it all reminds me of what we lost."

"I know." He laid a hand against her cheek.

"I don't think you do." Still she didn't move away.

"You were thinking about the baby."

She turned her head slightly toward him. "Am I that transparent?"

"To me." He traced the curve of her jaw with his forefinger. "I was there with you, Christie. I know how you feel."

"You don't really know me, Joe. Not anymore. You have no idea who I am, what I want, where I'm headed."

"People don't change."

She lifted her chin and met his eyes. "You're wrong." Her laugh was bitter. "People change, and there isn't a damn thing you can do about it."

"Circumstances change," he persisted, "but we don't."

"You're a fool, Joe." She said it without anger. He would have preferred anger. "Don't you ever get tired of chasing after lost causes?"

"No."

The night air carried the scent of her perfume. She lowered her head. "I'm too lost even for you. Go back to Marina. That's where you belong."

Tell her, McMurphy. She was your wife. You can trust her. . . .

"Things aren't what they seem, Christie. Marina doesn't—"

"Understand you? I've heard that before, Joe, maybe a thousand times from a thousand different men."

That knife in his gut twisted deeper. "Says a lot about your social life."

"No," she said with a trace of her old fire. "It says a lot about my *lack* of a social life. If you knew me as well as you think you do, you'd know I'd never spend time with a man who'd say that."

He grinned. "I didn't say that."

"I know you didn't." She paused a beat. "Were they upset?"

"That you stormed out on them?"

She nodded.

Joe shrugged. "They chalked it up to jet lag, but I wouldn't try it again tomorrow night."

"I don't think I'll make it to tomorrow night." She closed her eyes for a moment. "I'm thinking of going home in the morning. Terri said I could stay with her until my apartment's ready."

He ruffled her hair the way he used to back when they were married. Strange how a long-forgotten gesture could seem so familiar, so right. "You'll make it through the party."

She arched a brow. "How can you be so sure?"

"You love Sam and Nonie," he said. "And having you here for the party means the world to them."

"You make it sound so simple."

"It is. You belong here, Christie."

"I've never belonged here. Right from the start I was the odd one out. Nothing's changed about that."

"Bull."

"You don't know what you're talking about."

"This place is part of you. Everything you are, everything you'll ever be, it's all right here."

The silence was painful. It telescoped out until he wondered if he'd ever see the end of it.

"Shouldn't you be getting back to your wife?" she finally said.

"Soon."

"How about now? I came out here to be alone, Joe."

"You knew I'd follow you."

"I knew no such thing." He could hear the hope in her voice . . . or was he hearing six years of emptiness echoing inside his head?

"You know I want to tell you the whole story, Christie, every damn bit of it."

"What's to tell?" Her tone was brittle. "You're a happily married man."

"You're half right."

She pulled away from him. "I don't want to hear this. You're not being fair to me and you're sure as hell not being fair to Marina."

"It's not what you think it is between Marina and me." He knew he was crawling out onto a particularly shaky limb, but danger had never seemed more inviting. "We're not sleeping together."

"That's not any of my business." There was a light in her eyes that wasn't there before.

"Yeah?" A burst of hope, crazy and illogical, filled his heart. "I think it is."

She looked at him.

He looked at her.

She hauled off and punched him in the gut.

"Jesus Christ!" he sputtered. "What the hell was that for?"

"I don't sleep with married men, Joe. Not even if the man is my ex-husband."

"Trust me, Christie." His voice was urgent with the need to make her understand. "You know me, you know what I am. I wouldn't—"

"You're married," she repeated, looking to escape.

"There's nothing between Marina and me," he repeated, "but you're going to have to take me on faith."

"I don't take anyone on faith, Joe, not even myself."

"But you want to," he said, pushing. "Admit it, Christie. You want to believe me."

She jumped to her feet. "Yes, I want to believe you, but what difference does it make? It doesn't change anything. It doesn't make you any less married. It doesn't make me into the kind of woman you need. It doesn't change one damn thing."

"I don't love her."

Her eyes grew soft with unshed tears. "God, Joe. For her sake, I hope she doesn't love you."

"She can't stand me."

"They why did you marry her?" she persisted. "This sounds crazy, even for you."

"You've gotta trust me on this, Christie." He stood up and pulled her into his arms. She didn't resist. "I'm not going to hurt you."

"Sure you are," she whispered, tilting back her head to meet his eyes.

Her lips were soft, slightly parted. He took that as an invitation. His mouth covered hers in a kiss that was equal parts revenge and longing and wonder. Her arms were pinned against her sides. He could feel her heart thudding against his chest, hear the quick staccato of her breathing, smell the scent of her perfume filling his head with dreams.

He knew the sounds she made in the back of her throat when she came, the way her body shuddered with the aftershocks. And it was still there, all of it, waiting for them to give in to the heat.

Marina watched them from the shadows. She felt their longing in every fiber of her being, felt it the way she felt her longing for Zee. That bone-deep, aching void inside her heart that was as much a part of her as breathing.

Life was so unfair, and it was all her father's fault. Christine and Joe belonged together. The only thing keeping them apart was this sham of a marriage, same as it was keeping her away from Zee.

She moved father into the shadows. A twinge of pain flared in her lower back, and she rubbed it absently. Lately she felt so old and brittle, as if the bits and pieces of flesh and bone that held her together were breaking apart. American magazines attributed every ailment to the cumulative effects of stress. She'd never given much thought to such a thing. When you're fighting for your existence, the simple act of keeping alive tended to put life's problems into perspective. But since marrying Joseph, she'd found herself plagued with all manner of things, from sleeplessness to stomach pains.

Christine broke the kiss and rested her forehead against Joe's shoulder. Tears welled in Marina's eyes. They looked so right together, as if the hand of God had destined them for each other. Then, as suddenly as this rush of empathy came over her, it was replaced by a dizzying sense of injustice.

Christine and Joe were together in an embrace beneath a benevolent moon. Marina and Zee were separated by her father's arrogance and greed. Christine had everything: beauty, wealth, acclaim, a man who quite obviously would walk across hot coals simply to be near her. Marina had nothing but the growing certainty that she would never see Zee—or her homeland—again unless she took matters into her own hands.

Everything she needed was back in New Jersey. Surely she had accumulated enough property to pay for a plane ticket. There was nothing she could do trapped here on the Cannon ranch, but once they returned to the house in Hackettstown she would find a way to reclaim her own life. Even if it meant she had to take Slade into her confidence in order to do it.

The thing to do was avoid Joe.

Christine locked herself in her room that night and was tempted to throw the key out the window. He was an occasion of sin, that's what he was, and she was a good Catholic girl who knew all about such things. She'd made a lot of compromises in her life, some harder to justify than others, but she'd never compromised her stand on married men. She wasn't about to start now.

Marina deserved better from the two of them, and, frankly, so did Christine.

It didn't matter why he'd married Marina. The fact that he had spoke volumes. Sure, Christine could sleep with him, but where would that get her? That was one trip down memory lane she could do without. Sex between them had always been both passionate and explosive. There was no reason to think it would be any different now.

She sat on the edge of the bed and waited for the fire in her blood to cool. She was angry and sad and everything in between, but beneath all of that wild emotion she was also alive. Vibrantly, deeply, wonderfully alive.

And wanting Joe more than ever before.

Sleeping together would only complicate an already ridiculously complicated situation. She'd start dreaming of happy endings, believing in the impossible, wondering if love really was lovelier the second time around.

She was too smart for that. You didn't get to be heiress apparent to Barbara Walters by making stupid mistakes. She'd worked too long and too hard to blow it now by getting herself involved in something that would only break her heart . . . and maybe Marina's along with it.

Not that she should give a damn about Marina. The girl was nothing to her. Less than three weeks ago she hadn't even known the little thing existed. These maternal feelings she'd been experiencing toward her ex-husband's new wife were downright bizarre.

When things were back to normal and she was settled into her New York apartment, she intended to buy herself a cat and let all of her maternal feelings channel themselves toward the lucky feline.

"What are you looking at?" Joe asked Marina as he stripped down to his shorts. He was tired, still hungry, and unable to stop thinking of the way Christine's mouth had felt beneath his.

"What do you think you're doing?" Marina looked horrified. "Put those trousers back on immediately."

"Listen, kid, sleeping on the floor's bad enough. I'm not going to sleep in my clothes."

"You slept in your clothes in New Jersey."

"I slept in my shorts in New Jersey."

"But you took your trousers off in another room."

"I don't see the difference."

"There is one," she said. "Watching you drop your trousers is too intimate."

"So close your eyes," he suggested. What difference did it make if he dropped his pants in front of her or dropped them in the bathroom, the hallway, or the rooftop? There was only one woman he wanted, and she wasn't the one he was married to.

Marina was sitting on top of the bed, wearing one of her plain gray nightgowns with the buttons down the front. She seemed lost in its voluminous folds.

"Don't you ever wear anything that fits?" he asked as he lay down on the pallet he'd set up near the window.

"I have more important things with which to concern myself."

"Not planning anything that requires a passport, are you?" The look in her eyes made him uneasy.

Her expression didn't vary so much as a millimeter. "I will do whatever it is I decide to do."

"Very cryptic, grasshopper," he said. "Feel like speaking English?"

She lay down on the bed and closed her eyes.

"For what it's worth, I wish this was over, too, kid."

He wasn't sure, but he thought he saw her smile.

"This was a wonderful idea," Christine said as her father started up the truck a few mornings later. "We haven't had nearly enough time together since I arrived."

He fixed her with a look. "Been thinkin' you might be avoiding me, Christie."

"How can you think such a thing?" She upped the wattage on her smile.

"Don't be givin' me that TV smile, daughter. You might fool your big city friends with that, but you can't fool your pa."

"I'm not trying to fool you," she said with a shade less certainty than before. "You must admit things have been hectic."

"Nothin' unusual about that."

"You know what I mean, Daddy." The truck lurched forward, and Christine grabbed for the dashboard. "With the party and all, there's been a lot going on."

"Seems to me you been spendin' more than your fair share of time on the telephone."

"I explained to you and Mom that I have to keep in touch with the office. With the show getting ready to premiere, there are a lot of balls to juggle."

"I thought you had people to do your juggling for you."

"It's my show," she said as they bounced down the dirt road, "which means I do most of the juggling." Not entirely accurate, but it seemed the safest explanation.

"What's with that English boy?" He downshifted. "He carries that camera all around with him, but I ain't seen him taking that many pictures."

"I suppose he's waiting for the party."

Sam shot his daughter a sideways glance. "Seems he's been spendin' a lot of time with Joe's wife."

"I hadn't noticed."

"Seems like you've been spendin' a lot of time with Marina's husband."

She swiveled in her seat. "What's that supposed to mean?"

"It means what it means," said her father. "A blind dog could see that marriage ain't long for this world."

She started to laugh. "They're newlyweds," she pointed out. "They're getting acquainted."

"Marina and that English boy are getting acquainted. Joe's been with you when he's not helpin' us replace the windows in the bunkhouse."

"You're getting old, Daddy," she said lightly as they turned onto the main road. "Letting your imagination run away with you."

He screeched to a stop, sending the truck angling across the road. "Hellfire!" he roared. "Don't you go patronizing me, girl. There's nothin' wrong with my eyes or my brain. I know what I see, and what I see spells trouble. You're still in love with him."

"Is that a question?"

"Don't smartmouth me, Christie. This is your daddy you're talkin' to. I deserve better."

She sagged back against the torn leather seat, scarcely noticing the broken spring poking against her fourth vertebra. "You're right," she said. "You do deserve better. I'm sorry." He reached out and patted her on the shoulder, and to her horror, she began to cry. "He—he says they're not . . . really married, that there's a whole big story that he can't tell me about right now, but I—" She buried her face in her hands.

"I believe him," said Sam.

She peered through her fingers. "You do?"

"I do," Sam said with obvious conviction. "I know that boy through and through, and I know he loves you now the way he loved you the day you two tied the knot."

"A lot's happened since we tied the knot, Daddy."

"Maybe, but that don't change the fact that you two belong together."

"Next thing I know you'll tell me you read romance novels."

"Ain't nothing wrong with romance. Got your ma and me through some tough times."

"Seven children," she said. "I would suppose you and Mom found time for romance."

"More to life than children," he said, meeting her eyes.

"I know that," she whispered.

"I'd've loved your ma no matter what."

"You can't know that for sure."

"The hell I can't. When it comes down to it, nothing means anything without your ma by my side."

Nice words, but Christine was unconvinced. Whether or not her father admitted it, his family was his world. The very survival of the ranch depended on the effort of every member.

With the exception of Christine.

"This is pointless," she said. "Joe's married and not to me. Case closed."

"Case ain't closed. Not until the two of you sit down and hash out your differences."

"We don't have any differences, Daddy. We don't have anything at all."

"You have the best thing of all," said Sam. "You two got a past."

"Maybe so," she said, "but Marina is his future."

"You don't believe that any more than I do."

"I don't know what I believe anymore, Daddy. My heart says one thing, my head says another." She laughed hollowly.

"That ain't a love match, Christie, not by a long shot. Whatever reason he's got for marryin' the girl, it's got nothing to do with love."

"So what do you think it is?" Christine asked Slade after dinner as they took a walk near the pond.

"Sex," said Slade, snapping a picture of her reaction.

"Baloney," she said, splashing water in his direction.

His Nikes were covered with a layer of dust. No walks like this once he got the Guccis. "The Boy Scout's telling you that he's playing the celibate groom?"

"Joe hasn't told me anything at all. I'm relying on women's intuition."

He wasn't buying it. "I'm the one next door to the newlyweds," he reminded her.

"And you're probably the one with his ear pressed up against the wall."

"You wound me, love. I'm much more subtle than that." And a great deal more dangerous.

He watched, amazed, as cool Christine Cannon struggled to get control of her emotions. What was it about this dreary, godforsaken land that made these Yankees drop their guard?

"I haven't noticed much . . . affection between

them, have you?" she asked, trying to act as if it didn't matter a damn.

"Wouldn't know, Chris love. I'm more interested in you."

She met his eyes and flashed him her big, wide, perfect smile. "Not much longer," she said with a toss of her blond hair. "The party is at the end of the week, and I promise we'll leave the next morning."

"Don't rush for me, love," he said easily. "I'm becoming a regular cowboy."

They both laughed at the absurdity of the statement, but there'd been more truth to it than Christine would ever know. Every day he came closer to the truth, and he'd be goddamned if he left before he knew all of their secrets.

13

The Church of the Sacred Heart was located thirty miles from the Cannon Ranch. Father Bill had volunteered to drive out to the house to perform the ceremony, but both Sam and Nonie were adamant.

"A church wedding," said Nonie firmly.

Sam agreed with his wife. "After fifty years, it's time we made it legal."

Everyone had laughed at that statement, but for Sam and Nonie it was the plain truth. No fancy cruise or trip to Europe for them. Renewing their vows before their family and friends was all they wanted.

"You don't have to do this," Christine repeated on the morning of the wedding as she handed Slade one of her father's ties.

"Naff off, love," he said pleasantly as he looped the oblong of silk around his neck. "I'm the best photographer in town. Why shouldn't I record the event for posterity?"

She kissed him on the cheek. "You're not half as bad as you pretend to be," she said, wiping a smudge of lipstick with the tip of her finger. "Mom and Daddy are over the moon about the video."

"Remember that when you're bitching about the *Vanity Fair* photos."

"Me bitch? You must have me confused with someone else."

"I know that look in your eye, love. It's time to get back to work."

She laughed but she didn't deny it. She was tired of bumping into memories every time she turned a corner. It had happened again just this morning. She saw herself as a little girl, sitting on the porch with a Nancy Drew book, while her brothers and sisters mucked out stalls and learned how to rope calves. *She ain't like the rest of you,* neighbors used to tell her parents. *That girl's got other things on her mind.*

For a long time she'd thought herself a changeling, dropped into the bosom of the Cannon family by a fairy with a sense of humor. She didn't like the great outdoors or dust or talking bloodlines around the corral. She wanted excitement, new faces, newer places, the chance to be someone besides one of the Cannon kids.

She loved her family and would lay down her life for them, but she'd always known in her heart of hearts that fate had other things in mind for her. It all came so easily for her brothers and sisters. Love, marriage, childbirth . . . predictable as night follows day. And the strangest thing of all was that they knew what riches they'd been granted and they thanked God for their blessings every single day.

Christine had seen it in Natalie's eyes. Oh, Nat loved hearing about the latest Hollywood gossip, the scoop on the D. C. follies, but Christine knew Natalie wouldn't trade a second of her hardworking life for an instant of Christine's glamorous existence.

"Finish knotting your tie," she said to Slade. "I'm going to change my earrings."

He was too perceptive, and her emotions were too close to the surface. He'd captured it all with his camera, and she'd find her heart exposed in the pages of *Vanity Fair* for the entire world to see.

You can handle this, she thought as she walked down the hallway. This time tomorrow she'd be on her way back East, back to her real life. A life she could control. She was ready to get back to work, get back to a world she understood, to a job she was good at. She didn't need these emotional entanglements, this quicksand feeling.

She hadn't told Joe yet about her plans. She'd done her best to avoid him the past two days, and it hadn't escaped her notice that he'd done the same. As far as she was concerned, he could have the house in Hackettstown. Yesterday she'd made a few calls, offered a few outrageous bribes, blessed Terri for being such a good friend, then breathed a sigh of relief that her Manhattan apartment would be ready for her to move in by the end of the week. Offices Extra was more than willing to pick up their equipment for a substantial fee, and the moving men would handle the rest.

She was done with living in the past. There wasn't one damned thing to be gained from it. The life her parents and brothers and sisters lived wasn't for her, and it never would be. Fate had determined that fact long ago, and it was about time she made her peace with it.

"Aunt Chris!" Franklin's daughter Hallie popped into the hallway. "I can't fasten my dress."

"Oh, Hallie," Christine whispered, looking at the young girl in her very sophisticated teal blue dress. "You look beautiful!"

"Do you really think so?"

"Absolutely." She stepped back and surveyed the outfit from shoes to hair. "I need four people to put me together half as well."

The girl's cheeks reddened, and she looked down at the floor. Eighteen and still able to blush. There was hope for the future. Christine smiled and placed her hands on the girl's shoulders.

"Spin around, Hallie," she said, "and let me fasten you up."

You're getting sentimental in your old age, Cannon, she thought as her fingers moved their way up the row of tiny pearl buttons. *Don't go telling the poor kid about the way you used to change her diapers and powder her behind.*

"There you go, Hallie."

Hallie turned around and grinned. Christine swallowed hard. She saw her father and her brother in that grin, and she saw the future stretching out before Hallie, all shiny and new and filled with hope.

"Are you okay, Aunt Chris?"

"Fine," she said, tossing back her hair. "I was just thinking there's one thing missing from your outfit."

"The shoes!" Hallie said with a groan. "I knew I'd picked the wrong shoes."

"Your shoes are perfect," Christine said, patting the girl on the shoulder. "What you need is something pretty around your neck."

"But I don't—"

"Yes, you do," Christine interrupted. "Wait right here."

She dashed back to her room and rummaged in the top drawer of her old dresser. Tucked in the far corner was a velvet pouch, a bit the worse for the wear, but that didn't matter. It was what was inside that counted.

Moments later she was fastening the locket around Hallie's slender throat. "Your Grandpa Sam gave it to me on my sixteenth birthday. It's very special to me."

"It's beautiful, Aunt Chris," said Hallie, looking down at the oval of gold. "I promise to give it right back after the party."

"No," said Christine, clearing her throat to hide the catch in her voice. "I want you to keep it."

"I can't! You said it was very special to you."

"And it is. That's why I want you to have it. I don't get to see much of you, honey, but that doesn't mean you're not in my heart." *One day you'll give this to your own little girl, Christie, and you'll think of your pa when you do.* There wasn't going to be a little girl for her, not now or ever, but giving the locket to her niece had gone a long way toward easing the ache inside her heart.

Hallie hugged her, then hurried away to show off her treasure.

"Damn!" Christine whispered, dabbing at her eyes with her fingertips. Why couldn't she be as cool and controlled as her TV persona, weeping only during sweeps month . . . and then only when the camera was zooming in for a close-up.

"Nice gesture."

She jumped at the sound of Joe's voice behind her. "How long have you been there?" she asked.

He stepped out of the shadows. "Long enough."

Christine met his eyes. "She looked beautiful, didn't she?"

"So do you."

She struggled to ignore the flutter of recognition

his words called to life. "When was the last time you wore a string tie?" she asked, summoning up a shaky smile.

"Our wedding," he said.

"Sorry I asked," she said lightly. He had no business having such a beautiful mouth. Lower lips like his should be declared a danger zone.

He didn't touch her or move closer, but she felt as if he had. "The sun was shining, the lupine was in bloom—"

Her heart beat hard against her chest. "Daddy's toast. I didn't think you'd remember."

"Best day of my life, Christie."

"Not exactly a testament to your second wedding day."

He said nothing. It was all in his eyes, the intensity of his gaze, the sense of destiny that was making her feel suspended in time.

"Beep-beep!"

They jumped as her nieces Charlotte and Alice Ann raced down the hallway in fancy pink party dresses and sock feet.

"The house is bursting with kids," Christine said as they watched the two giggling little girls head for the attic stairs. Not to mention aunts, uncles, cousins, and assorted friends, all of which were crammed into the main house and the two bunkhouses. It was hard to tell ranch hands from family.

"I tripped over a tricycle last night on the way to the bathroom. Lucky I didn't break my damn neck."

Impulsively she touched his forearm and felt a current zap its way north, south, east, and west. *Big mistake, Cannon. You're getting in over your foolish little head.* She pulled back. "I should see if Mom needs help getting ready."

"Yeah," said Joe. "Maybe Sam needs a pep talk."

It was a weak joke, but they both laughed politely. Something was happening between them, something deep and frightening, and Christine knew he was every bit as aware of it as she was. What they both needed was a dose of reality.

"Did Marina like the dress I found for her?" It didn't get much more real than that.

"The dress is great, but she's boycotting the party."

"Boycotting the party or her husband?" She instantly regretted the words. They sounded waspish and petty. Feeling that way was one thing; sounding it was another. "Sorry I said that."

"So am I."

She'd been looking for a mood breaker and she'd found it. It should have made her happy, but instead she felt as if she'd lost something very special. "Want me to talk to her? I can be very persuasive."

He looked less than enthused. "It won't do any good."

"Let me try," she persisted, as if that could somehow make up for everything that had happened between them. She didn't wait for him to say no.

She strode down the hall to their room and tapped on the door. "Marina?"

No response.

She tapped harder this time. "Marina, I'd like to talk to you."

The door swung open. "As you wish."

Marina was still in her nightgown, a sad beige affair. Christine noted the way it overwhelmed her painfully thin body as Marina led the way into the room. The girl's brown hair stuck up at odd angles, and her face was the color of the bedsheets. The dress she'd borrowed from Suzanne hung from the back of the closet.

Christine fingered the deep ruffle at the neckline. "Not your usual style, hmm?"

Marina shrugged her bony shoulders. "I am not inclined toward excess."

"So you've said before."

Marina sat down in the middle of the bed. The girl motioned for Christine to sit, but the idea of sitting on the bed Joe shared with his bride was more than Christine could bear. She stood near the window.

"Joe said you're not joining us today."

"Yes," said Marina. "That's right."

Christine smiled. "I know a fiftieth anniversary party must not sound terribly exciting to you, but you might be surprised. Cannon parties are legendary. Lots of good food, good music, dancing—"

"I will stay here, thank you."

"It's your choice, of course, Marina, but can't I convince you to—"

"I know my own mind," Marina declared firmly. "I shall stay here."

Against her better judgment, Christine approached the bed. "Are you feeling okay, Marina? I haven't seen much of you the past few days."

"I am fine."

"You're looking pale."

Marina said nothing. Morning sun spilled through the bedroom window, glinting off the gold of her wedding ring.

Christine looked away.

"My stomach," Marina said, then stopped.

Christine looked back toward her. "Are you in pain?"

Marina shrugged. "I—I don't know."

"Discomfort?"

The girl nodded.

"Have you told Joe?"

"It is none of his business."

So that was the way the wind blew. "If you would like to see a doctor, I'd be happy to take you."

"I have no need for a doctor, thank you. It is—I believe this is a woman's problem."

All of this angst, and they were only talking about her period. "There's Midol in the hall bathroom and Advil in my room if you need it. My mother swears by her heating pad. I'm sure she'd let you—"

"No." The girl managed to sound arrogant and childlike at the same time.

"Fine," said Christine. "Suit yourself."

Marina's mask fell as soon as the door closed behind Christine. She curled up into a fetal knot, drawing her knees in close to her chest, letting herself give in to the fear that had been clawing at her chest like a wild animal struggling to break free of its captor.

The pain had returned last night. She'd slipped from bed, careful not to step on Joseph, then locked herself in the bathroom where she could pace the length of the tiny room in privacy. Not that pacing helped alleviate the pain. In truth, nothing had. Pain was her constant companion.

Christine had seemed so warm, so understanding, that for one foolish moment Marina had wanted to forget their differences and beg for her help. She felt her life spinning out of control, and there was nothing she could do to stop it.

She'd heard the news reports of fighting in the mountains of her homeland, and despair engulfed her with the sudden fury of a flash flood. She'd begged Joseph to find out everything he could about the situation, but he turned up nothing. She wondered if he'd even tried.

Thousands of miles away her father and the man she loved were locked in deadly combat, and here she was, trapped in the middle of a land so vast and empty she felt more insignificant than ever. Before long she would vanish altogether, and she wondered if anyone would even remember her name.

"Sorry about this," Christine whispered as Joe escorted her into the church. "My family suffers from the Noah's Ark syndrome."

"Don't worry about it."

"It wasn't my idea."

"I never said it was."

"I didn't want you to get the wrong idea."

He followed her into the front pew. "Trust me. I don't have the wrong idea."

"I'm glad," said Christine.

"Good," said Joe.

"Good," she repeated.

"Place is packed," Joe said, craning his neck to check out the crowd.

"Probably all relatives. You know what they say in these parts: Scratch a cactus, find a Cannon."

An odd expression drifted across his face. "I've really missed them."

"They missed you, too. You could've visited them."

"No," he said slowly. "I couldn't have."

It was less what he said than the way in which it was said. Christine had a sudden understanding of his own loss, an understanding that cut so deep it stole her breath. When she walked out on him she'd done more than deprive him of a wife and bedmate. She'd stripped him of a family, a network of love and support that he'd never known before—and probably hadn't known since.

She cleared her throat. "I wish it could have been different."

He met her eyes. "It could have."

"We keep going over the same ground, Joe. It's pointless to do it again. I've made my peace with the past. I advise you to do the same."

"You owe me, Christie."

She arched a brow. "I don't owe you anything at all."

"Not even an explanation?"

"Like your explanation about Marina?"

"That's different."

"That's what I thought you'd say." She didn't want to feel this way, all open and hopeful and scared. Every time she saw Joe, each time she heard the sound of his voice, she was catapulted back to the girl she'd left behind. The one who, for a little while, believed in miracles.

They sat in silence, listening to the music, the excited whispers of the guests filing into the church, the sound of their own heartbeats, separate and distinct. Franklin and his family shared the pew with them. Hallie made sure she sat next to Joe, and

Christine felt a sharp pang as she watched the way the girl ducked her head and looked up at Joe through tangled lashes. Hallie was a lot like Christine had been at that age, hungry for everything life had to offer, yet still innocent enough to appreciate it.

I used to look at you like that, Joe. Do you remember?

For the first time since he arrived in Nevada, Joe wanted to run. It was all coming down on him, as fast and hard as the long-ago avalanche that had got him into this mess in the first place. Past, present, future—it was all converging in this country church, on this morning, and Christine was at the heart.

Did she have any idea how much Hallie resembled her? The high, proud cheekbones, the beautiful mouth, the set of her jaw. They even had the same blue-grey eyes, wide set and curious. But there was one significant difference, and that difference tore at his heart: Hallie's eyes shone with optimism while Christine's, hidden behind the bright blue contact lenses, held the shadows of disappointment.

A few weeks ago he wouldn't have believed it possible. She had a prime-time weekly show on tap, the cover of *Time* in her back pocket, and the world at her feet. He'd spent the last six years hating her for walking out on their marriage . . . and hating himself for still giving a damn. She'd gone on to bigger and better things than marriage to some schmuck who made his living tilting at windmills, and if she ever gave him a thought it was only to thank her lucky stars that she'd been smart enough to move on.

Suddenly he wasn't so sure. The loneliness in her eyes was unmistakable. Christine Cannon, a lost cause? He'd be laughed out of town for a statement like that. Most people would say she was one of life's golden girls, but Joe liked to think he wasn't most people—and that he saw what other people didn't.

The pieces were beginning to fall into place. Three weeks together in Hackettstown, and he'd never heard her call a friend to say hello, and he sure as hell hadn't heard any friends calling her to shoot the breeze. She talked business and she talked finance, but she never talked about any of the other things that mattered. That snotty Brit photographer was the closest thing she had to a friend, and Joe had no doubt the bastard would sell her out to the highest bidder given half the chance.

Maybe it was the smell of orange blossoms in the air or the strains of the Wedding March, or maybe it was just that he was tired of being alone, tired of wondering what might have been, tired of looking for someone to take her place when he knew damned well there was no other woman on earth who could make him feel the way Christine had simply by being his. Whatever the reason, he knew things couldn't go on the way they were.

Nonie and Sam took their places at the altar.

The priest cleared his throat. "My dear friends, we are gathered here today . . ."

Joe looked at Christine.

". . . to celebrate one of life's most mysterious wonders . . ."

Christine's eyes misted over with tears.

". . . the miracle of marriage between a man and a woman . . ."

He reached for her hand.

". . . who have invited us here today to join them as they . . ."

She looked at him through a tangle of lashes as he laced his fingers with hers.

". . . show us all that love can triumph over the adversities of life. . . ."

She squeezed his hand.

He squeezed back.

If love had a sound, it was the chorus of angels singing inside his heart as he sat there on that hot summer morning with Christine's hand in his.

Weddings did foolish things to a woman.

Weddings made you believe in the impossible. They made you believe in happy endings and rose-covered cottages and that there was no braver act in the world than that of a man and woman tossing in their lot together and facing an uncertain future with nothing but love on their side.

She watched as her parents fearlessly made those promises for the second time in their lives. Her mother's lined face was aglow with happiness. Her father's rugged countenance seemed lit from within. Their married life had been a tapestry of hard work on the ranch, the heartbreak of losing two children in infancy, the day-to-day grind of staying one step ahead of adversity.

And still they stood there, backs straight, voices strong, and spoke those vows with the same passion and certainty she imagined they'd exhibited the first time.

When times were tough, they'd turned toward each other, taking comfort in sweet familiarity, trusting that in the grand scheme of things love would see them through.

She'd always thought them the luckiest people on the face of the earth but now she wondered if she'd been wrong. Was it luck that had kept them together, or was it the fact that they'd worked just as hard at loving each other as they had at being good parents and good citizens and good landowners? A few weeks ago she might have run from that question but now she found herself longing to dig more deeply.

A magazine reporter had once asked Christine how you know when you're finally an adult, and she'd said it was a question of illusion. Once the last of your illusions was stripped away and you found yourself facing life without the buffer of optimism and the shield of dreams, you'd finally crossed the boundary into adulthood. They'd both agreed it was a damn shame.

But as she sat there with her hand in Joe's, she could feel the ache inside her chest, and she wondered if it was love or its absence that would break her heart in two.

14

"Praise God!" said Amelia Sweeney as she clutched Christine and Joe to her bony chest. "Your ma must be beside herself to see the two of you together again!"

"As I live and breathe!" declared Buzz Wyman, pumping Joe's hand up and down. "Always knew you'd be back one day." He turned to Christine and winked. "You, too, missy. Real glad to see you worked things out. Better late than never, I always say."

Buzz wasn't alone. Every time Christine and Joe turned around, another well-meaning friend or relative swept them up into a bear hug and congratulated them on getting back together.

"I should have told them you're married," Christine said as the Mallorys, her cousins twice removed, hurried off to spread the news. "Actually, *you* should have told them you're married."

"Why ruin it for them?" Joe asked with a good-natured shrug of his broad shoulders. "Besides, it's your parents' day. Might as well let people hang on to their fantasies a little longer."

"Christie!" Her brother Mark's voice boomed across the crowded yard. "Come on over here and say hey to Walt Dailey."

"Who's Walt Dailey?" Joe asked. "I don't remember him."

"Neither do I," said Christine.

Joe took her hand. "Let's mingle."

She could have pulled her hand away from his or said something, but she did neither. The afternoon had taken on a surreal quality that made her feel as if she were floating through space. She was incapable of saying or doing anything that would break the magical spell she had fallen under back at the church. And why should she? None of this was real. Tomorrow morning she'd be on her way back East, and this interlude would be nothing but another memory to add to the stack of memories filed away inside her heart.

Walt Dailey turned out to be the rancher who bought the old Jackson spread that adjoined the Cannon ranch to the north. Dailey was one of the new breed of ranchers, well educated, environmentally aware, but still grounded in the time-honored traditions. Even better, he shared Joe's opinions right down the line. The two men launched into a spirited discussion on using government lands and were quickly joined by her father and brothers and assorted other friends and relatives.

"Stay," Joe said as she took her hand from his.

Christine shook her head and drifted off toward the house. She bumped into Natalie and Hallie near the buffet table.

"You're lookin' wilted," her sister said, handing her a cup of lemonade. "It's hot as the dickens out here."

"Thanks." Christine took a sip, then sighed in appreciation. "It's wonderful. Don't say anything, but it's better than Mom's."

Next to her Hallie beamed. "I made the lemonade, the punch, and the cole slaw. I wanted to prepare sushi rolls, but Mom said that was dangerous territory."

Christine put her arm around the girl. "You start Penn State in September, right?" Hallie nodded. "I'll send a car for you one weekend, and we'll do Manhattan. There's a place on Columbus Avenue that does the best sushi in town."

You'd think she'd offered the girl her weight in diamonds. Hallie whooped with delight, hugged Christine, then dashed off to make her brothers green with envy.

Christine turned to Natalie. "Why is it I don't think the boys are big on sushi?"

Natalie gave one of her full-bodied laughs. "Sometimes Hallie reminds me so much of you that I have to remind myself that I was the one with the fourteen-hour labor."

"I meant what I said before. I'd love to keep an eye on her while she's at Penn."

"I know you're going to be real busy with the show and all," said Nat, "but it's real nice of you to offer."

Christine laid a hand on Nat's forearm. "Really, Nat. I know you haven't seen much of me the past few years, but that doesn't mean I don't love all of you. Hallie's a great kid. I'd like to help her out if I can."

"Well, I'd really appreciate that. Hallie's a dreamer. The world isn't kind to dreamers."

Suzanne, heavily pregnant, strolled past with little Bree's hand in hers.

"I'm glad I delivered all of mine in the spring before the dog days settled in. Good thing Marta used her head."

"Marta? Do you mean—"

Natalie's face reddened. "Daddy always said I have a mouth the size of the Grand Canyon. Marta and David weren't plannin' to let the cat out of the bag until later tonight."

"I won't tell a soul," Christine promised, trying to dwell on the fact that life was seldom fair. Marta was almost forty-five. With all the miracles available for women of childbearing age and beyond, you'd think there'd be just one small miracle left over for her.

The two women grew silent, sipping their lemonade and listening to the commotion in the yard. Joe's voice rang out over the combined male rumble from the ranchers.

". . . what you need is visibility . . . a voice where it counts . . ."

"Seems like he never left, doesn't it?" Nat remarked.

Christine nodded. "He always did fit in here better than I did."

"What a crazy thing to say. This is your home."

"It hasn't been my home for a long time, Nat. I'm not sure it ever really was."

"You're a Cannon. This land belongs to you as much as it does any one of us."

"I'm not like the rest of you. I'm not good with horses, I don't like the outdoors, and I—" She stopped abruptly.

"Don't have kids?"

She met her sister's eyes. "Yes," she said, lifting her chin. "I don't have kids."

Natalie gestured toward the score of children racing around the front yard. "Seems like we have more than enough to go around."

"You know what I'm talking about, Nat."

"I guess I don't," Nat said slowly. "Not really. I

never gave a lot of thought to how it would feel not to have them."

"Why should you? That's like questioning the fact that you breathe."

"You're happy with your life, aren't you, Christie?"

The question surprised her. "I suppose so." She paused for a moment. "Of course I am."

"You don't sound that sure."

"Your question surprised me, that's all."

"If you surprised me with a question like that, I'd still know the answer."

She smiled at her older sister. "I'd know the answer, too, Nat. You're a happy woman. It shows in everything you do."

Natalie didn't disagree. She glanced toward Joe, a thoughtful expression on her face. "Something's wrong when you can't remember that a man's a newlywed."

Christine smiled.

"Nothing to say, Christie?"

"Not a word."

"Can't help wondering what brought Joe and that girl together."

"I know," said Christine with a long sigh. "I've been wondering the same thing myself."

"He still loves you."

She tried not to acknowledge the fierce elation Nat's words called to life. "Doesn't much matter, does it?"

"It does if you still love him."

Of course she didn't still love him. She'd put those feelings aside years ago. She loved her work and she loved her independence and she loved Cristal champagne. The one thing she didn't love was Joe McMurphy.

"Stop looking at him like that." Slade popped up at her elbow a few minutes later. "He's a married man."

She gave him a disgusted look and stalked off toward the stable.

"Touchy, aren't we?" Slade fell into step with her. "At least I didn't take a photo."

"I'm not in the mood for this, Slade."

"Definitely touchy." He considered her thoughtfully. "PMS, I'd say."

"Mind your own damn business."

"Did you forget something, love? You *are* my business . . . at least for the time being."

"I saw you with that redheaded cowgirl with the pneumatic breasts. Didn't look to me like you were conducting business."

"Just trying to figure out how the West was won." He leaned against the fence. "So where's the bride?"

"In her room. She's not feeling too great today."

"Kind of gives you a free hand, so to speak, doesn't it, love?"

She used that free hand to slap him across the face. Hard.

"You're losing your edge, love," he said, rubbing his cheek. "A few weeks ago you would have laughed."

He's right, she thought, turning away from him. What he didn't know was that she'd been losing her edge for months now, wondering why on earth the things she'd been working for seemed so unimportant now that they were within reach.

Whether or not she was willing to admit it, the truth had been staring her in the face from the moment she opened her eyes and saw Joe standing over the bed. It was more than her edge that she was losing. She was losing her heart as well.

Christine stood at the edge of the makeshift dance floor in the old bunkhouse and watched as her father and mother twirled to music piped in from the stereo in the main house. Age had done nothing to diminish her parents' beauty; it had only enhanced their love for each other, as well as for the world around them.

She wrapped her arms across her chest and stepped deeper into the shadows as her brothers and sisters and their various spouses took the floor with Sam and Nonie. The women wore full-skirted dance dresses in all the colors of the rainbow, while the men were decked out in full western regalia.

"You belong out there, too, Christie."

She started at the sound of Joe's voice behind her, yet on a deeper level she wasn't surprised at all.

He stepped closer. She could sense his nearness in the way her body seemed to gather heat and make it her own. And there was his smell, so familiar, so intoxicating, so much a part of him that she'd carried a sense memory of it through all their years apart. *Those foolish, wasted years . . .*

"They're asking for you out there." His arm slipped around her waist.

"They don't even know I'm missing."

"Not true. You're one of them, Christie."

"There's a problem," she said. She could feel his breath on the back of her neck. "I have no one to dance with."

His laughter sent a shiver of delight up her spine, rippling along her nerve endings, as his body began to sway to the music. "We always were good together."

She turned to say something to him, but the words, whatever they might be, died in her throat. It was like one of those dreams where you're standing in the center of a wildly spinning universe of possibilities, trying desperately to hang on to what's left of your heart.

One moment she was standing alone at the edge of life, and the next she was dancing toward it in the arms of the only man she'd ever loved. The magic circle seemed to part just long enough to make room for them. They merged with the others, their laughter rising up into the soft night air and reaching all the way to the stars.

She was part of the earth beneath her feet, the reddish brown hills beyond the ranch, the canopy of sky, the rush of wind through trees. But more than that she was part of these people. In the deepest part of her heart she knew their hopes and dreams. Their blood flowed through her veins. She could travel to the ends of the earth and never find people who would love her more . . . or a place where she felt more welcome.

"People are going to talk," Joe said as they danced in the moonlight.

"I don't care," Christine said, resting her head against his shoulder. This was the truth she'd been fighting for longer than she could remember. She belonged there in Joe's arms, in that place, surrounded by her family and the friends of her youth. She knew it couldn't last forever, that whatever magic spell she was under would vanish with the dawn, but it no longer mattered. This moment, this exquisite moment, would make everything that came after worthwhile.

She didn't know how long they danced. Time didn't matter. Nothing mattered beyond the strength of his arms, the strong beating of his heart, the certainty that they were moving toward something she was incapable of stopping.

The party gained a second wind around midnight. Everyone converged on the house as Nonie invited one and all inside for an impromptu supper of steak and eggs and home-baked bread.

"I'm not hungry," said Christine.

"Me, neither," said Joe.

They exchanged a look and without another word they slipped from the circle of light in the yard and into the shadows. Their need to be alone was a living thing, drawing them closer together with each second that passed. She stumbled over a rock, and he took her arm to steady her. She leaned against him, savoring his strength and warmth, and let her hands rest against the solid wall of his chest.

Laughter floated toward them from the house, carried on the night breeze. The moon, obscured by a passing cloud, emerged again, raining silver on the landscape. A benediction, she thought. Together they walked toward the barn, merging with the shadows and the darkness.

"Alone at last," he said as they stepped into the cool stillness of the building. She knew his voice so well. The husky tremor spoke volumes.

"I don't want to talk." Her words caught in her throat.

"Neither do I."

He pulled her close.

She melted against him, pressing kisses against the side of his neck, the strong curve of his jaw, his ear. *I love you,* she thought. *I never stopped loving you, not once during all these years.* She wanted to tell him. She wanted to drop the last of her defenses, let them go crashing to the floor, and lay her heart at his feet.

He pushed her hair off the side of her neck and buried his face against her throat. Heat moved slowly through her body, through her arms, her legs, outward from her chest and belly. This was what it was all about, this painful wonderful sensation of being alive down to the last cell, the last neuron.

He'd long since discarded his tie, and with trembling fingers she unbuttoned his shirt. Lowering her head, she tasted him, breathed him. She circled his nipple with her tongue, glorying in his shuddering response. She wanted to pile sensation upon sensation, storing it all away deep inside her heart against the time when she'd be alone again.

"This isn't enough," he said, sliding down the zipper of her dress. She felt the cotton fall away from her body. The night air against her bare back made her shiver. The sensation brought reality into sharper focus, if only for a moment.

"Marina," she managed through the haze of desire. "I don't want to hurt her."

"She won't be hurt."

"I want to believe you, Joe, but it's hard. This situation is anything but normal."

"I'd tell you everything if I could, but it's not up to me. You have to—"

"Joe, please! Don't say—"

"Trust me, Christie."

"That's what I didn't want you to say. It's a cliché. Empty words."

"Not this time." He drew her closer. "Not with me."

He'd never lied to her, not once during all the years

she'd known him. Everyone knew there was something peculiar about his marriage to Marina. The only heart in danger of being broken was hers, and she'd welcome that over the empty loneliness that had been her companion for longer than she cared to remember.

"Trust me," he said again.

"I do," she whispered. "The whole thing's crazy, but I do."

He kissed her hard and long. They fell to the ground, then Christine yelped as the handle of a pitchfork caught her in the leg.

"Too dangerous," she said.

He tossed the pitchfork aside. "Not anymore."

She gestured toward the door. "Not that. I mean, someone might walk in."

He got to his feet. "The hayloft."

Laughter bubbled up inside her. "Another cliché? You overwhelm me, Joe."

"That's what I want to do, Christie. Overwhelm you."

She shivered again, but this time it had nothing to do with the cool night air. It had to do with the fact that he was a man and she was a woman, and it had been a very long time since such a simple truth carried with it so much meaning.

They climbed the ladder to the loft.

"Alone at last," she said, in a soft voice she barely recognized as her own.

She struggled with his shirt. He had trouble with her bra. The button on his pants flew off and pinged against the window while one of her shoes bounced off the ladder and fell to the first floor with a bang.

"We're not very graceful," she said.

"We make up for it in enthusiasm."

"I'm out of practice."

"It's like riding a bike." They both broke up with laughter.

"Cliché number three."

He moved against her. "I try harder."

"So I see."

He was right. Instinct took over. That basic, primal need to join with the man you loved, would always love, in the oldest way possible. She took him in her hand, feeling his strength and power, the way the blood throbbed beneath the skin. He caressed her, teasing her sensitive flesh, prolonging his fingers' exploration until she thought she would die from pleasure.

They lay together on a bed of clothing and hay, and she opened both her heart and her body to him. There was nothing graceful or romantic about their coupling. No soft music or candlelight, no flowers or welcoming bed. Just the two of them, naked and greedy, in a blaze of passion and need and sorrow for what they had lost. She felt a sting of pain but welcomed it as proof that she was alive and eager for all the wonders life had to offer.

He filled her.

He overpowered her.

He forced responses from her that came from the darkest part of her soul.

She held him fast when he climaxed, and a long answering wave of sensation rocketed through her. She cried out, sharp and high, as the last of her defenses shattered.

Afterward they lay on their sides, face to face, bellies pressed together. She saw herself reflected in his eyes, and in that reflection she found the woman she'd lost a long time ago.

"I feel you everywhere," she whispered against his lips. "In every part of me."

"Because you belong to me." His voice was rough, unbearably sexy. "You always have."

He moved inside her, and she caught her lower lip between her teeth.

"Did I hurt you?"

"A little," she said.

"You should have said something."

"Then you would have stopped, and that's the one thing I didn't want you to do."

"It's been a long time for you, hasn't it?"

"A very long time."

"I'm glad."

She smiled. "So am I."

"I don't sleep with Marina."

"So you said before."

"I don't love her."

"I know that."

"She doesn't even like me."

"Everyone knows that."

"I want to tell you the whole damn story—"

"It doesn't matter, Joe. I believe you."

His expression shifted, darkened. "Like I believed you years ago."

The pain inside her heart made it hard for her to breathe. "You believed what I wanted you to believe. At the time that's all that was important to me."

"It was never just about the baby, Christie. I knew I'd lost you, too, and I couldn't find a way to get you back."

She pressed her face against his shoulder. "I didn't want to come back, Joe. I needed to leave . . . for both of us. I wanted you to find someone you could laugh with, someone who could give you all the things I couldn't." She had needed to leave the pain behind and create herself anew, with people who didn't know how very much she had lost.

He took her again. Fast and hard and without preliminaries. She absorbed his anger and his pain and found in his release her own absolution.

They didn't talk afterward. Joe held her close and wondered if sanity would return or if he was condemned to feel this strange combination of anger and joy forever.

He'd lost control, and it scared the hell out of him. She'd walked out on their marriage, on their dreams for the future, and she hadn't given him a chance to make things right because she didn't believe he could.

He was Joe McMurphy, world-class champion of the underdog, and he hadn't even realized his beautiful young wife was drowning right before his eyes. He'd bought into the illusion same as everyone else had, that because she was beautiful and bright, because she'd been born into a loving home, that nothing life threw in her path could possibly harm her.

He should've known. The clues were all there if he hadn't been too blind and too drunk to see them. His own pain had taken precedence, and he'd waited for Christine to hold him in her arms and make things right. When she didn't, when she withdrew into her own loss, he'd found himself stripped of everything that mattered. She was his home and his family, and without her he had nothing left but anger.

They lay together for a long time, listening to the sounds of music and laughter coming from the house, followed by the rumble of engines as guests climbed back into their cars and trucks for the drive home.

"We should go back in," Christine said as the world fell quiet once again. "They're going to notice we're missing."

He kissed her quiet.

"I'm serious, Joe," she said, pushing him away. "I don't want anyone to be hurt by this."

It occurred to him that the two hearts most in danger were theirs, but he had the feeling that wasn't the right thing to say. He helped her to her feet, and they laughed as they brushed away bits of hay stuck to their skin and tangled in their hair.

"Dead giveaway," he said, running his hands through her silky blond hair. "There's no way to explain hay."

"You're right." She brushed his back then gave him a firm smack on the butt. "A dead giveaway."

He told her what he wanted to do to her . . . for her . . . and she ducked her head in an attempt to hide the pleased expression on her face.

They dressed quickly, then he helped her down from the loft.

"We can't go back together," she said. "That'll get them talking for sure."

He shot her a look. "You don't think they're already talking?"

"I hope not."

How she could look so wide-eyed and innocent after what they'd done in that loft was beyond him, but it was part of her appeal and always had been.

"They're already talking," he said, cupping her chin.

"Oh, God," she said softly. "Do you think so?"

"Count on it."

"What about Marina?"

"I'll take care of her."

"I'd hate to see her hurt."

To his surprise, so would he. She was Ric's daughter, after all. Hell, she was young enough to be *his* daughter. It had to be tough, married to a stranger, then sent away to a foreign country with no friends or family for support. The thought wouldn't have occurred to him a few weeks ago.

"I'm going to want answers," she said in a quiet voice.

"You'll get them, Christie, but not yet."

"I have to know the truth."

"You will," he said. "Just give me a little more time."

They kissed once, sweetly, before they separated to return to the main house.

Love must be making them mellow, he thought, watching as Christine combed her hair with her fingers, then snapped her public smile into place. And it was love. There was no doubt about that. Not in his mind and not, he hoped, in hers.

15

⚬∾⚬

"Christie!"

All eyes turned toward the door as Christine entered the kitchen. *They know,* she thought wildly. *Everyone knows.*

"Where's Joe?" Her father asked over his cup of coffee. "Been lookin' for the two of you ever since the dancing ended."

This is just like doing television, she told herself, strolling into the room. Keep smiling, keep talking, give away nothing. "I was about to ask you the same thing." She sat down between Sam and Marta and poured herself a cup of her mother's coffee. "I haven't seen him in a while." She took a sip. "Delicious."

"Trace and I saw you near the barn," Suzanne said, oblivious to the undercurrents at the table. "I called you, but I guess you didn't hear me." She winked at Christine. "If you two weren't divorced, I'd think you were sweet on each—ow!" She spun around to glare at her husband. "What was that for?"

Marta cleared her throat. "Do you have any more of that cinnamon bread, Mom? I forgot that eating for two gives me this big an appetite."

Everyone relaxed, and conversation resumed its normal pattern. Christine chatted amiably with her family. She sipped her coffee and munched on some bread, and she prayed nobody realized how close she had come to disaster. Poor Suzanne looked horribly embarrassed. She wanted to give the girl a hug and tell her not to feel that way. It wasn't Suzanne, after all, who'd just made love with another woman's husband.

"Anyone for poker?" Sam pulled a deck of cards from the buffet behind his chair. "I'm feelin' lucky tonight."

The groans could have been heard all the way back in Hackettstown.

"Git ready to kiss your money good-bye," said Franklin.

"You're the best poker player in the family next to Daddy," Nat said to Christine. "You goin' to uphold our honor?"

Christine stifled a yawn. "Not tonight, I'm afraid. I don't know about the rest of you, but I'm so tired I can't see straight." She leaned over and kissed her father's ruddy cheek. "It was a greaty party, Daddy," she said. "I'm very glad I was here."

He hugged her hard, and she saw the glitter of tears in his faded blue eyes. Christine caught the familiar scent of soap and vanilla as her mother enveloped her in a hug as well.

"I'm making breakfast in the morning," Christine told her mother. "Eggs Benedict for everyone."

"You're a guest," Nonie protested. "I can't have you fussin' around doin' my work for me."

"No back talk," Christine said, using her mother's favorite phrase.

She floated down the hallway to her room, aware of her skirt swirling around her knees, the sway of her hips and breasts. She felt female, powerful, part of everything and everyone. It had been a very long time since she'd felt connected, soul and mind and body, and the sensation was intoxicating. Returning home had brought her back to life in ways she couldn't have anticipated.

The door to Joe's room was slightly ajar. She hesitated for a moment, wondering if he had slipped into the house while she was sitting in the kitchen with her family. She supposed she could peek inside the room, but considering the fact that he shared it with his wife, that seemed the wrong thing to do.

She noted that the bathroom door farther down the hall was closed. She heard the sound of running water and something else. A keening sound like someone crying. Marina? It was none of her business if the girl was crying, but she couldn't just walk away. She tapped on the door. "Marina?"

No answer, just the low, keening wail from inside. She tapped again. "Marina, is everything okay?"

She waited but still no answer. "Look, I'm sorry," she said, opening the door, "but call me a worrier. I have to make certain you're—" Her words died. "Oh, God!"

The girl was curled on the floor near the clawfoot tub. The spreading crimson stain was a terrifying sight against the pale beige fabric of her nightgown and the pallor of her skin. The high sweet smell of blood filled Christine's nostrils, and she swallowed hard against nausea.

She was beside the girl in a flash. "What happened?" she asked, struggling to keep her voice calm. "Did you fall?" There were no signs of injury except that ghastly bloodstain.

Marina's voice was a terrified whisper. "I didn't

fall. It's—I hurt. . . ." Her words faded away as she clutched Christine's hand. "Please help me! I don't know what's happening to me."

If the girl didn't fall or cut herself, there was only one other possible explanation. She helped Marina sit upright, leaning back against the tub. "I think you're hemorrhaging," she said, maintaining her calm tone of voice. "Have you periods been heavy lately?"

"N-not really." Marina thought for a moment. "Actually they've been very light."

"Does this feel like your period?"

"Yes . . . no—I don't know. It's like a terrible pressure. . . ."

A dreadful notion occurred to Christine, but she pushed it an arm's length away. It was impossible. It had to be. "Is Joe in your room?"

Marina shook her head. "I have not seen him since this morning."

Christine grabbed three fluffy white towels from the towel bar and tried to bunch them up into pillows to make Marina more comfortable. "Don't move," she ordered, standing up. "I'll be right back."

She hated to leave the girl even for a minute. That wide-eyed look of fear touched a chord of memory deep inside. One she would give anything to forget.

"I need help!" she said, bursting into the kitchen. "Marina's in trouble."

"Where's Joe?" Sam asked.

"I don't know."

Natalie stood up. "What's wrong?"

"She's bleeding." Christine hesitated a beat. "I think she's hemorrhaging."

"Sweet Jesus," Natalie whispered. "I'll take a look at her."

"You're a vet, for God's sake, Nat."

"I know anatomy and I'm all you've got." Natalie turned toward her husband. "Warm up the truck. We'll take her to Central General."

"Someone find Joe," Christine snapped over her shoulder as she followed Natalie down the hall to the bathroom. "He needs to be here."

"He *is* here."

Christine stopped in her tracks as he strolled through the front door looking as if he hadn't a care in the world. Natalie continued down the hallway to Marina. Joe's smile faded as he met Christine's eyes.

"What's wrong?" he asked.

"I think you're wife is having a miscarriage." Her words were cold, blunt. He didn't deserve anything more.

"Come on," he said, raking a hand through his hair. "That's—"

"Impossible?" She spat out the word like snake venom. "You can do better than that, Joe." He *had* done better than that. He'd made her believe they had a chance to get it right.

"She can't be pregnant."

"A virgin birth? That's been done before."

He grabbed her by the forearm. "I'm telling the truth, Christie. I've never slept with her."

"It's not the sleeping that worries me, Joe," she said, her voice on the edge of hysteria. "It's what comes before."

"I need help!" Nat shouted from the bathroom. "Now!"

I'm not going to think about it, Christine told herself as she searched for sanitary napkins and a clean nightgown for Marina. *I'm going to think about the girl.*

"Are you coming with us?" Nat asked as Joe helped Marina into the truck.

"No," Christine said, avoiding Joe's eyes. "I'm not."

"Christine!" Marina's voice was shrill with dismay. "You must come."

Christine's stomach twisted in on itself. "Joe and Natalie will be with you."

"Please!" Marina tried to climb out of the car, but Joe held her fast. "I want you."

"Get in!" Natalie ordered. "They're waiting for us at Central."

I can't, Christine thought. *Don't ask me to do this.* She'd been there herself. She knew how it felt to be bleeding and terrified.

But she hadn't been alone. . . .

"It's going to be okay, Christie," Joe said, holding her hand tightly in his as they drove through the dark Nevada night to the hospital.

"You don't know that," she said, choking back her tears. "You can't promise me that."

"I can promise you that." If he was scared, it didn't show in his voice or in his manner. Maybe things weren't as bad as she thought. "Remember what we read in the book about Braxton-Hicks contractions. That's what this is."

She needed to believe him. She was only in her fifth month. If this was premature labor, the baby would never survive.

"I can't lose this baby, Joe." Her voice trembled

with fear. "This was a miracle. You know we'll never have another chance."

"We won't need another chance," he said fiercely. "Everything's going to be all right."

She'd clung to him through that terrible night, through the parade of doctors, through the agonizing tests, through the endless wait for someone, anyone, to tell them that there was nothing to worry about and she would have a beautiful, healthy baby four months from now.

But the pains came faster and they came closer together and they kept on coming until she couldn't breathe and she couldn't think and the very last thing she remembered was a voice saying "I'm sorry" and her husband's tears. . . .

They reached the hospital in record time. Nat wheeled into the driveway in front of the E.R. door, and seconds later Marina was on a stretcher and being wheeled into an examination room. There was a brief flurry of excitement as a pair of doctors recognized Christine and a crowd gathered around her, but Christine managed to be friendly and polite and still let them know this wasn't the right time for signing autographs.

Nat disappeared down the quiet corridor in search of a pay phone, leaving Christine and Joe alone. The waiting room was empty. A television droned in the far corner.

"Mind?" Joe asked, reaching for the switch.

"Be my guest," said Christine.

"We need to talk," Joe said as the room fell quiet.

"You need to to talk," Christine shot back. "I don't need to listen."

"I need to explain."

"I don't particularly give a damn what you need, Joe. Maybe you should be thinking about what your wife needs."

"The doctors are with her. She's in good hands."

"You're despicable." Her voice was low with fury. "She's a baby having a baby. How can you be so callous?"

"If she's pregnant, it's not with my child."

"You bastard. The game's over. The least you can do is level with me."

"It's not my baby."

Shaking with anger, she stood up. "Don't talk to me. Don't follow me."

He didn't. Joe leaned back against the wall and closed his eyes. *You asked too much of me, Ric,* he thought. *Why the hell didn't you tell me there was a baby?* Of course there was the possibility Ric didn't know any more than Joe did. Jesus, she was skinny as a rail. She barely ate enough to keep herself alive, much less a baby.

And, damn it, why did it have to be happening here? This hospital was filled with memories. He saw them walking down the hallways, he heard them echoing through the corridors. This was where it had ended, where he and Christine had ended. All those dreams, all those plans for the future, gone in an instant.

Christine stood near the window, head bowed. He could feel her pain across the room, see the way it was pulling her down deep into despair. She hadn't wanted to come to Nevada in the first place. She'd done her damnedest to avoid it, but he couldn't let it alone. He'd hammered at her until she finally gave in, and now her worst fears were coming true. The memories she'd tried to avoid for almost seven years had her in a stranglehold, and there wasn't a damn thing he could do to ease her pain. Not without risking Marina's life.

"Mr. McMurphy?" He jumped as the doctor, a young woman named Serrano, approached. "Your wife is resting comfortably."

"Was she—is she . . ." He couldn't find the words.

Christine, however, had no trouble. "Is the baby all right?"

The doctor looked at Joe.

"You can talk in front of Christine," he said.

"Her blood pressure is higher than I'd like to see, and there's some concern about her cervix. I'd like to keep her overnight for observation."

"Sure," Joe said. "Whatever you say."

The doctor looked at him with open curiosity. "Your wife seemed . . . surprised to learn of the pregnancy."

"That makes two of us," Joe said, aware of Christine's intense scrutiny.

"Be that as it may, Mrs. McMurphy is at the start of her third trimester and—"

Christine gasped. "Her third trimester? My God, she's not even showing."

"I don't know where you've been looking," said the doctor in a sharp tone. "But the young woman is most definitely at the start of her seventh month, and she'll be needing a great deal of support until she delivers." It was patently obvious from the doctor's expression that she believed Marina was in less than capable hands. Joe wouldn't blame her if she brought him up on charges of child neglect. "I'd like to see her in a week for a thorough examination."

"We're not from here," Joe said. "Can Marina travel?"

Dr. Serrano sighed deeply as she took down the particulars. "When you know your flight number, I'll make the necessary arrangements."

Christine straightened her shoulders. "Can I see Marina?"

Serrano looked from Christine to Joe. "Perhaps her husband first—?"

Too bad her husband hadn't thought of that.

Christine was everything Joe wasn't. She sat beside the girl, holding her hand, talking quietly about nothing and everything, while Joe paced the small room, wishing he was any place on earth but where he was.

Marina looked pathetic, lying there against the white sheets, with the IV drip and the fetal monitor and a loneliness even he could see. He felt small and inadequate. Everything he said sounded either banal, insincere, or heartless. He wanted to grab her by her narrow shoulders and ask her what the hell she thought she was doing, hiding a pregnancy under baggy sweaters. Risking her life and her baby's. Taking his life and throwing it up for grabs.

"So who's the father?" he asked, unable to stand it any longer.

Marina said nothing, just kept her gaze trained on a "Mary Tyler Moore" rerun on the TV suspended from the wall.

"Marina." He stood at the foot of the bed, blocking her view of the television.

"Leave her alone," Christine snapped.

"I just asked her a question."

"Don't ask her anything. She's been through a lot today. Don't add to it."

"I'm not adding to anything. I'm looking for answers."

"You're not going to get them tonight."

"The hell I'm not."

Christine stood up and went toe-to-toe with him. "You're not going to ask her again tonight."

He started to say something, but Marina chose that moment to burst into noisy tears.

"I hope you're happy," Christine snapped.

"Ecstatic," he snapped back. "Nothing like making a pregnant woman cry." He felt like a bastard, that's how he felt, and there didn't seem to be a damn thing he could do to change it.

He left the two women together, bonding or whatever the hell they were doing. He regretted telling Nat to go home. Right now he could've used a friendly face. Not that he could have told her his troubles. He'd made a promise to Ric, and he still couldn't see his way clear to break that promise. Now that his temper had cooled, he realized Ric probably hadn't known anything about his daughter's pregnancy. No way would the guy have compromised his kid—or his grandkid. Ric still would have engineered this marriage, but he would've made damn sure Marina got the medical care she needed.

The thing was, how could he get in touch with Ric to let him know the situation had changed? The guy was hiding somewhere in the middle of a war zone.

He stopped a nurse. "Where's the pay phone?"

"In the lobby near the snack machines."

Unless Ric had a cellular phone tucked in his bunker, Joe was going to be shit out of luck. But, damn it, he had to do something or he was going to go nuts.

"Good to see you, love." Slade was sitting on the front porch when Christine arrived back at the ranch late the next morning. "How's the little mother?"

"Fine." Christine sank down onto the bottom step and rested her head in her hands. "I'm exhausted."

"You look it." He made a show of looking her over. "Thought about concealer?"

She didn't laugh. "She almost lost the baby."

"The Boy Scout must be relieved."

She said nothing. Slade already knew more than he should about the situation, and she trusted him even less than she trusted herself. Right now the only important thing was Marina.

And the baby.

The last thing Christine wanted was to care about Marina. Wasn't it enough that a colossal twist of fate had put her in the position of playing nursemaid to her ex-husband's pregnant bride in the same hospital where she'd lost her own baby? She'd intended to turn away after the danger was past, to rein in her emotions the way she always did, and let Joe take care of his own wife. But she couldn't do it. She made it halfway to the hospital exit where she was ambushed by flashes of memory that almost brought her to her knees.

You can't leave her. She's not out of danger yet. Get her back to New York, give her your gynecologist's name, then you can put the whole thing out of your mind.

She had nothing to fear; her heart was already broken in two.

". . . must be chuffed about the kid."

Christine looked up. "What was that?"

"I said you ex must be chuffed about the kid."

"Most men would be," she said noncommittally. Someone to carry on your name, your bloodline. Wasn't that the Holy Grail for a man?

"How do you feel about it, love?"

Dangerous territory. She had to be careful. "I'm glad Marina is well."

"How about the baby?"

"What are you driving at, Slade? I'm too tired for games. Of course I'm glad she didn't lose the baby."

"Puts a different spin on their marriage, wouldn't you say?"

"Their marriage is none of my business."

"So why did you stay there at the hospital?"

"Because Marina wanted me to."

"How about the Boy Scout? Did he want you there, too?"

"I don't like where you're taking this, Slade," she said carefully.

"Just looking out for you, love." He flashed a smile that inexplicably made her blood run cold. "That's what friends are for, right?"

She could have left. She had the plane ticket and she still had time to get to the airport for the flight. There was nothing to stop her from packing her bags and leaving everything and everyone behind. She was good at that. She'd done it before. It was a tried-and-true method that never failed.

Joe's wife was pregnant. The implications of that were clear to every single member of her family. They were clear to Dr. Serrano at Central General, and they were clear to Slade. If Christine used the brain she was born with, she'd put as much distance between herself and Joe as possible.

They had no future. That much was obvious. Maybe for a few hours in the hayloft she'd let herself believe they had a chance, but she'd come to her senses. Marina's pregnancy had seen to that.

Still there was a part of her brain, one tiny irrational part, that clung to the stubborn hope that things weren't quite the way they seemed.

16

Three days after the Cannons' anniversary party, Slade found himself aboard a jumbo jet headed back to Newark Airport. No plummy first class this time around. He was a tad put out to be sitting back in coach with the polyester crowd, but the Airfone helped him pass the time.

"They arranged for an ambulance to be waiting for them at the airport," he told the woman on the other end of the connection. "They're taking her to—" He looked down at his notes, scribbled along the margins of *People* magazine. "St. Claire's Hospital near Hackettstown."

"She shares her husband's last name?"

"Far as I know."

"Maiden name?"

"Sorry, love. Haven't the foggiest."

"You're not giving me much to go on, my friend." The woman sighed. "Not even the name of the country she's from."

"Best I could do, love. I only had a few minutes to go through the girl's things. Those clippings were all I could come up with."

"Still at the same phone?"

He repeated the Hackettstown number and a warning that he shared the telephone with the people involved. "Move fast before the Boy Scout puts paid to the whole situation."

"You'll be trading those plimsolls for Guccis before long, dear boy."

"My thoughts exactly."

The original plan was for Joe to accompany his wife to the hospital, but Marina flew into such a fit of rage when she heard Christine wouldn't be with her that they quickly came up with a new plan.

"Doesn't the little bride want her husband with her?" Slade asked in a tone of voice that set Christine's teeth on edge.

"It's a female thing," Christine said. Lame, yes, but it beat the truth. No matter how she and Joe felt about the situation between them, both agreed that leaving Slade alone in the house was an invitation to disaster.

So Christine went to the hospital with Marina and held the girl's hand through a battery of tests designed to bring a woman to her knees. Technology had advanced light-years in the seven years since Christine had traveled that particular road, but that peculiar sense of being in a situation beyond your control was everywhere.

She could see in Marina's eyes that the girl felt it, too. When the doctor pronounced Marina well enough to go home, she sagged against Christine as if the weight of relief was more than she could bear. Every gut-level instinct in Christine screamed for her to put as much time and distance between herself and this mess as she possibly could, but still she sat there, holding the girl's hand and wondering how this whole thing would end.

*   *   *

"We'll need to hire a new housekeeper," Christine said to Joe after they'd settled Marina in.

"I liked Mrs. Cusumano."

Christine lifted a brow. "I rather doubt Mrs. Cusumano likes us all that much." Most housekeepers were a tad defensive about being falsely accused of petty theft.

"Did you ever find your jewelry?"

"No." Actually she hadn't even thought about the missing items until that moment. Her life had been in such turmoil these past few weeks that recalling her own name took extra effort.

"I've been thinking of hiring a part-time nurse to take care of Marina."

"That's your business, Joe. Not mine." She pushed back her chair and rose to her feet. "I have a meeting in the city tomorrow. I think I'll turn in." It was time she remembered she had a career, and a damn good one at that. Something she could count on and control.

Something that wouldn't let her down.

She didn't sleep well that night. So much had happened since they were last under that roof. Each time she closed her eyes she felt Joe's arms around her, the muscled strength of his body, every nuance of sensation right down to the rippling climax that had left her exhausted but deeply, wonderfully satisfied.

There was a karmic justice to it all, she thought as she rode into Manhattan the next morning. Her brain was empty of original thought. Circles ringed her eyes. She felt fuzzy and out of step with the world, as if her body had returned to New Jersey and forgotten to tell her soul.

This was her punishment. She'd slept with another woman's husband—even if the husband in question had belonged to her first—and she deserved everything she got. A fourteen-year-old kid wouldn't have bought Joe's story about it not being a "real" marriage. Reality had been staring her in the face, and she'd been too besotted, too lonely, too damned needy to even notice.

But what if he's telling the truth? What if it is a marriage in name only and the baby isn't his?

"Dreamer," she said out loud.

The limo driver met her eyes in the rearview mirror. "Ma'am?"

She forced a smile. "I said, would you wake me when we get to the studio?"

"Yes, ma'am."

She closed her eyes, but all she saw was the future stretching before her like an endless stretch of highway going nowhere.

"She's impossible, Ms. Cannon," said the nurse. "I tried to give her a sponge bath, and she kicked me in the hipbone."

Christine sank down onto the top porch step and buried her head in her hands. For the last ten days she'd been juggling staff meetings and interviews and research in Manhattan with the bizarre situation here in Hackettstown, and she was at the end of her rope. "You're quitting, aren't you?" Why should this nurse be any different from the three nurses who had preceded her?

"If she kicks me again, I will. Physical abuse isn't in my job description."

"God bless you," Christine whispered as the

woman went back into the house. Blessings on her and her children and her children's children. It was just a matter of time until Marina did something else to the woman, but a temporary reprieve was better than none.

Joe pulled into the driveway with Slade and a trunkful of groceries. Slade unloaded the beer and, claiming back trouble, climbed the porch steps and went inside.

"The bastard's back didn't bother him when he was doing pushups this morning," Joe said, leaning against the railing. "If he thinks—"

"I'm leaving." The words surprised her as much as they obviously surprised Joe.

"You're going out?"

"I can't do this anymore, Joe. I'm moving back to Manhattan."

He heard the words, but they didn't sink in. *Her eyes are gray*, he thought, staring at Christine. A deep, blue-gray, the color of the ocean on a stormy day. He couldn't stop staring at her.

"Joe." Her tone was sharp. "Did you hear me?"

"No," he said. "Not one word." Her hair was skimmed off her face with a headband. Her face was free of makeup, and she wore a pair of cutoffs and a T-shirt that said LIVE FREE OR DIE. She was the girl he'd fallen in love with on the steps of NYU, and he was falling in love all over again.

"I'm going back to Manhattan tonight."

He frowned. He liked it better when the words weren't sinking in. "Early meeting tomorrow?"

"I'm moving back for good. I can't do this anymore. It's too hard."

"Should I hire some more help?"

"That's not the problem, Joe."

Being around Marina was tearing her up inside, and he knew it. "We'll move. I kept the place on the West Side."

"That's ridiculous. My apartment is ready. It's not as if I planned to stay here forever."

The words lingered in the air between them. He wanted to grab her, climb into the car, and disappear. He wanted to forget Marina and the baby, forget everything but the fact they'd found each other again.

"What about Slade?" he asked.

She didn't answer.

His jaw tightened. "Isn't it time he found a place of his own?"

"He has a place of his own in L.A."

"So why isn't he in it?"

She sighed loudly. "You know about the *Vanity Fair* piece. When it's finished, he'll go home."

"He must have enough damn pictures of you by now."

"That's not any of your business."

He knew he had no rights where she was concerned, but that didn't stop him. "Don't sleep with him. He's not good enough for you."

Her laugh sounded high and tight. On the verge of being out of control. "Right," she said. "I'll make sure I stick to married men with pregnant wives."

"Jesus, Christine—"

"What do you want from me, Joe? Do you want to keep me on the side while you play proud father to Marina's baby? This is killing me, and I don't want to feel this way a minute longer."

She was in motion before he could react, tearing down the driveway, her bare feet kicking up pebbles.

What was it about him that made his wives take off that way? He had to hand it to Christine: That delicate flower look of hers hid the fact that she could give an Olympic track star some stiff competition. She was halfway up the street by the time he caught up with her.

"Chris! Stop . . . let me—"

She quicken her pace.

So did he. "We've gotta talk, Chris."

She lengthened her lead.

"Son of a bitch!" he roared. "I love you!"

"Go to hell!" She never was at a loss for words, his Christine.

There was only one thing he could do.

"Are you insane?" she yelped as they fell to the grassy shoulder. "You tackled me!" She pounded him on the shoulder with her fists.

"Ow!" He tried to roll out of reach, but she was relentless. "You trying to kill me or something?"

"I *should* kill you!" She didn't let up with the pounding. He quit fighting and let her take her best shot. Unfortunately she had a half dozen best shots, and each one hurt more than the one before. "You bastard! You rotten stinking bastard!"

He saw his opportunity, and he grabbed her hands, pinning them behind her back. "It was an arranged marriage, Christie. I met her thirty seconds before we said 'I do.' She needed protection, and I gave it to her."

"Protection?" She struggled to break free of his grip. "She's pregnant, damn you!"

"Not by me."

"Who? The tooth fairy?"

"Maybe. I don't know."

The expression in her gray eyes changed, sliding from utter contempt to something a shade less hostile. Call him an asshole, but he was starting to feel optimistic. "She's your problem, Joe, not mine. I don't want to be part of it."

"I never asked you to be."

"Marina did, and that's even worse."

"I'll explain it to her, about the baby and why you're leaving. She'll understand."

Christine kicked him in the shin. "You idiot! You don't tell a pregnant woman that your first wife miscarried. She has enough to worry about without living proof that bad things happen."

"She knows bad things can happen, Christie. Her mother was murdered in front of her a few years ago."

He felt the fight drain from her body. "Oh, God . . ." Then, "But that doesn't explain anything else, Joe. It sure as hell doesn't explain why you married her."

He hesitated. "It was an old debt."

"An old debt." She laughed. "Most men write checks to repay their old debts. You get married. What a crazy—" she stopped. He could see the light dawning.

"The avalanche story," she said more to herself than to him. "I wondered why you and Marina looked so uncomfortable when Suzanne asked about it." She met his eyes. "You found Ric?" The words themselves felt strange and unreal as they tumbled from her lips. Things like this just didn't happen in the real world. A boy doesn't get plucked from an avalanche to find himself married to his rescuer's daughter twenty years later.

Or did he?

Joe's expression never wavered. "I spent six months looking for Ric, and he finally found me an hour before I boarded the plane for home."

"What did he do, show up at the airport with a shotgun and his pregnant daughter?"

"Gimme a break, will you, Chris?" He shoved a hand through his thick dark hair.

"Sorry," she mumbled, embarrassed. "Force of habit."

"He sent two of his men, and they brought me to some bombed-out building in the center of town. You know the situation there. He's between a rock and a hard place. He's willing to give his life for what used to be his country, but he's not willing to give his daughter's. Not after losing Helena."

Christine looked down at her hands. "And you were the lucky guy."

"Yeah," he said, his voice heavy with irony. "And I was the lucky guy."

"Why marriage? Why not just bring her to this country?"

"Their immigration laws were drawn up in the Stone Age. She had to be married to emigrate." He dragged his hand through his hair a second time. "Preferably to an American."

Despite herself, Christine smiled. "A reluctant groom and a rebellious bride. That must have been a hell of a wedding."

Their eyes met. "Nothing like ours, Christie."

"No," she said softly. "I don't imagine it was."

All of her questions came a distant second to the sharp relief Christine felt as the realization that Marina was only Joe's wife and not the mother of his child finally sank in. She could have accepted his marriage, she could have accepted Marina as his lover, but the one thing she could never have accepted in a million years was another woman carrying his child.

She knew her feelings were irrational and unfair, based more on wild emotion than on anything logical or generous, but there they were. For years she had prided herself on the way she kept those emotions under control because that control made her loneliness somehow easier to bear.

But now she overflowed with emotion. Love. Desire. Fear. And a deep, unexpected compassion for the pregnant girl so far from home.

Joe went on to tell her that Marina's life was in danger from the radical element trying to keep Ric from ascending the throne, that the danger could reach all the way to American shores if Marina's whereabouts became public knowledge.

"I think he's wrong," Christine said. "Independence is tough all around. Why should his country be any different?"

She listened carefully as Joe outlined Ric's take on his country's future, and she had to admit the would-be king seemed right on target with his assessment. King Juan Carlos had proved to be the unifying element in post-Franco Spain, and he'd managed somehow to blend an old monarchy with a newborn democratic government, providing both stability and a sense of history.

"But why didn't you tell me before?" she demanded, her anger reasserting itself. "Didn't you trust me?" She waited for an answer. "Joe. Say something."

She could see the answer in his eyes. "I made a promise, Christine. I couldn't break it."

"Even if it meant we'd lose each other again?"

"She's my responsibility. I couldn't risk it."

"You don't trust me."

"I didn't say that."

"I don't hear you denying it."

"You want the truth, Chris? You got it. An exiled princess in a marriage of convenience would make a damned good opening segment for your show."

"You bastard!" She slapped him hard across the face. "Don't you know anything about me?" Did he really believe she would compromise the young girl in order to promote her own career? *Would you, Cannon? Are you absolutely sure you'll be able to pass this up?*

"You're ambitious, Christine." His tone was even, cool. "The problem is I don't know how far you'd go for your career."

"No," she said, "the real problem is you haven't gone far enough."

"We've always wanted different things. We have from the start."

"Only from our careers."

"Do you still want those other things, Christie?" he asked. "Home and family and everything that goes with it?"

She met his eyes and opened her soul to him. "More than you could ever know."

Being pregnant made Marina feel like a small country surrounded by hostile nations. Someone was always pushing against her boundaries, and she found it necessary to defend her independence against attack.

"Take this away!" She pushed the tray of food back toward the nurse. "I hate fish. Bring me some chicken without sauce and vegetables."

"I'm a registered nurse, not a Cordon Bleu chef." The nurse turned around and stormed from the room.

Marina had to admire the nurse's self-possession. She didn't even flinch when the bedroom slipper crashed into the doorjamb. The last one had run crying to Joseph, saying she had never been treated so harshly in her entire privileged life.

The baby kicked against Marina's belly, and she absently moved her hand across the swollen mass. Knowing you were pregnant was one thing; actually believing that a small human being was growing inside you was another. Joe had asked her how it was she hadn't realized what was going on, but the truth was she hadn't a clue. She had none of the usual symptoms, not even a missed period. The doctor's pronouncement had shocked her every bit as much as it had shocked Christine and Joe.

"This has to stop, Marina."

She looked up to see Christine in the doorway.

"I hate fish," she said, feeling her cheeks redden beneath the woman's disapproval.

"You have to think of the baby."

"My baby will not like fish, either."

"Very funny." Christine crossed the room and sat on the edge of Marina's bed. "Listen, kid, I've seen you put away four slices of pizza and some calzone. Don't tell me you can't find room for an innocent filet of flounder."

"Doesn't anyone hear what I'm saying?" Marina snapped. "I want chicken, not fish."

"And last week you wanted lamb instead of chicken."

"I'm pregnant," Marina said, lifting her chin. "I'm allowed my cravings."

Christine sighed and rested her head in her hands. "How long have you been pregnant?" she asked, peering at Marina through her elegant fingers. "Two, three years?"

"It seems that way. I am more a prisoner now than ever before."

"That's tough," said Christine, not looking at all sympathetic. "I'm afraid the most important thing is your health . . . and the baby's."

Marina considered Christine carefully. There was something different about her, something she couldn't quite put her finger on. "Your eyes!" she said after a moment. "They're gray."

"Blue-gray," said Christine.

"I like this color better than the other."

"Well, television likes the other color."

"You would change your eye color for a job?"

Christine laughed. "You make it sound as if I'd sold myself into prostitution."

"Isn't it the same thing?"

"I don't think so, Marina. There's nothing wrong with making changes in your appearance."

Marina tugged at her lank brown hair. "I wouldn't know where to begin."

"A good haircut, for starters. You have beautiful thick hair."

"It's straight as a stick."

"A good cut would release the wave."

"Do you really think so?"

"Trust me," said Christine. "I'm an expert on these things."

"I have no patience with cosmetics."

"That's because you don't know how to use them."

"My mother was quite clever with them."

"Joe told me she was a beautiful woman."

"Everything I'm not."

"You have your own appeal." Christine patted Marina's belly. "Obviously someone thought so."

Marina blushed. "Zee loves me for my mind."

"So that's his name."

"What?"

"Zee," said Christine. "I've been wondering who he was."

"I didn't mean to tell you."

"I know that, but I'm glad you did."

In a strange way, so was Marina. She'd been carrying secrets around for so long there were times she thought she would collapse under the weight of them. "It was not my intention to cause difficulties for you and Joseph."

"Joe and I have more than enough difficulties between us. This was just one more to add to the stack."

"But you are no longer angry with each other."

Again that beautiful smile that Marina so envied. "We are no longer angry with each other."

"He loves you," Marina said, tracing circles on her belly with the palms of her hands.

"How do you know?"

"It is in his eyes each time he looks at you. I saw it that very first night in your bedroom."

"I think what you saw was surprise."

Marina shook her head. "No."

"And what about Zee?" Christine asked. "Is that how you look at him?"

"I dream of him," she said slowly, "and of my country." A strange sensation gathered in her chest, a heaviness that pressed against her lungs and made it difficult to draw a breath.

"And the dreams make you sad?"

She shook her head. "The dreams are good. It is just the feeling I have that I will never see either one of them ever again." To her shame, she started to cry, big ugly gulping tears that streaked down her face and made her nose run. She reached for a tissue on the nightstand.

"You'll go home again," Christine said. "As soon as the situation is more stable. That's one of the things Joe wanted to check on while he's down in Washington."

"I know," said Marina, "but how can he possibly find my father when my father is in hiding?"

"You'd be surprised what Joe can accomplish when he puts his mind to it."

"I know so little about him despite the fact that we are—"

"Married. You can say the word," Christine said with a slight smile. "I understand the situation now, but I don't think you understand the kind of man Joe is."

Marina listened as Christine, with obvious pride, listed Joseph's many journalistic accomplishments and awards.

"But he is not rich, is he?" Marina asked. "In America I thought riches invariably followed accomplishment."

"Unfortunately that isn't always true. You see, your husband has a soft spot for the underdog even if it means he can't pay his bills."

"I didn't know that about him," Marina said, turning the information around in her mind. She knew that he wrote for an important news magazine and that there was talk about a book in the works, but beyond that it was all a blur. "Apparently there is much to admire about him."

"More than you could possibly know," said Christine. She cleared her throat. "I promise that you'll see your country and Zee and your fa—"

"You don't understand," Marina persisted. "This isn't just a dream. It's a premonition."

"You think something terrible is going to happen to you."

"Yes," Marina said, leaning forward as far as her belly would allow. "Something awful."

Christine patted her hand. "That's perfectly natural," she said with irritating good cheer. "All pregnant women feel that way."

"You don't know what you're talking about."

"I do."

"That's not possible."

"I've done thousands of interviews with pregnant women."

"But that is not what you mean, is it?"

"No," Christine said softly. "It isn't."

Marina's tears flowed again. "You and Joseph—?"

"It was a long time ago."

"The baby . . . what happened?"

Christine hesitated. She looked toward the door as if plotting her escape. "I was at the end of my fifth month," she said in a voice so low Marina struggled to hear it. "The baby—I miscarried a little boy . . . a perfect little boy."

Marina's hands began to shake. She thrust them behind her back. "I'm so sorry."

The haunted look in Christine's eyes changed to one of compassion. "Oh, honey, please don't misunderstand. The baby—I have some physical problems that caused the miscarriage. It won't happen to you."

The last thing Marina wanted to do was cause Christine another moment of grief. She summoned up a smile and said that she really wasn't worried at all, that she was just feeling emotional and foolish, and Christine shouldn't give her a second thought.

Christine seemed convinced. "I'll go see if there's any chicken in the fridge."

"I can do that." Marina swung her legs from the bed.

"Not on your life." Christine gave her a fierce look. "Unless you want to fight."

Marina did as told. She waited until Christine's footsteps disappeared down the hallway, then stood up. A pad of paper and pen rested atop the dresser, and she gathered them up and hurried back to bed.

The world seemed a more dangerous place than ever, she thought as she wrote a short statement on a sheet of lined paper. She read it over, trying not to think too clearly about what it represented. Satisfied at last, she folded it and slid it into her underwear drawer beneath her maternity bras and tried to put it from her mind.

But it was there, hiding in the shadows.

Waiting.

17

"Coffee, sir?"

Joe looked up at the smiling flight attendant on the D.C.-to-Newark shuttle and shook his head. "I'm in caffeine overdrive already, thanks." He watched as the guy turned his practiced smile onto the next passenger, a power type in an expensive navy pin-striped suit that screamed lobbyist.

After three days in Washington, Joe had gotten pretty damned good at spotting lobbyists. Look for a trendy haircut, fine leather briefcase, and an attitude, and five'll get you ten you were going eyeball-to-eyeball with someone who peddled influence for a living.

Not that Joe had anything against influence peddling. When you needed something done, the lobbyists were the ones to turn to. Small ranchers had a fairly effective lobby, and Joe had come away with a stack of notes and phone numbers that alone made the trip worthwhile. He'd also managed to corner the junior senators from Nevada and Oklahoma who both agreed to give Joe formal interviews when they were in Manhattan next week for the annual press dinner at the Plaza.

Too bad things hadn't gone as well over at the State Department. He'd hung around the halls for a while,

schmoozing with old friends and downing a couple
gallons of coffee, until he spied the undersecretary
heading for the elevator.

Amazing how much an intrepid journalist could
accomplish between floors. The undersecretary told
him that the fighting in Marina's country was so
intense between the socialist insurgents and the
democratic monarchists that U.N. observers didn't
believe it could last more than another month. Who
would win was anybody's guess.

"I can't promise anything," the undersecretary said
as Joe followed him into the cafeteria, "but I'll see
what the guys in Geneva can come up with."

Joe leaned back in his seat and closed his eyes.
He'd told the undersecretary he wasn't looking for
miracles, but it occurred to him that a miracle was
exactly what he needed at the moment. It was going
to take one to find Ric in the middle of a civil war; it
was going to take an even bigger miracle to find Zee,
the guy Marina loved.

But if there was one thing Joe'd learned in the last
month, it was that miracles happened. He and Christine had found each other again, and if that wasn't a
miracle, he didn't know what was. The timing was
wrong, the circumstances were bizarre, but the feeling that a benevolent fate had him in the palm of its
hand was impossible to deny.

If he wasn't already married to a plain-faced
pregnant princess, he'd throw Christine over his
shoulder and drag her to the altar.

He couldn't help grinning at the absurdity of the
statement, but the truth was he'd grown fond of Ric's
kid. She had a lot of guts, more than he'd originally
realized. He knew what it was like to fight for the

underdog, but he'd long ago lost the certainty that he could help make the world a better place. Not so Marina. She burned with the flame of commitment, and she believed that she—and her rebel boyfriend— could make the impossible happen.

The pregnancy had thrown her for a loop, but she fought any signs of weakness in herself with the same fierce determination she'd used to plan her many escape attempts. You had to admire the kid's guts. Thousands of miles away from home, pregnant by the man she loved, married to a man she barely knew—the kid was stronger than any ten men. Joe included.

He and Marina were still sharing the guest bedroom each night. With that damn Brit photographer nosing around, they couldn't afford to take any chances. If Slade got even the slightest hint that he and Christine were lovers, Joe knew they'd find their kissers plastered across the front page of the *New York Post*, and that was only for starters.

Truth was, he'd been glad to get away, even for a few days. The tension of being in the same house with Christine and not being able to touch her or hold her or say the things he wanted to say to her was pushing him to the breaking point.

What they needed was to be alone, away from Slade and Marina and even their house in Hackettstown. Someplace where they had no past so they could find out if they had a future.

"I shouldn't be doing this," Christine mumbled as she pressed the buzzer to Apartment 9D. The anonymous phone message had come in around noon. *Ratings guaranteed. 6 p.m. Sources verified.* She didn't recognize the West Seventy-second Street address.

The reporter in her couldn't resist even if she was only three days away from the premiere of her show and stressed to the limit. "We're looping tomorrow morning," her producer had said as she gathered up her belongings to leave. "Matt wanted to do a run-through tonight."

She'd waved the yellow message at the producer. "Hot lead, Sandy. This might be the story that pushes us over the top."

The past few weeks were a chaotic blur of meetings, deadlines, and Lamaze classes. When Marina first asked her to be her labor coach, every instinct in Christine's body had told her to run, but she'd taken a deep breath, summoned up a smile, and promised the girl she'd be there for her. She'd arranged for Marina to have a private coach at home while she would take classes in Manhattan under the guise of doing research for the show.

And in the midst of the chaos was Joe. Part of her soul but not able to be part of her life. Not with Slade living there with them. She found herself spending more time in Manhattan, if only to ease the exquisite tension she felt each time Joe walked into the room, all male exuberance and beauty. She wanted him and needed him and longed for him in a way that defied logic. He was her soul mate and her friend and the object of every heated fantasy she'd ever enjoyed and, thanks to their impossible situation, they hadn't shared more than a lingering glance in the hallway since coming home from Nevada.

Even miracles needed more help than that.

She buzzed again. The intercom crackled to life,

then abruptly died. She waited, tapping her foot against the marble floor. *You've been had, Cannon,* she thought. *Somebody's idea of a joke.* Turning, she was about to leave when the door buzzed. A minute later she was in the elevator on her way to the ninth floor. The elevator overshot by a good six inches. She slipped out of her three-inch heels and jumped from the car, twisting her ankle in the process.

She slipped the shoes back on, tried to take a step, then realized her folly.

"Damn it," she said, hobbling toward Apartment 9D. What a great impression she was going to make. Famous television personality arrives barefoot and in search of a hot lead. Her ankle hurt like the blazes, but it felt marvelous to be out of her heels.

Three minutes, she thought, pressing the doorbell. One hundred eighty seconds to get the story, or she was out of there. She was tired and hungry, and she wished she never had to put her shoes back on again as long as she lived. Or have an intelligent conversation. Or have her hair streaked. Or worry about contact lenses, camera angles, or Q-ratings.

The door swung inward, and she found herself face to face with Joe. He wore a pair of tight-fitting jeans and a work shirt open at the neck. His feet were bare, his hair looked freshly washed, and the look in his beautiful blue eyes was everything she'd always wanted and never thought she would have.

He grinned the way he had that first day on the steps of the library.

She grinned back, feeling the way she had all those years ago.

"So are you gonna stand there all day or are you coming inside?"

She pretended to check the apartment number. "I don't suppose you're the guy with the hot story."

"Could be."

She gave him her best professional smile. "So why don't you invite me in?"

He threw her over his shoulder and closed the door behind them.

"Put me down, Joe!" she ordered, laughing, as he carried her into the living room. "You'll give yourself a hernia."

"You're too damn thin."

"Better for the camera."

"That's what you said about the contact lenses." He peered at her. "Still not wearing them."

"I will be."

"I like you better this way."

"You're in the minority."

"Good."

He tossed her onto the couch and covered her body with his own. She was his captive, his willing prisoner. She met his eyes, and the years they'd spent apart vanished as if they'd never happened. This was her husband.

"I've missed you so much." She kissed his mouth, his nose, his forehead, trying to imprint the smell and feel of him on her heart. "It's so hard seeing you and not being able to touch you."

"I know," he said with a groan. His fingers found the buttons of her blouse, then slid both the blouse and silk teddy off her shoulders.

"Oh, God, Joe." She arched her back as his mouth closed over her nipple. She was pure sensation, sweet fire and dangerous need. He sucked hard at her nipple, and she felt her response deep in her womb, a hard pulling contraction that became the center of her existence.

She pulled his shirt from the waistband of his pants, hungry for the smell and feel of his bare skin against her mouth, against her body.

He stopped her as she reached for the snap of his pants.

"Not here," he said.

"Yes."

"The bed."

"Now."

Somehow they found their way into the bedroom . . . to the wide and welcoming bed near the window. They shed their clothing and their inhibitions, coming to each other the way they had years ago, the very first time, with hope and joy and the certainty that no two people had ever loved or would ever love quite this way again.

Later they sat together on the living room floor, eating Chinese food from the cartons and watching the evening news. Christine, fresh from the shower, wore a pair of panties and one of his white shirts. He never thought he'd envy a shirt, but there it was. Her wet hair was slicked back from her flawless face, and he found himself wanting her again.

"Moo shu pork or kung po chicken?" she asked.

He sat down on the floor next to her. "You."

"I'm not on the menu."

He traced the curve of her calf with his tongue. "You should be."

"You're insatiable," she said with a pleased smile.

"Any complaints?"

She took a bite of kung po chicken and shook her head. "Not a one."

"Stay here tonight, Christie." He heard the need in his voice and did nothing to disguise it. "We might not get the chance again for a long time."

She put down her fork and met his eyes. "What are we going to do, Joe?" she asked, her voice soft. "What's going to happen to us?"

"We're going to be together," he said, drawing her into his arms. "That's the one thing you can count on."

She stiffened and pulled away. "We can't count on anything. There's Marina and the baby and Slade . . . God only knows how this is going to end up."

"Happily," he said. "That's how it'll end up."

Her smile was tinged with sadness. "Still believe in miracles, do you?"

"We're together, aren't we? If that's not a miracle, I don't know what is."

"Staying together's the miracle."

He leaned back against the sofa and cradled her to his chest. "We're not going to make the same mistakes."

"How do you know?" Her voice was muffled. "We still have the same problems."

"Kids?"

She nodded. "I can't have them. You deserve them."

"I can live without them."

"You don't know that for a fact."

"I want to spend the rest of my life with you, Christie. If not having kids is part of the bargain, so be it."

"What if you change your mind?"

"I'm not going to change my mind."

"You can't be sure of that."

"If I wanted kids, I'd have them by now. It's been six years. I could've started a family." She flinched at his words and ducked her head. "Goddamn it." He pushed her away so he could see her face. "I love you. I've loved you from the first moment I saw you standing on the library steps. Nothing's changed, Chris, not one goddamn thing in all these years."

Her eyes glittered with tears, but that didn't stop him. He couldn't have stopped now if his life depended on it. "You left me. I didn't leave you." He stood up, feeling the years of anger building inside his chest, threatening to explode. "You took our marriage and tossed it aside like so much garbage. It wasn't me, Chris. I was in it for the long haul. You're the one who bailed out."

His chest felt constricted, and he strode toward the window, trying to pull a deep breath into his lungs.

"I did it for you," she said, walking toward him. "I did it so you could have the life you deserved."

"Who the hell are you to decide what I deserve? We lost a child. We didn't need to lose our marriage as well."

"You wouldn't talk to me, Joe. I needed to talk about the baby, but you just wouldn't let me inside your head long enough to understand what you were feeling."

"What did you think I was feeling? He was my son, too. I loved him as much as you did."

"You should have told me."

"You should have known."

His words caught Christine off guard, and she

struggled against an onslaught of emotions that seemed to be bombarding her from all sides. "I—I never thought about it," she admitted slowly.

"I know," he said. "That was part of the problem."

She reached for him, but he moved away. Her hand dropped to her side. "I wish I'd never gotten pregnant. It hurt so much to come so close, then lose . . . everything."

"You shut me out, Christine. Your grief went so deep that I couldn't find a way to reach you, and it scared the hell out of me. You had your friends and your family to help you. You didn't need me."

Her voice was choked with tears. "I needed you more than anyone, Joe, but you weren't there. I'd lie awake at night, waiting for you to come home so you could hold me and tell me everything would be all right, but you—"

"Didn't come home," he finished for her. He raked his hand through his hair and looked toward the window. "I was too busy closing down every Irish pub in Manhattan."

"I wondered if you'd found someone else. . . . I almost hoped that you had."

"There's never been anyone else, Christine."

"I know that now," she whispered.

"That's why you made me believe there was another man?"

She nodded miserably. "I wanted to make it easier on both of us, end it all before it became ugly."

"I wanted to kill you," he said in a voice that made her shiver. "When I thought of you in the arms of some other guy, I wanted to find you and wrap my hands around your throat—" He cut off his words as if their power was too terrible to be borne.

"Say it," Christine urged. "I want to know how you felt. If we're going to have a future, if we're going to make things work, we need to be honest with each other, right from the start."

"I found a woman the night after you left me," Joe said. "She was blond and beautiful and she let me have her for the price of a drink and a few sweet words."

"You slept with her?" She had no right to feel what she was feeling. She'd given up the right to jealousy when she walked out on him.

"I tried." He met her eyes. "You're a tough act to follow, Christine Anne Cannon."

She glanced away. "I don't want to talk about this anymore."

"You haven't been celibate all this time."

It was a statement rather than a question. The weight of her mistakes lay across her shoulders, and she couldn't shrug it away.

"Yeah," he said after a moment. "That's what I thought."

The silence in the room surrounded them both, and for a few moments Christine wasn't sure if it would break them apart or bring them closer together.

"I never stopped loving you, Joe," she said when the silence grew too painful for her to bear. "Not even for a minute."

"I tried to stop," Joe said, dragging his hand through his hair in the familiar gesture of his, "but you were always there, just beyond reach, reminding me how right it could be."

"But do you love me?" she whispered.

"Didn't you hear me a few minutes ago?"

She dismissed it with an impatient gesture. "Not

then," she persisted. *"Now.* At this moment in time, at this place?"

"Damn it, what do you think?"

"I don't want to think. I want you to tell me. If you love me, I want to hear you say the words before we take this any further—"

He grabbed her to him. His fingers dug into the soft flesh of her upper arms, but she didn't feel the pain. All she felt was the violent pounding of her heart and the wild surge of hope that flooded her body. "I love you, Christine. I always have and, goddamn it, I always will."

She rested her forehead against his shoulder. Her nostrils twitched at the scent of soap. His skin was hot to the touch. She felt as if she could stand there like that for the rest of her life and die happy.

"We never did finish the Chinese food," Christine said the next morning as she tossed the cartons in the garbage. "Good Morning America" droned on in the background from the TV at the far end of the counter.

Joe winked at her over his cup of coffee. "Regrets?"

She smiled back. "You must be joking." She stepped around the counter and wrapped her arms around his neck. "I hate to leave you."

"So don't."

"I have to. I can't show up at work wearing the same clothes."

"People remember those things?"

She rolled her eyes. "You wouldn't believe how much they remember. Besides, Slade will be there.

He's too observant by half. There are times I think he knows more about me than I know about myself."

Joe's brows knotted. "I don't like the sound of that."

She kissed the top of his head. "You're jealous," she said. "How wonderful!"

"I'm not jealous. I just don't think you can trust that SOB."

"Slade's not so bad," she said, slipping into her jacket. "He's ambitious, and he's poor, and he's talented."

"Bad combination."

"And he likes me."

"Even worse."

She grabbed her purse from the countertop. "You have nothing to worry about."

"It's not me I'm worried about, Christie. It's you. He's a user."

"Oh, for God's sake, Joe. Why don't I—"

They saw it at the same time. Ric's picture, out of focus but recognizable, filled the TV screen.

"What the hell—?" Joe leaped forward to raise the sound.

". . . whereabouts is unknown. Since the rebels took control of the city last night, information has been sketchy and difficult to confirm. More on the Evening News tonight with Peter Jennings."

"Marina," Christine said. "I hope she didn't hear this."

Joe turned off the TV. "I'll drive out to Hackettstown right now."

"I'd go with you but—"

He kissed her hard. "Go to work. I'll take care of it."

*   *   *

Her producer was waiting for Christine when she arrived at the studio. And so was Slade.

"Where the hell have you been?" Sandy roared. "All hell's breaking loose around here, and you don't bother to call in for messages?"

"I was off on a wild-goose chase," she said calmly with a quick smile for the photographer. "I had a hot lead, and it took me most of the night to track it down."

Sandy's eyes lit up. "Something good?"

"I thought it would be, but it didn't pan out."

"Damn it," said Sandy, lighting up a cigarette. "We need something to bump up the show. It's just not where I want it to be."

"The show's fine," said Christine. "Especially that piece on the First Lady's stand on abortion."

"Too soft," said Sandy.

"The hell it is. That was major stuff."

"Not enough juice. We need something like the casting couch piece you did back in L.A."

"I thought you said that was sleazy."

Sandy thumped her fist on the desktop. "Damn right I did. Let me tell you, we could use a touch of sleaze right about now."

Christine barely suppressed an urge to punch her producer's lights out. They all knew sleaze translated into Nielsen ratings, but she'd hoped for more bang for her journalistic buck. "I thought the original concept was celebrity news with a social conscience, more like what I was doing in print."

"That's what the affiliates said they wanted," Sandy conceded, "but I'm telling you it'll never play in Peoria."

"This is a hell of a time to change direction, Sandy." She tried to ignore Slade's avid interest in the conversation as she glanced at the wall clock. "We debut in less than thirty-six hours."

"Look," said Sandy, "I'll give it to you straight. We showed a rough cut last night to *TV Guide* and *USA Today*, and we didn't hit a home run."

"You did what?" Christine exploded. "Why wasn't I consulted?"

"Check your messages, Cannon," the producer fired back. "We gave it our best shot. You could've been here. You didn't respond."

She sidestepped the fact she hadn't checked her messages. "Let's put back the sex-on-daytime piece. Soap stars always bring out the viewers."

"Not good enough."

"Okay. There's the sex and pro tennis story. The video's been edited. All I'd have to do is tape the voice-over and write an intro. It's do-able."

Sandy pulled a face. "Maybe next week. We need something hot and current. Slade was telling me about a rumor he heard that tied in with the lead story on this morning's 'GMA.' Now if you could manage to dig up something on this disappearing princess, we might have something."

Christine's stomach clenched violently. *Stay cool, Cannon. You've been in tougher situations than this.* Smiling, she turned toward Slade. "Princess Anne hit the road again?"

"No," he said, unfolding his lanky body from the chair and rising to his feet. "Something a little closer to home."

Bile burned her throat. "Don't hold out on me,

friend," she said, meeting the challenge in his eyes with one of her own. "Let's hear the dish."

"Nothing concrete, love. Just bits and pieces."

"Stay on it," she said. "Never know what you might uncover."

She excused herself ostensibly to go into the studio to finish looping the piece on the First Lady, but raced down the hallway to her office and the telephone. Marina was still asleep, the housekeeper was at the grocery, and the nurse said Joe hadn't arrived yet.

"Can I take a message, Ms. Cannon?"

"No," she said, feeling more frantic by the minute. "I'll call back." This message had to be delivered personally. Movement at the doorway caught her eye, and she looked up to see Slade leaning against the jamb.

"Jesus!" She struggled to recover her composure. "How long have you been standing there?"

"Not long," he said, stepping into her office.

"So," she said with a practiced smile, "come to take a picture of the struggling TV star in search of ratings?"

He took a seat and swung his feet up onto her desk. "Actually I came to ask what took you so long, love."

"Good grief," she said with a brittle laugh. "Be late for work one day, and the world comes to an end."

"That's not what I meant."

"Somehow I didn't think so. What, then?"

"The pregnant princess. I wondered how long it would take for you to put the pieces together."

There was no point in lying. "How long have you known?"

"Two weeks." He grinned. "You look surprised."

"Only that you've kept it to yourself."

"You're not going to undercut me, are you, Chris love? It's a big story. We can pool our resources and break it together on your show."

Christine was cool in the face of his fire. Loyalty wasn't his strong suit. Ambition was. So be it. She was ambitious, too, and she'd be a liar if she said she wasn't tempted by the world-class story that had dropped into her lap.

"Seems to me we'd be jumping the gun," she said carefully. "We couldn't possibly get enough information on the story to lead tomorrow."

"She's living in your house," Slade pointed out. "You can call the shots."

"Her pregnancy," Christine reminded him. "I want this story as much as you do, but I don't want a miscarriage on my conscience."

"You're letting your personal life cloud your judgment, love. I'm disappointed."

She got up and walked toward the window. The ground seemed a long way down from the fortieth floor. He was right and she knew it. This was the kind of story that ratings gold was made of, guaranteed to get those Nielsen households tuning in.

She could let Slade break the story, then do a follow-up "my side" feature on her own show that would protect Marina and cement her place at the top of her field. Damn it, she wasn't the one who married the girl and brought her to the United States, land of soundbites and paparazzi. Joe must have known he was taking a chance by letting Marina live in the same house with a celebrity journalist and an ambitious photographer.

If the story was going to be broken anyway, why shouldn't she be the one to do it?

Her intercom buzzed. "Sound is ready for you, Christine," her assistant said.

"So what's it going to be, love?" Slade asked. "Do we go for the brass ring, or do I get all the gold for myself?"

"I need time," she said. "Let me finish the looping and the affiliate interviews."

"The clock's ticking, love."

"Four o'clock," she said, grabbing up her notes and her purse. "My apartment."

"We're cut from the same cloth," he said in a matter-of-fact voice. "If I don't break the story, I know you bloody well will, and I won't get a thing out of it."

"Trust me, Slade," she said, kissing him on his narrow cheek. "I won't let you down."

Slade watched as Christine vanished down the hallway, enjoying the way her short navy blue skirt twitched with each step. Too bad most of her fans had no idea she had the best ass in the business.

"You just don't get it, do you, love?" he said out loud to the empty office. She didn't call the shots this time, he did. She had the name, but he had the photographs, and those photographs were going to make him a very rich boy.

He'd been trying to hold off as long as he could before breaking the story, but greed was getting the better of him. Stories like this didn't come around every day, and the last thing he needed was for some other hungry photographer to pull the plum from the pudding, right under his bony English nose.

That black reporter, Terri Lyons, thought he'd sell his mother to the tabloids if the price was right, and maybe he would. In fact, if it were anybody but

Christine, he would have been on the phone with the tabloids right now, talking six figures for the rights to the story. But it was Christine, and that muddied the waters.

He didn't like seeing her tangled up with the Boy Scout. The dumb sod thought he was doing a bang-up job of hiding the way he felt for Christine, but a blind man could see the sparks flashing between the two of them. Damn waste, if you asked him. She could do a hell of a lot better than some burned-out foreign correspondent. But that was her choice. He hoped the sex was better than the prospects for the future.

Christine had confirmed his suspicions about Marina, but he needed some good solid proof before he blew the story open, which was another reason he'd agreed to give her time to consider her options.

Whether Marina turned out to be the center of a juicy ménage à trois with Christine and Joe or a real, live princess with a baby princelet and a sexual history to rival Stephanie of Monaco, it didn't much matter to Slade.

Either way, his future was assured.

18

"Christine!" Marina looked up from the couch in the living room. "What are you doing here?" Her face was fuller than it had been a few days ago, and the added weight softened her features.

"Thought I'd drop in for lunch." She sat down on the arm of the sofa. "You look wonderful, Marina. How're you feeling?"

"Fat," the girl said, brushing her hair off her face. "The doctor said I'm just about where I should be."

Christine felt a tiny pang of envy but pushed it aside. "Is Joe around?"

"In the kitchen." Her smile faded. "Is something wrong?"

"Absolutely not. I just needed to run something past him."

"I saw an advert for your new show on the telly last night. It looks wonderful."

"From your mouth to God's ear," Christine said, heading for the kitchen.

Joe was standing by the window eating a peanut butter and jelly sandwich. "What's wrong?" he asked as soon as he saw her.

"Everything. Slade knows."

"You've got to be kidding."

"Afraid not."

"How much does he know?"

"Enough to take it to the papers and have them believe him."

"Did you confirm it?"

"Not in so many word, but he had me dead to rights, Joe. He wants me to break it on my show."

"What about you?" he asked. "Would be one hell of a debut, wouldn't it?"

"Yes," she said, not looking away. "Guaranteed ratings."

"Tempted?"

"You bet I am. That's why I'm telling you to get out of here as fast as you can and take Marina with you."

"You sure?"

"Never more sure of anything in my life." She could see it in his eyes: love and something else, something unexpected. Respect. "I'm as surprised as you are, Joe. I didn't know I had it in me."

There'd be time later on to bask in the glow of approval, but they had more important things to discuss. Marina's survival, for one. The bombing of the World Trade Center had made most Americans aware of the fact that terrorism wasn't limited to Third-World nations. Ric had feared for his daughter's safety; that was why she'd been sent away in the first place.

They concocted a plan in the time it took Joe to finish his sandwich.

"For all I know, Slade's on his way out here," Christine said as she threw Marina's clothes into a suitcase. "I'll do my best to keep him off your tail, but you have to hurry."

Joe tossed his gear into a duffel bag while Christine went to break the news to Marina.

"What about you?" Marina asked, starting to cry. "You and Joseph love each other . . . and I—" Her voice broke, and she buried her face in her hands. Her sobs tore at Christine's heart.

"Don't cry, honey. This is going to work out. You'll see."

"I cannot do this without you. You're the only one who understands what I am feeling. Please," she said, choking back tears, "when my time comes, will you—?"

Christine hugged the girl close. The baby kicked hard, and she felt an answering response deep inside her own flat belly. "If I have to move heaven and earth to do it. You have my word."

Christine ran out to meet Slade in the driveway when he pulled up a little after one o'clock. "The son of a bitch is gone!"

It wasn't the greeting he'd expected, all things considered. "You're having me on."

"The hell I am. Look around, friend. You don't see his car, do you?"

"Maybe he's out."

"He's out, all right." She glared at him fiercely. "He took his clothes and his wife."

He climbed from the car and put an arm around her. "Better off without him, love. Boy Scouts don't make good husbands."

"Tell me something I don't know," she snapped.

They walked up the porch steps together with Slade's arm still resting on her shoulders. She was coiled so tightly he could feel tension pulsing through her body. There could be a lot of reasons for that tension, reasons that had nothing to do with her ex-husband and his pregnant wife running out on her. It occurred to him that this could be an elaborate ruse designed to knock him off track, but that kind of thing was more his bailiwick, not Christine's.

Christine was ambitious, but he'd never known her to lie. That was usually his territory. Still, something about the situation didn't feel right, and he was determined to get to the bottom of it.

"Sit down," he said when they stepped inside the house. "You need a cuppa."

"Good God," she said, her voice trembling with emotion. "The last thing I need is caffeine. I'm afraid I'll explode." With that she started to cry, ugly sobs that seemed to come from her gut.

Slade had never seen Christine lose control like that before. It was like watching a perfectly beautiful marble statue shatter right in front of you. He mumbled something vaguely comforting, then popped into the kitchen to brew up some tea.

"Drink up, love," he said a few minutes later as he handed her the mug of Lipton's. "It'll do you good."

She did as told, taking big gulps of tea between sniffles.

"Wh-what are you doing here?" she managed after she polished off the cuppa.

"Could ask you the same thing, love."

She dabbed at her eyes with the corner of a paper napkin, then looked him straight in the eye. "I came here to tell Joe you knew the whole story."

"Blunt, aren't you, love?" he asked, knocked breathless by her honesty.

"Why not?" she retorted, regaining a tad of her usual fire. "He's gone. It hardly matters anymore."

It mattered, and they both knew it. The question was, what was she willing to do about it?

"He was all wrong for you, love," he said while she recovered her composure. "You should have known that after the first go-round." And she definitely should have known it after the little poppet turned up preggers.

"At least I'm consistent," she said with a bitter laugh. "The same damn mistake over and over and over again."

Slade grinned, beginning to see a light at the end of this particular tunnel. "Should've taken me up on my offer. Younger men have a lot to recommend them."

"I don't want to think about sex again as long as I live," she said vehemently. "Sex is what's wrong with this world. I'm going to be celibate."

"Seems a waste to me, love."

"Not to me it doesn't. I swear to you, Slade, no man is ever going to make a fool of me ever again."

He saw his opening, and he went for it. "I'm going to break the story, Christine."

"Where?" she asked, throwing him a pitying look. "In one of those tabloid rags you're so enamored of? Don't waste my time."

His hunger sharpened. *"Vanity Fair?"*

"You must be joking. I'm going to break it on my show, Slade, and I'm going to break it so big Joe and Marina won't be able to show their faces anywhere."

"And where do I fit in?"

"Isn't that clear? You're the only one with pictures . . . and you're the only witness to what went on. You'll be on the show to tell your side from your point of view. We'll run your photos."

"Not good enough," he said. Not nearly good enough. "I want more than fame, Christine. I want some cold hard cash."

"And you'll get it. As soon as the show airs, you're free to do what you want with your photos. Sell them. Give them away. Sell the whole damn story to every sleazy tabloid in the universe. I don't care. Just let me break it first on my show, and I'll give you a media launch that'll put you permanently in orbit."

He didn't make it easy on her, but in the end he gave in. Christine's emotions were shaky at best. If he pushed her too far, she'd cut him out without a penny, and he'd be back where he was before he hooked up with her. No *Vanity Fair* article. No first-class flights. No entrée to bigger and better things.

For a smart woman, Christine was amazingly dense when it came to herself. You'd think with all of her experience mining for celebrity gossip, she'd know the big one when she saw it. Hell, Slade didn't give a rat's ass about one of those starving eastern European countries. Everyone knew they didn't matter a damn in the scheme of things. Who cared if some ersatz princess was married to a second-rate journalist?

But blowing the roof off media babe Christine Cannon—that was another story. Blond bombshell TV star, her lover (who also happens to be her ex-husband), and her lover's very pregnant wife. It didn't get much better than that.

The longer she took to break the story on her show, the juicier it was going to get. Yeah, he'd wait awhile longer. No matter what happened, Slade knew he couldn't lose.

A few years ago Joe had done a favor for one of the editors at Long Island *Newsday*, and it was time to call in the marker.

"A friend would do this for you?" Marina asked as they settled into the small garage apartment in Floral Park, just over the border in Nassau County.

"You know about reciprocal trade agreements?" he asked, hanging up her clothes in the closet. "Same thing, but on a more personal basis."

"You must be well liked," his wife observed.

He grinned at her over his shoulder. "You sound surprised."

"I suppose I am," she said, obviously considering her words with great care. "You were not the most agreeable of men when we first met."

"You weren't a bundle of charm either, kid."

She smiled, hesitantly at first, then with more conviction. "The circumstances were hardly conductive to friendship."

"I don't think Ric gave a damn about us being friends. He was more concerned with getting you safely out of the country."

"I was in no danger."

"I'm not your father, Marina. I was there. I know what was going on. Once the rebels came down from the mountains, you'd have been first in line for kidnap or murder."

"I was one of those rebels," she snapped. "Zee understands much more about what the people need than my father ever could."

Joe felt his eyes popping out of his head. "You were

up there in the mountains with the revolutionaries?"
He smacked his head with the heel of his hand. "Shit,
kid, now you tell me. I could've been halfway to a
Pulitzer with that kind of inside information."

"I have no inside information."

"If you were up there in the mountains, you have
more information than anyone else in your country
combined."

"What I saw is of no importance now," she pointed
out with an impressive display of logic. "The situation has changed dramatically."

"You could give me background."

"It would have no relevance."

"That's my problem."

"I probably shouldn't."

"You tell me your story," he said with a grin, "and
I'll tell you mine." His grin widened. "Maybe even
the avalanche story if you play your cards right."

She ducked her head and smiled.

"You should do that more often. You look pretty
when you smile."

Her smile vanished as quickly as it had come, and
he cursed himself for commenting on it. She sighed
deeply. "I'll never be beautiful. Not like Christine."

"Life comes with compensations, kid. Christine is
beautiful, but it's taken her a long time to be happy."

"It's because of the baby, isn't it?"

He stopped what he was doing and walked over to
the couch where she was propped up against a stack
of pillows. "You know about the baby?"

Marina nodded. "Christine told me."

He didn't know what to say, so he just stood there,
staring out the window.

"Are you going to marry Christine?" Marina asked.

He tugged at a lock of her soft brown hair. "Can't have two wives at the same time, kid. I thought you knew that."

Marina made an impatient gesture with her hand. "This will not last forever," she said. "One day I'll be gone, and you and Christine can be together again."

"Don't be in a rush to leave us," he said, feeling an unexpected but very real rush of affection for Ric's daughter. "Christine and I can wait."

"You shouldn't have to."

It was an odd thing to say, strangely urgent from someone so young. "We have plenty of time," he said after a moment. "The main thing now is to see that you have a healthy baby. I want to be able to tell your old man that mother and child are doing well."

"The baby will be perfect," Marina said.

He waited for the next sentence, but it never came. He sat down next to her on the sofa, wishing Christine was there to give aid and comfort. "Are you afraid?"

She shrugged. "Only of the unknown."

"I found a good doctor for you, someone who'll make sure both of you come through with flying colors."

She suddenly looked very young and very trusting. "Christine will be with me?"

"Damn right she will. Both of us, kid, right next to you." He rose to his feet then, to his surprise, bent down and kissed the top of her head. "You'll be fine, Marina," he said gruffly. "Didn't I promise your old man I'd take care of you?"

*   *   *

Christine's show debuted on Thursday night. She caught the last half of it at Terri's apartment after Lamaze class.

"It stunk," she said, sinking deeper into the couch. "Really stunk."

"I liked it, Aunt Chris." Celina looked up from her Latin homework. "It didn't make me think too much."

Terri cleared her throat. "Why don't you and Julius Caesar study in your room?"

Celina grumbled, but she did as her mother asked.

"Out of the mouths of babes," Christine muttered. "You shouldn't have asked her to leave, Ter. She was only telling the truth." Narrowing her eyes, she peered closely at her friend. "Wasn't she?"

Terri drew in a deep breath then nodded. "She was."

"So it stunk."

"It was lightweight."

"It was awful."

Terri nodded. "For you it was awful."

"Oh, God." Christine buried her face in her hands. "Damn, damn, damn. I had a winning formula. Why did I let them mess with it?"

"Maybe you had other things on your mind."

A wild laugh broke through her fatigue. "Maybe I'm losing my edge."

"Wait until the overnights come in tomorrow, Chris. Let the public decide."

The next morning found Christine seated in her producer's office with a slew of network reps huddled around the table looking as if they were planning D-Day redux.

"So what's the verdict?" she asked as she took her seat at the round table.

Sandy held her hand out flat and moved it from side to side. "Moderate. You didn't hit a home run and you didn't strike out."

"*Mediocre*'s the word you're looking for, isn't it?" Christine asked, a sharp note to her voice.

One of the network reps cleared his throat. "Good solid, middle-of-the-road ratings. Definitely a good foundation for the show."

"Damn it!" Sandy broke her pencil in half, then chucked the pieces into her wastebasket. "We were looking for a smash."

Another network rep jumped into the fray. "Magazine programs have . . . uh . . . historically got off to a slow start. '20/20' took a year or two to hit its stride, while 'Prime Time Live' had to split up the anchors before it found its audience. I—"

"Ancient history," Sandy said, glaring at Christine, who was doing her best to remain cool. "You guys don't give shows time to hit their stride these days. Can you guarantee us the full twenty-six weeks?"

"Nothing's written in stone," said the first rep, "but you know we'll do our best to find the right slot for Ms. Cannon's talents."

Ms. Cannon's talents. It took all of Christine's self-control to keep from laughing out loud. The final version of the show had been an enormous disappointment to her. The interview with the latest Hollywood rave piqued viewer interest but apparently not quite enough to make an appreciable dent in the Nielsens.

You let it happen, Cannon. You let them package you into something you're not.

She was comfortable with celebrity journalism. That wasn't the problem. Her print interviews had been known for their bite and sting. She'd even managed to retain those qualities in Los Angeles when she worked at a local station. Somehow both her bite and her sting had been lost in the translation to network television. There were affiliates to consider, competition to outflank, sensitive egos to be stroked. And whatever made Christine Cannon a name to reckon with had vanished in the process.

"We're going to re-tool," Sandy said after the network reps left for another meeting. "Maybe bring out some of the big guns."

"We did the First Lady," Christine observed. "How much bigger do you get?"

"That piece on drugs in Hollywood," Sandy said, shuffling papers on her desk. "Let's get moving on that."

"That's been done to death. Everyone's heard the latest rehab story."

"We'll go inside a rehab center and get the real nitty-gritty."

"That's invasion of privacy."

"Celebrities give up their right to privacy when they step into the limelight. It comes with the territory."

Your own words, she thought, *coming back to haunt you*. How many times had she said the same thing about a movie star publicly whining about life in the public eye? *Doesn't feel too good, does it, Cannon?*

She'd been more than willing to be put up there for public scrutiny, but it had never occurred to her that the sharp glare of the limelight would hurt the people closest to her. Slade was out there trying to track down Marina and Joe, and if he found them, Christine would find her life and the lives of those she loved spread across the front pages of tabloids coast-to-coast.

The second show gained a point in the ratings. Sandy attributed it to the piece on sex in the movies. The network brass credited the green contact lenses they made Christine wear. "Blue-eyed blonds are a dime a dozen," one of them had said. "But green eyes—that's an innovation."

"It was the weather," Christine told Joe when they talked on the phone that night.

"Rain equals ratings?"

"When it's raining from Omaha to New York, it does."

People stay in and watch TV, and Christine thanked her lucky stars the show they watched was hers.

The third show was postponed a week thanks to a Presidential press conference, which gave Christine time to keep Slade occupied following her around.

"*Vanity Fair* wants a meatier article than we first thought," she told Slade over dinner that night at Tavern on the Green. "Something to do with disappointing ratings. Hate to break it to you, friend, but you're stuck with me for another week." She took a sip of wine. "Any luck finding Joe?"

"The bastard disappeared into thin air," said Slade, swallowing a gulp of Dom Pérignon. "But I'm working on it."

She willed her heartbeat to return to normal. "Any leads?"

"Someone thought they saw him at a market in Queens, but that's not bloody likely, is it, love?"

"Not terribly," she agreed. "I lean toward D.C. myself. Most of his connections are in government."

Slade polished off the champagne and stood up. "Excuse me, love, but if I'm going to make the last shuttle to D.C., I'd better get moving."

Christine was still smiling long after he left.

"Don't count your chickens," Terri warned her over Szechuan food that night. "Slade's a shrewd customer. He might be stringing you along."

"He's not stringing me along," Christine said, grabbing a shrimp with her chopsticks. "He's too hungry for that. He thinks he's on to something in D.C."

They chatted about office politics and a major anchorman's latest face job, then finished off the meal with another pot of tea and fortune cookies.

Christine snapped her cookie in half and extracted the thin white slip of paper. She laughed when she read it. " 'Good things come to those who wait.' " She tossed it down on the table and met Terri's eyes. "The question is, how long are you supposed to wait?"

"Speaking of waiting, how is Marina doing?"

"Pretty well. She's gained weight. Her mood's improved."

"When's she due?"

"In fifteen days." She sighed. "Give or take a millennium."

"And then?" Terri's voice was soft.

"I don't know," Christine whispered. "I just don't know."

*   *   *

The phone woke Christine a little after three in the morning. Groggy, she reached for the receiver and mumbled, "Hello?"

"It's time, Christie."

She sat up straight, heart thundering. "Marina?" she asked. "The baby?"

"We're on our way to North Shore." Joe sounded tense and with good reason. "The pains are ten minutes apart."

She pushed her hair off her face and stifled a yawn. "I'll meet you there as soon as I can."

"Where's Christine?" Marina gripped Joe's hand as another contraction twisted through her body. "She . . . she promised."

"She'll be here, kid."

"You called her? You didn't forget to call her, did you?" She tried to remember what he had said the last time she asked, but couldn't.

"I called her before we left the apartment. You've gotta concentrate on your breathing, Marina. Come on!"

She tried, but it was like trying to ignore the fact that a thousand demons from hell were tearing at her belly. "I want to push."

"Oh, no, you don't," said the nurse as she attached the fetal monitor to Marina's exposed belly. "The doctor will tell you when it's time to push. You have a long way to go." The nurse hurried off to check on another patient.

"A long way?" She tried to sit up, but Joseph pushed her back down against the pillows. "What does she mean, a long way to go? I can't bear this another second, Joseph! You must do something right now."

"Have some ice chips."

She swatted them away. "I can't believe God meant women to suffer this way."

"It's biology," Joe said. "Men have heart attacks, women have babies. It all works out down the line."

He was talking nonsense, but somewhere through her pain she recognized that he was doing his best to ease her mind. It wasn't Joseph's fault he had the misfortune to be born a man. How could he possibly understand what she was going through, how it felt to give birth?

She needed Christine. Christine would understand.

She wanted to be back in London again, back in the world she'd known before it all changed, back with her mother and her father with things the way they used to be, safe and—

Another contraction bore down on her.

"Oh, God," she cried. "Christine!"

Christine would know what to do. . . .

"What if I pass out?" Joe asked as he scrubbed up at the sink.

"You're not going to pass out," Christine said, rinsing her hands under the hot water. "You'll be fine."

"You know how I feel about blood."

"I know what you're doing, Joe," she said, "and I appreciate it, but it isn't necessary. I'll be fine."

"Am I that transparent?"

"To me you are."

"You're okay with this?" he asked.

She nodded. "It's the closest I'm ever going to come

to a miracle. I'm glad Marina wants me here with her."

They donned scrubs and followed a nurse to the delivery room.

"Christine!" Marina gasped as a contraction eased. "Thank God! I—" She struggled for breath.

"Don't talk," Christine said, taking her position at the foot of the table. She grabbed Marina's hand in hers. "I'm here."

"Another contraction's coming, Marina," said the nurse-practitioner. "Try to relax . . . just ride with it."

"I c-can't . . . I—" Marina's back arched, and a low guttural sound tore from her throat.

Christine didn't flinch as the girl clutched her hand hard enough to break bones. She was vaguely aware of Joe standing behind her, but most of her concentration was focused on Marina. *Let the baby come soon,* she prayed silently. Marina's hips were so narrow, her belly so huge—she seemed too young, too tiny to suffer so much pain.

"You're fully dilated," the doctor told Marina. "It won't be much longer."

Thank you, thank you, thank you, Christine said to herself. It was almost over. In just a little while the pain would be only a memory, and Marina would have a beautiful little boy or girl in her arms, a baby to love and protect and—

"Doctor." The nurse's voice was low, urgent. "BP's spiking."

Time seemed to slow down, drifting around Christine in waves of sound and motion. She gripped Marina's hand harder than before. She'd felt this way before, but when?

"What is it?" Joe's voice joined the wave. "Is something wrong?"

The nurse rounded the foot of the table. "You'll have to leave."

"Leave?" Joe's voice rose. "I'm not leaving until—"

The nurse met Christine's eyes. "Please go with him," she said. "Marina's blood pressure is higher than we'd like. We may need to do a C-section."

"We're prepared for a C-section," Christine said.

"Get them out!" the doctor roared. "Now!"

Moment's later they found themselves standing on the other side of the door.

"Everything's going to be okay," Christine said, feeling sick to her stomach with fear. "They're just following hospital regulations."

"I don't like this," Joe said, trying to peer through the glass window near the top of the swinging door. "She needs us. She's too young to go through this alone."

"I know," she whispered, wrapping her arms around his waist. "But she's a strong girl. She knows we're right outside."

"Damn it! Why don't they tell us something?"

"We've only been out here a minute or two, Joe. A C-section takes longer than that."

Again she had the sensation of being suspended in time and place, floating above the scene but not really part of it. *We're sorry, Mrs. McMurphy, but we did everything we could . . .*

"Oh, God," she whispered, suddenly cold to the marrow. Not again. The baby was only two weeks away from being full term. Surely nothing could go wrong at this stage.

Two orderlies raced down the hallway, pushing huge carts of ominous-looking equipment. Christine and Joe watched in mounting horror as the orderlies smashed through the swinging doors and vanished inside.

"It's bad," Joe said. He began to shake, and she held him tighter, as if physical closeness could drive the demons away.

"They can perform miracles today," she said, grasping at straws. "It's not going to be the way it was for us, Joe. She's going to have a healthy baby. I know she will."

The minutes passed with excruciating slowness. Ten minutes. Fifteen. She relived her miscarriage a thousand times over and she knew Joe did as well. Marina was going to deliver a healthy baby, and before too long she'd be back in her own country with her father and the man she loved and a whole wonderful life stretched out before her.

"Mr. McMurphy."

They both jumped at the sound of the doctor's voice. She held Joe's hand as he cleared his throat. "How is she? Is the baby all right?"

He's not smiling, Christine thought as she watched the doctor's face. *Dear God in heaven, he's not smiling.*

As if on cue, a quick tight smile flickered, then faded away. "You have a healthy baby girl, Mr. McMurphy."

Christine sagged against Joe in relief.

"That's great!" Joe pumped the doctor's hand as if he really were the proud father. "That's really terrific! How's Marina?"

"I'm sorry, Mr. McMurphy," the doctor said, those deadly awful words, "but I'm afraid your wife is gone."

19

❧

"Just one more set of papers to sign, Mr. McMurphy," said the nurse with the kind eyes. "We're sorry it's necessary to bother you at such a terrible time."

"I understand," Joe said, watching himself go through the motions as if from a great distance. He glanced around the quiet corridor.

"Where is she?"

The nurse shifted position. "Your—your wife is being cared for."

Cared for. There's a euphemism for you. Joe cleared his throat, trying to banish the image of Marina, cold and alone, from his mind. "I meant my friend."

The nurse's expression brightened. "Oh! Ms. Cannon. I'm a big fan of hers," the woman gushed. "And she's even more gorgeous in person than on TV. But you must already know that. She's in the ladies' room. She'll be back in a minute, I'm sure."

He signed the stack of papers the nurse put in front of him. He could have been signing away his life for all he knew or cared.

It was so goddamn unfair, so wrong, that he couldn't find the words to give voice to the rage that burned inside his chest. All of the doctors said it was a one-in-a-million occurrence. Marina was so young, so basically healthy—she should have breezed through childbirth with no trouble at all. Even her blood pressure, problematic back in Nevada, had been under control right up until that last moment when an aneurysm in her brain burst and caused a fatal stroke.

One young life ended as another life began.

He supposed there was a karmic symmetry to the whole thing, life renewing itself, but right then he felt too bruised, too sorrowful, to take any comfort from the thought. He bowed his head, trying to hide his tears from the concerned nurse. He had no right to his pain. Ric had that right, the man Marina loved had that right . . . and most of all the newborn baby girl who would never know the woman who'd given her life.

"Joe." Christine's voice was soft as she rested her hand on his shoulder. She sat down on the bench next to him, and he turned toward her. Her hair was scraped off her face with a white headband. Her face was scrubbed clean of makeup as if she'd been trying to wash away the evidence of tears.

"You've been crying," he noted.

She nodded. "In the bathroom. Privacy's hard to come by these days."

"What the hell happened, Christie?" he asked, dragging his hand through his hair in an impatient, desperate gesture. "I can't find Ric, I don't know who the hell the baby's father is—" He stopped, struggling for control. "Jesus. What in hell am I going to do?"

"We're going to do whatever it is we have to do," she said, her voice choked with tears, "and the first thing is, we're going to see the baby."

"My name is on the birth certificate," he said, shaking his head. "They all think I'm the baby's father."

"Let it be for now, Joe. This is between you and Ric, not the hospital staff."

She was in the first incubator near the window on the left-hand side of the nursery. MCMURPHY, BABY GIRL, the sign at the foot of the crib read.

"She's beautiful," Christine murmured, touching the glass with her forefinger. "So perfect."

"Look at that chin," Joe said, chuckling despite himself. "She's Marina all over again."

The attending nurse looked up, saw them standing there, then hurried to the door.

"Good heavens," she said, all friendly hustle and bustle, designed to make them feel better. "You haven't held your little girl yet, have you, Mr. Mc-Murphy? Well, let's remedy that right this minute."

He didn't want to hold the baby. He'd never known exactly what to do with infants besides find someone else to take them off his hands. But she was so little, and she looked so much like Marina, that when the nurse handed him the precious bundle the pain in his heart eased if only for a moment.

"She's smiling," he said, blinking back tears.

"That's gas," Christine and the nurse said simultaneously.

It felt good to laugh. An hour ago he wouldn't have thought it possible, but the human spirit was an amazing thing, especially when faced with the future in the guise of a newborn baby girl.

"She looks like you," the nurse said. "Same wavy dark hair."

He and Christine looked at each other, a moment of such intense and total understanding that it made his knees weak. This was the opportunity they'd been denied years ago, and the irony was lost on neither of them.

"Ric's a grandfather," he said, shaking his head in amazement. "He's gonna love this kid."

"I placed your call to the Undersecretary of State," Christine said, opening her arms for the baby. "They said they'll do their best."

"I'll call him later," Joe said, placing the baby in her waiting arms. "At *home*."

In a way he was almost glad. How did you tell the man who once saved your life that there had been nothing you could do to save the life of his only child?

"Ohh." Christine exhaled on a sigh as the baby nuzzled close to her breast. "So sweet . . ." The baby opened her mouth to nurse, and Christine gave her her pinky to suck on. "I think she's hungry," Christine said to the nurse.

"Why don't you feed her?" the nurse asked Christine.

"Is it okay?" Christine asked. The look on her face was celestial. He'd never felt closer to heaven in his life.

"Sure is," said the nurse. "Why don't you all come with me?"

It was a simple enough act, a woman giving a bottle to a baby. One that was probably being played out in every town, in every state, in every country on earth. But the effect it had on him was both particular and profound. He couldn't put a name to the feelings battling inside his chest, but he acknowledged their presence.

And he wished he could make the moment last.

At ten o'clock on Monday morning Marina was buried in Joe's family plot at Calverton on the eastern end of Long Island after a short graveside service.

At two P.M. Christine and Joe left North Shore University Hospital in Manhasset with a stack of legal papers, some good wishes, and a six-pound, fourteen-ounce infant named Baby Girl McMurphy. Terri had seen to it that they had an infant seat and the essentials.

"She looks a lot smaller out here in daylight, doesn't she?" Joe asked as he carried the baby out to the car.

"I was thinking the same thing," Christine said, wiping her damp palms on the sides of her skirt.

It took them twenty minutes to get the baby safely strapped into the infant seat. Christine had never felt so clumsy and useless in her life.

At least not until the baby started crying on the Long Island Expressway.

"Oh, God, Joe," she said, leaning over the seat to stare at the squalling little girl. "What are we going to do?"

"I thought you'd know," Joe said.

"How would I know? I've never had a baby."

"I thought it was a woman thing."

"Breastfeeding is a woman thing. This isn't gender specific."

"Do you think she's hungry?"

"She ate before we left the hospital, don't you remember?"

"Maybe she needs to be burped."

"I did that," she said, making a face. "That's what happened to my silk blouse."

He sniffed the air. "Maybe she needs to be changed."

"Don't even kid about that."

He unrolled the window. "I'm not kidding, Chris."

They exited the Expressway and pulled into a diner on Queens Boulevard. Christine took the baby into the ladies room while Joe made another call to the State Department. She breathed a sigh of relief when she saw they had a changing table in the anteroom.

"You're going to have to cooperate with me, sweetheart," Christine said as she lay the baby down on an opened blanket. "I don't know any more about this than you do."

The baby squirmed as Christine undid the old diaper and disposed of it, then seemed to laugh as Christine cleaned and dried and powdered her.

"You like being naked," Christine said, bending over to kiss her on the tummy. "Just you wait until you're thirty-five and your breasts bounce against your knees when you walk down the street. You'll get over it."

The baby seemed unconvinced, and she resisted Christine's best efforts to diaper and dress her.

"Oh, no, you don't," Christine said, scooping the baby up and holding her close. "Don't you use those feminine wiles on me. I'm not going to fall in love with you."

That's the last thing she wanted to do. This was a temporary situation, a detour in the scheme of things. This baby didn't belong to her, she didn't belong to

Joe, and to pretend otherwise was surely an invitation to disaster.

Joe was sitting in a booth by the window when she and the baby left the ladies' room.

"We haven't eaten since last night," he said as they settled the baby into the car seat he'd brought in while she was changing diapers. "I ordered tuna sandwiches and coffee for both of us."

"Thanks," she said, sliding into her seat. "I didn't realize I was hungry until you said that."

A family with two little girls claimed the booth behind Joe. Christine found herself watching them with a sense of envy she hadn't experienced in more years than she cared to count.

"I don't want to feel this way," she said, looking down at her hands. "This hurts too much, Joe. I just want to get up and run as far and as fast as I can."

He reached across the table, and she watched her hands disappear beneath his. "You don't have to be part of this, Christie." There was no anger in his words, no hidden agenda. "This is my problem, not yours."

"It became my problem somewhere along the line and—" She stopped and composed herself. "I wish it hadn't," she finished simply. "I really wish it hadn't."

"Bail out, Christie. Whatever we found, it'll still be there when this is over."

The waitress dropped off the coffee and sandwiches, then hurried away.

"No guarantees," Christine said softly. "Life delights in making fools of us all."

He looked at the infant next to him, then back at Christine. "I can handle this."

"I know you can." She sighed deeply, then gave in

to the inevitable. "I want to be part of it." She smiled, really smiled, for the first time in days. "My life, Joe. My choice."

How long had it been since she'd felt so violently, painfully alive and open to the future? The last time she remembered this rush of pure emotion was the day she and Joe stood before her family and gave their hearts in marriage. Great joy often led to even greater sorrow, but after all these years of living with her emotions under lock and key, it seemed a risk worth taking.

She looked at Joe, then at Marina's baby, and knew a moment of towering joy that made everything else pale by comparison. She might end up with a broken heart, but she'd rather that than no heart at all.

Christine called in for messages before they left the diner.

"I told you there was a funeral today," she said a bit testily to her producer. The details were nobody's business but hers and Joe's. "I'll be in tomorrow."

"Not good enough," Sandy snapped. "I need you here now."

"Impossible."

"I'll pretend you didn't say that."

"Tomorrow morning," Christine repeated.

"The network's talking about a new time slot. We need a strategy meeting and we need it now."

"Damn it!" Christine exploded. "Don't you hear what I'm saying, Sandy? I just buried someone I cared for today. Your strategy meeting will just have to wait."

"You hung up on her," Joe observed as they climbed back into the car.

"I know."

"Was she pissed?"

"Royally."

"Regrets?"

"Not yet." She grinned. "But the day is still young."

They made good time and hit the Hackettstown exit on I-80 a little after nine P.M.

"I let the housekeeper go," Christie said.

"What about your pal Slade?"

"He's shifted his focus to Manhattan," she said. "Besides, he doesn't have a key to the house."

"You did a good job keeping him off my tail. I hear he was down in Washington, snooping around."

"He's good at what he does," Christine said. "Don't ever forget that. He usually gets what he goes after." She chuckled. "With one notable exception: One of his sources said you'd been grocery shopping at C-Town in Queens."

Joe paled visibly. "I shopped at C-Town our second day in the apartment."

"What did I tell you? Slade's ethics are questionable, but there's no denying his ambition."

"And you think he has the talent?"

"I know he has the talent. If he'd leave this tabloid junk behind, he could make a fine name for himself as a *real* photographer instead of a paparazzo."

They made the turn near the pizzeria, then the series of turns after the church. The evening air was cool and blessedly silent. The first of the autumn leaves crunched beneath the tires as they approached Marlborough Road.

Joe slowed as they turned onto their street. "What the hell's going on up there?"

Christine's gut knotted. "I see lights," she said, pointing in the direction of their house. "I think it's a camera crew."

"Shit," he muttered.

"Turn around," Christine ordered. "They haven't spotted us yet. We can—"

"The hell I'll turn around. Nobody's keeping me out of my own house."

"These people are relentless," Christine said. "They'll be shoving cameras at the baby, screaming questions. You don't know how awful they can be—" She stopped. "Trust me on this, Joe. I was one of them."

He swung the car into a tight U-turn.

"Don't speed up," Christine warned. "That's a dead giveaway."

"So's a U-turn."

"Don't compound things. Just cruise on out of here."

"You're good at this," he said. "I never knew how good you were."

"Thanks," she said as they headed toward Manhattan. "Too bad Slade is better."

Terri flagged them down a half block away from Christine's apartment building. "The place is crawling with reporters," she said as they idled at the curb. "Keep going."

Terri was right. A knot of reporters and paparazzi were camped out in front of Christine's apartment building.

"Forget this," said Joe. "Let's try my place."

"What makes you think they won't be there, too?"

"It's a sublet. They wouldn't be able to track it to me."

Joe said a quick prayer of thanks when he pulled up in front of the building and saw nothing but a doorman. "You and the baby go on upstairs," he said, helping them out of the car and handing Christine the keys. "I'll find a parking spot and follow."

When he got upstairs, Christine was in tears. So was the baby.

"She won't eat, Joe. She's so tiny—" She cried harder.

"You're exhausted," Joe said, taking the baby from her. "Get some sleep. I'll take care of the kid."

"You know what to do?"

"I know as much as you do."

A wavery smile broke through the tears. "That's not saying much."

"Sleep," he said. "There's enough for us to worry about tomorrow."

She stumbled down the hall toward the bedroom, leaving him alone with Marina's daughter.

"The world isn't this bad all the time," he said, settling down on the sofa with the infant. "I know it's hard for you to believe it right now, but it's gonna get better." He coaxed the bottle's nipple between her tiny lips. "First you eat, then you sleep. Once you master that, we'll talk about toilet training."

She began to suck greedily on the nipple, slurpy, milky sounds that made Joe grin.

"Way to go, kid."

His grin widened. He'd conquered bottle feeding before Christine. He wasn't about to let her live it down.

*   *   *

Slade was lounging against a parked car when
Christine left for the office the next morning. "Front
page," he said, shoving a copy of the *New York Post*
in her face. "You knew I'd get it sooner or later."

She saw a picture of herself, Joe, and an obviously
pregnant Marina that had been taken at the house,
then a picture of Christine and the baby taken
coming out of the diner. The headline read SHOT FROM
A CANNON. She felt sick to her stomach.

She pushed the paper back toward him. "You got
what you wanted, Slade. Now get the hell out of my
way."

"Touchy, aren't we? Surrogate motherhood's not
all you thought it'd be?"

"You bastard." She wheeled around to face him.
"How could you do that to me?"

"You screwed me. I screwed you." He folded the
newspaper in half and tapped it against his hand.
"Didn't have to be this way, love. We made a great
team before the Boy Scout came along."

The radio car she'd phoned for pulled alongside the
curb. She brushed past Slade and flung open the door.

"You can take that *Vanity Fair* assignment and
shove it," she said as she climbed inside.

"You'll get over it, love," he called out, "and I'll be
here when you do."

She was in a foul mood when she arrived at the
office. Confrontation was not her favorite way to start
the day, and she knew another world-class confrontation lay ahead when she found her producer.

As it turned out she didn't have far to look.

Sandy was sitting in Christine's office, behind
Christine's desk, and she didn't look happy.

"Make yourself comfortable," Christine said dryly as she dropped her briefcase onto a chair.

Sandy leaned back in the fancy leather chair and unfolded a copy of the *New York Post*. "Want me to read it to you?"

"No, thanks," said Christine. "I've already had the pleasure."

Sandy leaned forward, eyes flashing fire. "You owed us first crack at the story, Chris."

"That's not a story, Sandy. That's my life."

"If it's on the front page, it's a story."

"I disagree."

"You never told me your ex was married to a pregnant princess."

"Because it was none of your business."

"It's my business now."

"The hell it is."

"The network's giving us one more shot. They've put us on a two-week hiatus with orders to come up with the goods or close up shop. This is exactly what we need to put our name in lights."

How many times had she said the same thing to someone else?

"I'm not doing it, Sandy."

"Is that final?"

"It's final."

Sandy flung the newspaper across the room in a fit of rage. "Then consider yourself on suspension."

"No," said Christine, gathering up her briefcase. "Consider me unemployed."

"Ms. Cannon." The bartender crouched down next to the table and offered a friendly bartender's smile. "I think it's time to switch to coffee."

"Well, you just be my guest," Christine said, then burst into laughter. "As for me, keep those champagne cocktails coming."

Through a fog of booze, Christine saw Terri smile up at the bartender. "Coffee sounds like a good idea."

Christine wrinkled up her face. "Haven't you heard? You can't be too rich or too drunk."

"Yes, you can," said Terri, taking their glasses and placing them on the table next to them. "You're proof of that, kid."

The waiter appeared with a large pot of coffee and two fat white mugs. "On the house."

Christine squinted at the metal pot. "Doesn't look like champagne to me."

Terri waved the bartender away, then filled the mugs with coffee. "Drink this," she ordered, pushing a cup toward Christine.

"And get un-drunk?" She shuddered. "Not on your life."

Terri glanced around the dimly lit bar. "I'm all in favor of drowning your sorrows from time to time, but you don't drown them in public. Let's get you home."

"I sh-shouldn't have called you," Christine said, reaching for the champagne glass on the adjoining table. "You're no fun."

"I'm a lot of fun," Terri said, grabbing the champagne glass from her.

"I wish I liked Scotch," Christine mumbled. "I'd be drunk by now if I'd been drinking Scotch."

"You did just fine with champagne."

"I'm unemployed," Christine said, listening to the way the word sounded. "I haven't been unemployed since I was f-fifteen." She listened to the way those words sounded and shook her head. "Twenty years."

"You won't be unemployed for long," Terri said, her gaze straying toward the door. "Give them a day or two. They'll change their minds."

Christine snorted into her coffee mug. "I'm p-pathetic," she said. "Don't have a life . . . don't have friends . . . no family." She took a large swallow of coffee, dribbling some onto her chin. She didn't bother to wipe it away. "No job." By tonight her pathetic story would be on all the television stations, blasted across *Entertainment Tonight*," and ultimately on the front pages of the *National Enquirer* and *Star*. And damn it, they'd probably have the bare bones facts right but not the heart and soul of it, and that made her angrier than anything.

She grabbed her briefcase and rose shakily to her feet.

"Where do you think you're going?" Terri asked.

"Paris," she said with a hysterical laugh. "Maybe Hong Kong." Someplace where they didn't know her, where she didn't have a history, where she could forget the past few days had ever happened.

"Sit," Terri urged. "Drink some more coffee, and then we'll figure out where you're going."

She did as she was told. Mainly because she couldn't think of a good reason not to.

"Three days," she mumbled, resting her head in her hands. In one three-day period she'd welcomed a newborn into the world, buried a lovely young woman, tossed in her lot with her ex-husband, been betrayed by a colleague, and seen her career come to a screeching halt.

Was it any wonder she was trying to drown herself in a sea of booze?

She heard male footsteps approaching the table. "No more coffee," she said, not looking up. "Champagne or nothing."

"What the hell are you trying to do?"

Joe. She should have known.

She peered up at him between her fingers. "Trying to get drunk."

"Having any luck?"

"Not half enough."

"Terri told me what happened."

She looked over at Terri. "Terri has a big mouth."

"Slade's taking it to the press."

"Dirty rotten bastard," she muttered.

"I could've told you that."

She took a second look at him and the sleeping bundle cuddled against his chest. "This is no place for a baby, Joe."

"You're right," he said, taking her by the hand, "but I know a place that is."

She looked at Terri. Her friend's dark brown eyes glistened with tears. "Go, you fool," Terri said. "And don't look back."

20

Twenty-four hours later, Joe stood on the porch of the Cannon ranch, waiting for the sun to rise.

Inside the house, in their old room, Christine slept beneath a quilt her father's mother's mother had made not long after the Cannons settled in Nevada. She had been exhausted, a bone-deep weariness that required more than sleep to cure, whether or not she realized it.

She needed her family.

And they had been there for her, the way he'd known they would be. Without question. Without reproach. Waiting with open arms to pull her close and ease the pain. And the biggest miracle of them all was that they were there for him, as well, and for Marina's baby, the same way they had been there for him when he was a part of their family.

He leaned against the railing, listening to the sounds of the earth reawakening.

This was home. This unforgiving land. These very forgiving people. The woman he'd loved for longer than he could remember. The innocent baby girl who looked to him and Christine for her every need. It all mattered. More than career or money or any of the thousand other things that could vanish in the blink of an eye. This was what was real and lasting.

He'd always known it. Now Christine knew it, too.

If only it hadn't taken the death of a spirited young woman to make them understand the miracle they had right there for the taking.

"You're up early, son." Sam stepped out onto the porch as the first pale pink rays of dawn blushed the horizon. "Couldn't sleep?"

"Didn't want to miss this," Joe said, gesturing wide.

Sam nodded. "Somethin', ain't it?"

Joe met the older man's eyes. "Worth fighting for, I'd say."

Sam's smile was slow and steady. "Hear tell you've been doing some work for us in Washington."

"Laying the groundwork. There's a lot to be done. You ranchers are tough, but the government's one hell of an opponent." He gave Sam an overview of the fight over fees for grazing rights, then a quick prognosis for the future.

"They're fixin' to fight us tooth and nail," Sam said, "but that's all right. We've got plenty of time and a lot more patience."

"You're going to need patience," Joe said. "We're in for a real battle."

Sam clapped Joe on the back. "I like hearing you say that, son. We've missed you these past few years."

Joe gestured toward the house. "I don't imagine this is what you were expecting, Sam." He and Christine together again, but this time with a baby who didn't belong to either one of them and never would.

"When you get to be my age, you stop expecting things and you start accepting them. Makes life a whole lot sweeter that way."

"I love her, Sam," he said quietly, "and I want to marry her again if she'll have me."

"Can't speak for my daughter, son, but I'll have you know the rest of us are pullin' for you." He grinned just as the sun rose over the horizon. "So when're you going to ask her?"

"Just relax," Nonie said, handing Christine the bottle. "You worry too much. She knows what she needs, and she'll be sure to take it."

"How can she know what she needs?" Christine asked. "She's only three weeks old."

The baby reached for the bottle.

"See what I mean?" Nonie asked.

"I don't see anything."

"She reached for the bottle."

"That was a reflex action, Mom. She's too little to know what she's doing."

"Don't you be tellin' me my business," Nonie said in an amused tone of voice. "I raised up seven children and I know what I know. That baby girl was askin' for her bottle."

Christine watched as the baby drank noisily and with great abandon. "I stand corrected."

Nonie gave her shoulder a squeeze. "Don't you go makin' more of this than there is. Taking care of a baby is a matter of common sense, plain and simple. The good Lord gave us some pretty strong instincts when it comes to carin' for our young. Follow those instincts and you can't get into trouble."

"You make it sound so easy, Mom," said Christine with a sigh. "Is she eating too much? Is she eating too little? Has she gone through too many diapers—how on earth did you survive the lot of us?"

"Best years of my life," said Nonie, "raising you kids." She gave her daughter a meaningful look. "And the hardest work I've ever done."

"I believe it," said Christine, settling deeper into the overstuffed chair. "It's easier to put on a television show." And to fail at it, but that was another story. One Christine didn't intend to dwell on right now.

Her mother bustled off to load the washing machine, leaving Christine and the baby alone with her thoughts.

"You'll come back after you've licked your wounds," her attorney had said, after a marathon long-distance call to discuss possible litigation against her. "We'll get you back on track." The network had invested too much time and money in making her a success to let her walk out on it now. "They'll come around. Trust me."

In truth Christine didn't care if they came around or washed their hands of her permanently. There in Nevada with Joe and the baby and her family she felt connected to her life in a way she hadn't in longer than she cared to remember. The minutiae of everyday family living, the give and take between a man and a woman, caring for an infant—it all seemed suddenly natural. She didn't have to ask herself why she was there, what she wanted from the experience, or where she would be tomorrow.

For the first time she saw the beauty in the life she'd grown up with, the life she'd always taken for granted. Small ranchers like her father were an endangered species, and they needed all the help they could get. Joe had always known that. She was glad she knew it now, as well.

There was no denying that there were problems up

ahead, that this magical interlude would end sooner than she wanted it to, but none of those problems mattered. She was living in the present, passionately and completely, and the sensation was exhilarating.

All of the years of feeling as if she didn't belong drifted away, and she allowed herself to be a real part of her family, to love Joe the way he needed to be loved. The way she needed to love him. It hurt to have her heart exposed and beating for the world to see, but nothing good and wonderful came without risk, and love was the biggest risk of all . . . especially when you loved an infant who didn't belong to you. But the bottle had been uncorked. She couldn't stuff her emotions, her love, back inside and stash the bottle back in some forgotten closet. And she no longer wanted to.

Two days later Joe kidnapped her from the front porch, and they rode out to the pond south of the pasture. It had rained the day before, and the rich, fertile smell of earth and water softened the sharp tang of the autumn breezes. The sky was the deep clear blue you only saw west of the Mississippi. The sun was just past the midpoint, casting shadows across the smooth surface of the pond.

"Is this what they call a guilty pleasure?" Christine spread an old forest-green blanket down beneath a cottonwood tree and stretched out. "I feel decadent."

"Marta said she'd watch the baby." He sat down next to her. "Said she needs the practice."

Christine leaned on one elbow. "The baby," she said with a shake of her head. "That poor little girl needs a name."

"I know," said Joe, "but—"

He stopped abruptly, and Christine didn't pursue the topic. They were temporary caretakers, nothing more. To give Marina's baby a name seemed presumptuous when she had a father and a grandfather out there somewhere. And it was too beautiful a day to think of something as sad as giving up Marina's baby.

She smiled and snapped her fingers. "No serious talk," she said. "This afternoon is just for us."

"About that serious talk," Joe said, meeting her eyes. His hair gleamed in the sunlight, and she noted a random sprinkling of gray scattered near the temples. Pain, fierce and bittersweet, pierced her heart. Life seemed so precious, so miraculous, that she wanted to grab each second with him and hold it close. "There's something we need to work out."

Her pulse hammered in her throat. *I don't want this to end,* she thought, *not when it took so long to find.* "I thought you were enjoying yourself here."

"I am," he said, still looking too serious for her taste. "But there's one very important question we haven't dealt with."

"The fact that we're both basically unemployed?" she asked with a laugh.

"The fact that we're not married."

Her breath caught in her throat. "Joe . . ."

"You can't be surprised, Christie." He cupped her face between his powerful hands. "Where did you think we were going with this?"

"I knew where we were going with this," she whispered, "but with all that's happened—"

"Life is short," he said, mirroring her own thoughts. "I'll be damned if I'm going to live it without you. We wasted too many years as it is."

"This is all that matters," she said, pressing her mouth to his. "That we're here, that we're together, that I've never loved anyone the way I love you—"

"That we're married."

"Married didn't work so well for us before, Joe. Maybe we should try it a different way."

"Live together?" he snapped. "Keep our options open?"

"That's not what I mean."

"Damn it, then say what you mean."

"I'd rather lose you than know you had regrets. I love you too much to cheat you of your chance to be a father."

"I want you, Christie, and everything that comes with the package, good and bad. I already told you that. I don't know how to say it any plainer."

"That's pretty plain," she said, blinking back tears. "I just hope you know what you're doing."

The passion was there and the heat, but more than sex, more than desire, there was a deep sense of the inevitable, that this time there would be no turning back, no turning away, nothing but a future together.

"Come here," he said, motioning her closer.

A wicked grin broke through her tears. "Make me, cowboy."

With a wonderfully lusty growl he pinned her back against the blanket.

"We'll have to negotiate a new contract," he said, sliding his hands beneath her sweater.

"Maybe I don't want a new contract," she said, trying to ignore the way his hands felt against her skin.

"I'll make it worth your while." He moved against her. "Lots of fringe benefits."

"I might need them." She reached for the snap of his jeans. "There's a good chance my career is over."

"You'll land on your feet."

"There's no guarantee."

He cupped her breasts, drawing his thumbs slowly over her nipples until they hardened against him. "You'll go back into print," he said. "It's where you did your best work." He leaned back and met her eyes. "And you can lose those green contacts."

She eased his zipper slowly down. "Maybe I'll get used to unemployment."

"Not you," he said. "You're too good. It'd be a waste of natural resources."

"So are you," she said. "A natural resource, I mean."

His breath hissed as she found him with her hand. "So let's not waste it."

"My thoughts exactly," said Christine.

They didn't think again for a long time.

Sam was waiting for them on the front porch when they returned. Peering through the front window, Joe could see Marta, Nonie, and the baby silhouetted in the parlor.

"Hey, Sam," Joe called out to the rancher. "I told you I'd have her home by curfew."

Christine pointed toward the suitcases stacked up on the top step. "You trying to tell us something, Daddy?"

"Your phone call came," Sam said, looking Joe straight in the eye.

"The State Department?"

"Yup. I took a number. They said it's the real thing."

"Did they mention Ric? Is he—?"

"They didn't seem too fired up 'bout telling me much of anything, son. You best call them back and find out for yourself."

It sounded like a good idea. Hell, it was a good idea. So why was he so damn reluctant to do it?

"You'd better call," Christine said. "They're probably waiting for you."

"I know," Joe said, dragging his hand through his hair. He didn't know whether he hoped they'd told Ric about Marina or left the sad task for him.

The undersecretary was either unwilling or unable to give Joe much in the way of information beyond instructions to get himself and the baby to the airport ASAP and bring his passport with him. "I'm bringing more than a passport," Joe said. "I'm bringing my ex-wife."

Nonie and Marta had packed their things for them, including extra supplies for the baby.

"I had a small leather bag with Marina's belongings," Christine said as they made their good-byes in the front yard. "I think I left it in the bedroom."

"Right here," said Marta, pointing behind the suitcases. "We remembered everything."

The two sisters hugged, and Joe watched as Christine battled tears.

"You tell Nat and R.J. and Hallie and Suzanne that we're sorry we had to race off like this. Give everybody a kiss from me, will you?"

Marta nodded, sniffling loudly. "You take care of yourselves," she said, hugging Christine again. "And of that beautiful little baby."

Christine placed the palm of her hand against her

sister's slightly rounded belly. "Same goes for you, big sister."

"Come home soon," Marta whispered.

"I promise," Christine said.

Leave it to Nonie and Sam to grab hold of the situation, separate the two sisters, and physically herd Joe, Christine, and the baby into their rented car.

"Call us collect when you find a phone over there," Sam instructed them. "We want to know you're safe and sound."

"Geneva has plenty of phones," Joe said, shaking Sam's hand through the open window.

"You're due for a miracle," Sam said. "Just keep believin'."

"I love you," Christine said, waving good-bye as Joe started the engine. "Every single one of you." She looked over at Joe, eyes red with tears, and gestured toward his waist. "Seat belt."

"Same to you."

"Marina hated seat belts." They started down the road that led to the highway. "I always had to remind her."

He reached over and took her hand in his. A huge lump settled in his throat, and he didn't even try to speak around it. He glanced in the rearview mirror at the baby asleep in the car seat. *You're gonna love her, Ric,* he thought. *Maybe as much as we do.*

Lake Geneva was beautiful. That's what everyone said. Christine had no reason to doubt the truth of that statement, but as they drove toward the rendez-vous site, its beauty was lost on her. Maybe some day in the future she'd be able to look back and appreciate the sparkling sapphire-blue lake or the majestic splendor of the snowcapped Alps, but not today. Today she could only think of Marina, of a young life ended too soon.

And of a little girl who had become part of her heart.

It wasn't supposed to be this way. She'd known the dangers from the very start and she'd embraced them. Now it was time to pay the price.

"Where do you think they're taking us?" she whispered to Joe. The two of them and the baby were seated in the back of a chauffeured Daimler.

"I don't think they want us to know."

"Doesn't that make you nervous?"

"It did the first time. You get used to it."

"Funny," she said, "but I forgot how dangerous being a reporter can be."

"It's not something I spend a hell of a lot of time thinking about, but, yeah, it can be pretty dangerous."

She nuzzled the baby's sweet head. "A limousine but no car seat. What's wrong with these people?"

"It wasn't personal. They didn't think."

"They should have. Don't they know how vulnerable babies are?"

Joe said nothing. What could he say that made any difference? In a few minutes he'd be face to face with the man who'd saved his life twenty years ago, and he didn't know what in hell he was going to say. "I'm sorry" didn't cut it. He wasn't sure anything would.

The driver stopped the Daimler in front of a tall stone house on the outskirts of Geneva proper. At some point the stones had been whitewashed, but now only the palest shadow of paint remained, making the house blend into the surroundings.

They were met at the door by two men in uniform. The same way he'd been met at the door on that day months ago when his whole life had been turned on its ear.

"Please sit." One of the men pointed toward a pair of straight-backed chairs pushed up against the far wall. "The wait will not be long."

Christine, holding the baby tight, wrinkled her nose. "All the comforts of home," she drawled, scanning the spartan surroundings. She claimed a chair and gestured Joe to sit next to her, but he couldn't. His nerves were twitching, and the only way he could stay this side of sanity was to keep moving.

"Where's a punching bag when you need one?" he muttered, pacing the length of the small room.

He heard footsteps outside the door. Christine looked at him over the top of the baby's head. Her beautiful gray eyes were wide with fear. The door swung open, and Ric stood there on the threshold. He looked older, infinitely more tired than he had the last time Joe saw him.

He knows, Joe thought, moving toward his old friend. *He knows, and it's breaking his heart.*

They embraced in the clumsy but sincere way of men who couldn't find words for the deep emotions inside their hearts.

"It was out of your hands," Ric said as they broke apart. "An act of God."

He's comforting me, Joe thought. He couldn't imagine how he'd react in the same situation. With anger. Certainly with disbelief. But never with this almost fatalistic acceptance of an unimaginable loss.

"We didn't know she was pregnant." Joe stumbled over the words in his need to explain. "Maybe if—"

"There is no point to wondering," Ric said with more understanding that Joe could comprehend. "I railed against fate when I lost Helena, but nothing could bring her back."

"You've changed, old friend."

"In all ways," said Ric. He stood on the brink of leadership, and that leadership was taking its toll.

Ric turned toward Christine, and her heart went out to him. Yet, despite her compassion, she found herself holding the baby even closer to her chest.

"I feel as if I know you, Christine."

She nodded, offering a nervous smile. "The avalanche story is now part of my family's lore."

Ric's arms reached out for the baby, then he hesitated, as if fighting against the need to hold the child. Christine martialed her resolve and placed the infant in the man's arms, then turned toward Joe, who was standing near the window. He draped his arm across her shoulders. She rested her head against his chest. They stood like that for what seemed an endless time, looking out at the sparkling lake and towering mountains and seeing none of it.

Finally Ric cleared his throat. "She is a beautiful child," he said in a voice hoarse with emotion.

"And brilliant," Christine said, summoning up a smile. "My mother says it's impossible, but I'm sure she understands what we say to her." She quickly wiped away tears and reached for the small leather bag that contained Marina's belongings. "I thought you should have these."

The baby started to cry, reaching out her tiny arms toward Christine who ached to hold her.

Ric tried to open the bag but couldn't manage it with the baby squirming to reach Christine. "Maybe it would be easier if you held her while I looked."

Christine nodded. "Of course."

Joe grabbed the baby's foot and made silly faces at her, and she smiled giddily in return.

"We'll be okay," he said for Christine's ears alone.

"I know," she answered, "but it hurts so much."

Ric withdrew an envelope that had been sandwiched in with Marina's serviceable cotton underwear.

"What's that?" Christine whispered to Joe.

"I don't know," Joe said. "I thought you did."

Ric unfolded the letter and read it. Christine's heart ached as Ric turned away to recover his composure.

Christine and Joe looked up as one of Ric's assistants appeared in the doorway. "The plane awaits. We must go soon."

Ric nodded, still with his back turned.

This is it, Christine thought, nuzzling the infant, breathing in that magical baby smell.

Ric turned and held out his arms for the child. "She has Marina's eyes."

"And her chin," said Christine through her tears.

"And her temper," Joe added.

Ric smiled and then, to Christine's wonderment, handed the child to Joe.

"It is my daughter's wish."

"No," said Joe. "She's your granddaughter. She belongs with you." He didn't sound terribly convincing to Christine.

"She needs a home without bullets and the smell of death," Ric stated firmly. "She needs parents who

will help her to grow into a strong and compassion-
ate woman."

"But what about her father?" Christine asked,
afraid to hear the answer. "Can't he—"

Ric shook his head. "Zee was killed a few weeks
after Marina left for the States. That would have been
her fate if Joe had not agreed to intercede. This
beautiful child would never have been born." He
handed them the letter Marina had left behind. "It is
my daughter's wish. She came to love you both like
family, and I cannot disagree." He bowed his head
slightly. "I will return in a moment for your decision."

Christine and Joe were beyond words, too afraid to
hope that this wasn't a dream. Marina's letter was
simple, disarming in its directness. She'd loved them
and needed them as much as they needed this beautiful daughter she had left in their care.

The baby opened her eyes and smiled up at them,
and for the first time in weeks they laughed, really
laughed, as if the world and everything in it was
theirs for the asking.

Ric returned a few moments later. "You have
reached a decision?" He looked oddly vulnerable for
a man who was born to be king.

"We'll call her Marina," said Joe.

"If that's all right with you," Christine added.

Ric bent forward and pressed a kiss to Marina's
forehead. Christine saw the tears in his dark
eyes . . . and she saw the hope. It was the hope she
chose to remember.

Ric's assistant appeared in the doorway. "Now,
sir," he said more forcefully this time. "We must go."

"What about her future?" Joe asked as they made their good-byes. "She's in line for the throne."

"There won't be a throne when she's grown up," Ric said with certainty. "We're a dying breed, and maybe that's as it should be. Give her a real life. Show her a real future. Love her the way she needs to be loved."

With that he was gone.

"Tell me I'm dreaming," Christine said as the three of them stood together in the silent room.

"You're not dreaming," Joe said. "Remember what Sam said before we left?"

"Believe in miracles," she whispered.

Except this wasn't a miracle, this was her life . . . *their* life . . . and it was more than she'd ever dared to dream.

"Marina McMurphy," Joe said with a grin. "I like it."

"The McMurphy family." Christine met his eyes, and she knew she wasn't dreaming. "I like that even better."

"Come on," Joe said, reaching for the diaper bag. "It's time we went home."

Home.

She liked that best of all.